Breathe
AND
Count Back
from Ten

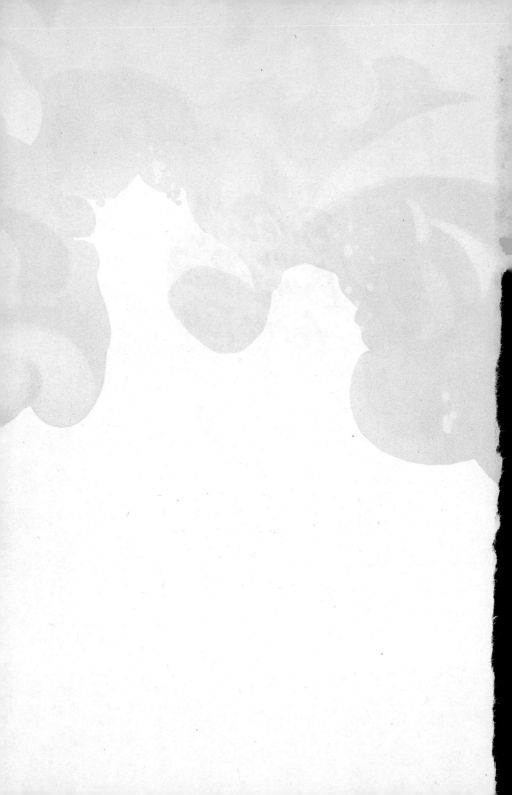

Breathe AND Count Back from Ten

by Natalia Sylvester

CLARION BOOKS
AN IMPRINT OF HARPERCOLLINSPUBLISHERS

When I started writing this book, I saw it as a story about a disabled immigrant teen's dreams and wishes, and the joys of encountering first love as she navigates her own relationship with her body. And while it is about all those things, they don't exist in a vacuum. There are parts of Vero's story that involve instances of bullying, ableism, slut shaming, and lack of consent, both medical and sexual. Processing them looks different for all of us, and there's no right or wrong way to do it. There's only what feels right for you, when and how you decide.

With love,

Natalia

Clarion Books is an imprint of HarperCollins Publishers.

Breathe and Count Back from Ten

Copyright © 2022 by Natalia Sylvester

www.epicreads.com

ISBN 978-0-35-853686-4

Typography by Karina Granda
22 23 24 25 26   PC/LSCC   10 9 8 7 6 5 4 3 2 1

First Edition

To all the HIPpies who've ever felt out of place:
together we are always home.

To Ceci y Ramón: por todo y por siempre.

Anesthesia: an·es·the·sia

1. (n.) a controlled, temporary loss of sensation or pain induced for medical purposes

2. (n. VR) a dreamless state; a nothingness in which you have no control

Chapter 1

WHEN YOU'RE ABOUT TO GO UNDER, the doctors tell you to breathe and count back from ten. Or they'll ask who the president is and what year we're in, the kind of things a time traveler would want to know. It feels like losing all sense of time, because I don't remember ever getting past nine or eight before the anesthesia numbs me and everything disappears. Everything switches. I blink and I wake, and I'm in another bed, another room, wrapped in a cast in another time. Six hours later, and I never even felt the emptiness.

Being underwater is the opposite. The faster I swim, the more time seems to slow down. I feel every ounce of breath inside of me. It's loud and it's quiet. It becomes a rhythm inside my body. Every four strokes, I tilt my head above the surface, long enough to fill my lungs, and not a milli-second or inch more. I practice twists, flips, and choreography if no one's watching, mimicking all the moves I've memorized over years of following Mermaid Cove's videos online. I hear my thoughts for once, clear as water.

It's the most awake I ever feel, and it's like I'm dreaming.

Except today there's a beeping. It's somewhere far away, but it's getting louder and more insistent. I swim to the edge of the pool and lift my head just enough for my eyes to clear the top.

It's not the construction truck I expected, but a moving truck, backing into a spot painfully slowly. A guy about my age stands by the curb, signaling to whoever's driving to come closer. Closer. Closer.

He waves both arms very suddenly for them to stop.

Too close, I guess.

The truck comes to a screeching halt and goes silent. I try to get a good look at the guy's profile, but it's hard from so far away. There's a whole tennis court between us, and it's old and cordoned off by a sky-high chain-link fence. Through the crisscross view, all I can read is his body language: hands on hips, shoulders drooping, chin up. Like he's tired of trying not to let his exhaustion show.

He disappears somewhere in front of the truck, and I go back to my swimming. I still have twenty laps to go, and if I hurry I'll finish before anyone else gets here. Now that it's summer, every parent in our apartment complex has decided this will be the year their kid learns to swim. Except they rarely use the kiddie pool like they're supposed to. They swarm into the lap pool with their noodles and flotation devices, splashing along the perimeter as they grasp at the pool's edges like they're support beams at a skating rink. I've been waking up two hours early every morning just to avoid the rush.

I finish my last stretch of laps in under six minutes, tugging off my goggles by the deep end. A pair of dusty brown boots collapse off the side of the lounge chair a few feet in front of me. The feet they belong to are still in socks, crossed at the ankles as the toes wiggle around.

Gross.

The guy from the moving truck sits up, legs straddling the long seat, looking startled, as if I wasn't here first. He's in jeans and a dark beige and white baseball shirt. The sleeves are bunched up around his elbows, but he tilts his head to the side and pushes them up further for no apparent reason. I feel sticky just looking at him. Sweaty, wearing-too-many-clothes-for-this-weather sticky.

"Can I help you?" I say.

"What? No. I didn't . . . I didn't mean to make you stop swimming. Please, pretend I'm not even here."

That's going to be near impossible, considering there's no one else on the pool deck right now, and of all the places he could've sat, he chose the chair where I left my things.

"My towel. It's on the back of your chair."

"Oh. Sorry." He twists and grabs my turquoise and purple beach towel. It's now a bundled wad that he passes distractedly from one hand to the other. "I just needed a quiet place to close my eyes for a bit. I wasn't watching you or anything," he adds hurriedly.

"I wasn't . . . thinking that. Until now." I dip my head back in the water to smooth my hair. When I come back up, he's leaning closer to the pool's edge. "Anyway you didn't make me stop," I say.

"How many laps did you do?"

"Fifty." I rest my arms over the edge and place my chin on my forearm. From this angle the sun's directly behind him, and all I can see is his dark silhouette, carved out by light. "This isn't exactly a quiet place, with all the splashing."

"I guess not. But you did me a favor." He turns his attention back to the moving truck. A man lifts the back open, and the door rumbles like a trash bin being dragged across uneven pavement. It's huge, one of those trucks people hire to move across state, and definitely bigger than any I've ever seen pull into Palmview Lakes. When my family and I moved from our one-bedroom across town into this bigger apartment eight years ago, Papi borrowed a pickup from a friend at work, and it only took two trips to bring over all our furniture. Mami packed all our other things into boxes she'd gotten from the loading dock at Publix.

"We brought way too much stuff," he mumbles, turning away from the truck. He runs his fingers over his hair in a dipping motion, like he's trying to hide his face behind his arm. Like maybe me seeing all his boxes is the same as being caught undressed. I look down and stare at my legs quietly flapping beneath the water.

"Where'd you move from?"

"Are you getting out?"

We break the silence at the same exact time, then both wait for the other one to answer. The quiet drags, and we let the questions drop like an overinflated dodgeball no one wants to touch.

I start growing cold in the water, but if I get out now, he'll see me in my bathing suit, and I know how this part of introductions will go. Eyes like a magnet to my scars. Silence stretching up my thigh and pelvic bone as he stares down every inch of them. Inevitably, the question, *What happened there?* Before he's even asked my name.

Sometimes I lie to people. I give them a story about a bizarre accident instead of the boring truth they're never comfortable hearing anyways. But this guy looks so sad and tired, I don't have the heart to mess with him. I contemplate asking him to pass me my towel, but now he's hugging it over his stomach like a security blanket and I'm not entirely sure he's noticed he still has it.

"Don't you need to go unpack?" It comes out sounding ruder than I meant it, and it seems to catch him off guard, because his jawline and temple pop. His face is all sharp angles and smoothness, and his long lashes move like butterflies as he blinks several times.

"The movers won't let me help. Apparently it's some kind of liability thing."

"Must be nice." Most people in our apartment complex don't exactly hire movers.

He lets out a half laugh. "Yeah. It's just that management—"

5

A deep Southern voice cuts him off. "There you are."

I don't have to turn to know it's Bob, our apartment's security guard, who is always nowhere he's needed and everywhere he's not invited. My best friend, Leslie, and I have spent nearly every summer begging Bob to let us drive his golf cart. He usually gives us rides around the complex instead.

"What'd I do now?" I say. There's always some new pool rule he teases me about breaking, though it's never actually enforced.

"Not you, Verónica. Him. I'm supposed to give this young man the grand tour today."

The *young man* finally releases my poor towel from his clutches and leaves it on the lounge chair as he gets up to shake Bob's hand. While they chat I take the opportunity to dart out of the pool and wrap the towel around my waist, forming a nice V dip just below my belly button. Bob calls for me to come over.

"Verónica, this here's Alex." So the young man has a name. "Alex's mom is our new property manager. How 'bout while she gets their things sorted in their new apartment, you show him around?" Bob slaps him on the shoulder with all the awkwardness of a drunk uncle. Alex raises his eyebrows into a look of quiet embarrassment.

"It's okay. You really don't have to," he says.

"It's just there's really not much to show . . ."

"Then it shouldn't take much of your time at all," Bob says.

Before either of us can respond, he's already rushing back to his cart. We watch him putter away until our eyes meet and redirect to the ground.

"That was really awkward. I'm sorry. It's just that management's set on giving us the VIP treatment, apparently."

"Must be nice," I say again, walking back to where I left my bag and change of clothes. I slip on a pair of jean cutoff shorts under my towel and pull on a yellow tank, then drape the towel back over the lounge chair for it to dry.

"It goes without saying, you don't have to listen to him," he says.

"Sure I don't." I grin and roll my eyes. It's not like I really have a choice. As much as Leslie and I like to make fun of him, Bob calls the shots around here, in a strange behind-the-scenes type of way. Draping my bag over my shoulder, I take another look at Alex and try to assess the risk factor. When my parents said they better never catch me at the pool with another boy *or else*, they meant it. Never mind that this would be completely different—my parents were so furious the night they caught me making out with Jeremy Bradley they haven't been able to see past their rage ever since. And they definitely don't see me. Not the way they used to, anyways.

I check the time on my phone. Mami and Papi will be at work by now, and besides, I'm just doing what I was told. Being nice, welcoming. Doing everything I can to not to be "desagradable." The second worst word in my family's dictionary, right after "promiscua." Heaven forbid an unpleasant or promiscuous daughter.

A tired sigh escapes me. I wrap it up with my most convincing smile. "Come on. I'll show you your kingdom, Mr. VIP."

Suelta: suel·ta

1. (adj.) loose; often used to describe a promiscuous girl
2. (v.—imperative VR) what I wish I could tell my parents to do—let go

Chapter 2

WE WALK TO THE RUSTED MONKEY bars and swing sets on the opposite side of the tennis courts. To the clustered mailbox unit that Mami constantly asks me to check, with its dried tiki hut roof that rustles at the lightest breeze, and then the faded hammock strung between two trees further down the road. Our apartment complex is, according to Leslie, a dinosaur—a giant, sprawling relic—but when we first moved in, my parents said we were lucky and we shouldn't complain. They said our apartment in Peru was a tiny box in a four-story building, no recreational facilities or pools, like here. I wasn't old enough to remember, but we lived right on a busy street that is practically a highway now. It's why Mami always says "At least it's not like Avenida Benavides" every time someone speeds through the main entrance. To which I usually respond that we should move to a unit closer to Leslie's.

It's quieter, and those apartments have three bedrooms, which is the natural next step in our migration pattern: studio in Lima, one-bedroom across town, two-bedroom here. So far, they're not exactly enthused.

Alex and I walk down the sidewalks and occasionally take a shortcut through the back of one of the buildings. There are eighteen total, lettered A through R, and the complex is bordered on one side by a canal and shaped like a snake, so we slowly make our way through its curves, meandering in one direction and then another. We end up talking this way, too, never staying on any one subject for long.

"So where'd you move from?" I ask, stepping onto the mosaic wall that lines the property. It grows from a few inches off the grass to several feet the further we walk, and I can tell he's nervous, watching me tower over him, stretching my arms out for balance.

"Texas. You sure you're all right up there?" He places his hand on the wall like it's a ladder he's trying to hold still for me, his palms resting against a row of seashell accents that line the edge.

I shrug and keep going. "It's not really that high."

"You walk like you've done this a million times."

I slow down, aware of his eyes on my steps. It makes everything feel less steady. "Definitely enough times to know my way." I try to think of where to take him next. "Do you play sports?"

"I was on the baseball team sophomore year." He looks

away from me, and I pick up the pace again. My hip socket cracks like Pop Rocks in an open mouth, sharp but soft enough that I'm sure he doesn't hear it.

"So you're a junior now?" I ask.

"Incoming senior."

"Same as me." I can't imagine transferring to a new school senior year, right before college applications are due. My parents would never uproot me and my sister like that. They're always talking about how leaving one country for another was hard enough, and now this—*here, the four of us*—is our home. It's why I'm only applying to the state schools closest to us. None of them are more than a three-hour drive away, and they're less expensive than if I went to college outside of Florida. It's lucky that I want to major in marine biology, though, and not, like, deserts or something.

I jump off the wall, landing on a soft patch of grass. My sudden dismount seems to surprise him, and for half a second, Alex hovers his hands over my sides like he was trying to catch me. We lock eyes for a beat past casual. Technically, I'm not supposed to be doing any of this—the doctors have always said no high-impact movements on my joints, and Mami would for sure kill me—¡aquí y al toque!—if she saw me practically leap into a boy's arms. They treat me like a fragile package no one should ever dare touch or open. All these rules, left and right, when I'm the one who knows what my body can and can't handle.

What my ego can handle is another story. It's still bruised

by Jeremy. Sometimes I swear his touch is a soapy residue on my skin that refuses to wash away. Even worse, I think my parents see it, too. They look at me like I'm sucia, impossible to scrub clean. They say they're *just so worried* about the kind of young woman I'm becoming.

"You good there?" Alex says. *His* concern for me, on the other hand, is kind of sweet.

"Million times, remember? This way, please." Ignoring the slight stiffness in my hip socket, I point both hands straight ahead in my best impression of an airline attendant.

As soon as we get to the beach volleyball court, Alex takes off his shoes and socks (this boy is in desperate need of a pair of flip-flops, the official footwear of Floridians) and dips his toes into the sand. He does a twisty thing with his hips, like he's trying to wedge himself in deeper.

"The sand is kind of shallow, actually. Maintenance hasn't refilled it in years," I say. "Every summer another tropical storm or hurricane depletes it more." Mami's tried to get them to fix it—she was captain of her high school's volleyball team in Peru, and my sister Dani's planning on trying out for ours this summer—but her requests go completely ignored. "You can't even dive for the ball. Look." I dig my foot in, exposing the concrete just a few inches deep. "I tried it last time my family and I played and practically scraped my whole knee off."

"Ouch. That sounds painful." He looks at my legs, and I want to kick myself for bringing attention to them again.

I can never tell if I've been limping, because it's usually really subtle until it's not. But if I have been and Alex has noticed, right about now would be the moment he asks why. I hold my breath, trying to think of a way to change the subject.

"Maybe I can tell my mom," he says.

"Your mom?"

"To add more sand?" His lips curve into a hopeful smile.

"Oh my God. Right. Of course!"

"Speaking of, I should probably head back. Just to see how things are going."

"Right."

And to think I was just starting to enjoy this whole tour guide thing. I make up for it getting cut short by pointing out small things on the way back to the pool, like the community bulletin board and the one apartment balcony that always goes all-out with a music-accompanied light show around Christmas. Nothing is really that impressive at Palm view Lakes, but Alex seems intrigued by everything I show him. I can't tell if he's sincere or just being nice, but I think it's endearing either way. He has a polite air about him, like he knows he's a guest in someone else's home. Even though this is now his home, too.

"Let me just check in to see if she needs anything," he says as we near his apartment. I wait by the sidewalk as he goes in and out. Even though it's been barely a few minutes when he returns, something about him seems different—

sad, almost. I ask if everything's okay, and he nods and makes some vague comment about his mom before letting his voice trail off. We head back to the pool to pick up my towel.

"Do a lot of kids from your school—our school—live here?" he asks.

I sweep one foot over a large grey stain that marks the path from the pool to the hot tub. "Some of them do. And a bunch of them who don't live here come over for the pool parties. See this? It's from the shaving cream fight a bunch of the juniors and seniors had on the night of the last day of school, a few weeks ago. It was huge."

"Shaving cream," he deadpans. "Sounds . . . slippery?"

"A total lawsuit waiting to happen," I say, echoing what Leslie said as a bunch of guys ran circles around our loungers. They had the whole deck reeking of a mixture of beer and Barbasol. When they finally settled down, a group of us got into the hot tub. Slowly, as the night wore on, people started leaving, until it was just me and Jeremy. Leslie was the last to go; she gave me a silent "you okay?" look, and I gave her a micronod while Jeremy wasn't looking. The hot tub is sectioned off from the rest of the pool by a wall, so I never saw what was coming before my parents stormed in and pulled me out of the water.

"Is that why the pool hours are . . . that?" Alex points at the RULES sign that hangs over the main gate. It's brown with white lettering, but the top line has a white patch of paper taped over it with new hours. Management *used* to look the other way, but leave it to our class to ruin a years-long tradition of parties by getting sloppy with the underage drinking and toiletry pranks.

I fold my towel and stuff it into my bag now that it's dried under the sun. "Basically, yeah. So now no one can swim past nine, just in time for summer." Not like my parents would let me swim at night anyway, after what happened. "You thirsty?"

We go to the vending machines that hug the wall of the leasing office, just outside the pool entrance. Unsurprisingly, they're all out of order, so I take him up to the second floor of the building, where there's a gym and a newish set of machines.

"The thing you should know about this place is nothing ever really works right," I say as we climb the stairs. My voice bounces off the cement walls, mixed with the sound of our steps.

"That's okay. I'm used to dysfunction."

I stop. With him standing only two steps behind me, Alex's eyes are almost level with mine and closer than I thought they'd be. They're the brown of an old wooden chair we have in our apartment, all these thin streaks of grain and light flooding through them.

"What part of Texas did you say you're from again?"

"I didn't. But Houston."

"And your mom's in charge of this place now?"

"Yeah. She wants to do all this community-building stuff. Happy hours and get-togethers, things like that. To help everyone feel more 'connected.'" His voice changes when he says that, as if he's imitating something she's said. He doesn't sound very convinced by it, or even happy, for that matter. I think of all the complaints my parents have ever brought to management. That there aren't enough guest parking spots. That there isn't even a few days' grace period for rent. That our front door doesn't have a ramp, so every time I've been in a wheelchair after my surgeries, getting in and out has been that much more difficult.

They're going to be so pissed if Palmview Lakes ends up hosting happy hours instead of addressing people's actual needs.

"What kind of drink do you want? It's on me. As a thank-you for showing me around," he says.

I push the buttons for a La Croix and he gets one, too, then we sit at the top of the stairwell sipping them. Knowing that my shorts will ride up and reveal the scar on my left hip, I sit to the right of him.

Our bodies are still warm from the sun. We're not even touching, but we radiate heat across the small space between us. I look at his hands and arms, the way he rubs them together nervously and squeezes them between his thighs like he's cold, like he's trying to make himself smaller. It must be ninety-nine degrees outside. His skin is a subtle bronze, but judging by how awkwardly he stretched out on the pool deck earlier, I'm guessing it's not from the sun. I want to ask where else he's from, but I don't. I figure he'll tell me eventually if we become friends, and besides, I hate it when that question is flung at me out of the blue. Our town's not even two hours from Orlando, but our population is barely a fifth its size, and being *born and bred here* is like a rallying cry of pride for some folks, a flag staked in the ground. The way our neighbors slip Peru into every and any conversation with us, pronouncing it PAY-ru, like it's a bouncy animal we owe money to, you'd think *we're* the exotic attraction here instead of the springs down the road filled with mermaids.

Beautiful. Wondrous. Mermaids.

Alex keeps his gaze fixed straight ahead. Through the slits of the stairs, we have a perfect view across the pool of the movers unloading the truck. They're maneuvering a large yellow leather sectional off the ramp and yelling directions at each other in Spanish. I try to catch glimpses of his parents, but they must be inside the apartment.

"God, I hate moving."

"Have you moved around a lot?"

He nods and takes a sip of his water, still not looking at me. "Within Houston, yeah. But this is the first time I've gone out of state. The drive was fifteen hours straight. And I did most of it."

There's a heaviness in his eyes I hadn't caught until now. When he blinks, he leaves them closed just a millisecond longer than most people, the way Papi does when he's covering the night shifts for another security guard at the university. Like he's just searching for one moment of calm.

"Do you have time for another mini tour?" I ask.

His face lights up with exaggerated glee. "There's more?"

"Just . . . trust me."

There are man-made ponds all over our complex, and some-times I think our apartment buildings were constructed around them instead of the other way around, like bread crumbs scattered down a winding path. Each pond—or lake, as management insists on calling them—has a fountain at the center, but the one that's just across the way from my bed-room window has two. I take Alex to the small hill that over-looks it.

"Sometimes I fall asleep with the windows open just so I can hear the water."

"I can see why. It's nice." He takes off his shirt, revealing a white ribbed undershirt splotched with sweat, and uses it as a pillow while he lies down on the grass with both his hands behind his head.

I check my phone again. It's barely past noon. No way my parents are anywhere near home, but my fear of getting caught in the vicinity of another boy runs deep. I stretch my towel several inches away from him and prop myself up on my elbows instead of lying all the way down.

The sky is a blanket of blue settling over our bodies. I can tell Alex is drifting into sleep by how his breath deepens, and after ten minutes or so, he stirs awake.

"Sorry about that. We've barely met, and I've already passed out in front of you."

I shrug. "The water has that effect on people. And it's much more peaceful here than by the pool." The wind picks up and blows the fountain's mist in our direction.

"God, that feels nice. I thought the Houston humidity was bad, but it's like y'all live in a swamp."

"I mean, we do. A few months ago, we even had a baby alligator living in this lake."

"Wait, what?" He looks around, startled.

"Yeah. It was, like, maybe three or four feet?" I demonstrate by holding my hands apart. "It was really cute."

"Cute? Those things can kill you."

"Rarely," I say, relishing how much Alex is so *not* from Central Florida. "Anyways, one time, my sister and I waved at it from my parents' car, and it moved its little leg, like it was waving back."

"Y'all are weird."

I chuckle and throw a handful of grass at him. It's nice, for once, to be called weird for being from Florida. Not for being born in a country that evokes nothing but llama jokes from everyone at school. Or for bringing "weird" leftovers to school for lunch instead of just buying from the cafeteria. Or for walking in a way that makes people look twice, think twice, as if something about me is just . . . off. Now that we're sitting up and I was careless about which side to sit on, I know Alex sees my scar. I know his eyes have caught on it the way a chipped nail catches on a new shirt, tugging at the most delicate thread in the fabric.

And yet he hasn't asked. Hasn't glanced my way like there's something wrong with me.

"Whatever. Animal control came and took the little guy eventually. Which sucked because he had become kind of like the Palmview Lakes mascot."

"Didn't an alligator kill a kid at Disney World a few years ago?"

"At one of their resorts. And yeah . . . that was a really horrible and isolated incident. We don't like to talk about it," I say. "It's too morbid and bizarre."

"Sorry. I won't bring it up again." He smiles apologetically and turns onto his side, head resting on his elbow.

"So, um . . . this town is pretty obsessed with water stuff, huh?"

"What?"

"The gators, the mermaid memorabilia everywhere. All the things that are shell shaped. The school mascot."

"Oh God, I was wondering if you'd seen that yet!"

"On our way into town? Oh yeah. It's kind of hard to miss a marquee with the Greek god of the ocean on it."

"So you're not a fan?"

He looks down and raises his eyebrows as he shrugs. They're so thick and dark, they make the whites of his eyes pop with intensity. I bring my knees as close to my chest as I can. He does the same, only he crosses his legs in front of him first. He makes it look so effortlessly comfortable, this twisting into a human pretzel.

"It's your mascot too now," I say, bopping my shoulder into his.

I actually used to love it, but then three years of pep rallies and our vice principal telling us to "show some Poseidon spirit" over the PA every morning made those vibes wear off real fast. There's nothing more tragic than describing a football team that's zero for twelve as the Mighty Poseidons. It doesn't even make sense. The god of the ocean, but in Central Florida, we're landlocked. The nearest body of water is the freshwater springs. Mami always jokes that it's unnatural; our family was born on the Pacific, and its cold salt water might as well run through our veins, yet we ended up here, in a town where the nearest body of water is a fresh spring.

"It's all because of Mermaid Cove," I say. "It's kind of this place's claim to fame. Your parents have to have known that before you moved here." Everything in our town is either water- or mermaid-themed, and generally, people either embrace it or can't wait to get away from it the second they graduate. Me, I'm obsessed. Right down to my tote that rests between us. It says I WANT TO BE WHERE THE PEOPLE ARE on one side and NOT on the other. It was a birthday gift from Leslie, the perfect blend of my Ariel obsession and her quirky snark.

"My mom," Alex says. "It's just me and my mom." His smile disappears into a grimace, as if he's stretching a sore muscle.

"Oh." I don't ask for the same reason he probably hasn't asked about my scar. Why push down on a place that's hurting? Instead I barrel through the silence, trying to bring the lightness back to our conversation. "Well, Mermaid Cove's been around since the fifties. It's a whole production. There's this troupe of women who dress up as mermaids and dance in the springs, and people view them through a glass in an underground cave." I'm about to tell him about the first time I saw them perform when he sighs.

"It sounds to me like another Florida-theme-park-manufactured fantasy."

He pronounces it Floe-ri-da, like my parents do, like each syllable's its own entity instead of sounds that run into each other. I want to tell him he's wrong: the mermaids and the dreams are real—at least to me they are.

But it's such a huge part of me to trust him with. I say the next best thing. "It's not as corny as it sounds. Believe me."

"If you say so. I mean, you're my guide. And I like everything you've shown me on the Verónica tour so far."

My cheeks flush. Did he mean the Verónica tour as in what I've shown him of the apartments, or the Verónica tour as in . . . me?

He looks down at his hands. "I was thinking maybe next time I'm trying to find my way around, I can text you?"

I tell him that's fine, and we exchange numbers. I do my best to act like it's no big deal. It's just me showing a new neighbor around to be nice, like Bob asked me to.

"So you come here a lot?" he asks, raising his eyebrows toward the lake.

"Not really." I shrug. "Just when I'm tired of my latest boy toy and need a hungry alligator to help dispose of the body."

"Wait, so I'm your . . . Interesting." And he leaves it at that.

I can't believe what I just said. I can't believe he called me on it. I was trying so hard to stay casual that the words sort of tumbled out of me like marbles in classic pseudo-flirt fashion—so clumsily I can't even pick them back up. I'm almost lightheaded from thinking of eight million comebacks when he smiles and lets out a little huff.

"I mean. I'm not objecting, is what I'm saying."

It grows so quiet, we actually hear a fish poke its tail out of the surface, quick as a shooting star.

"I gotta go," I say, getting up so fast I'm momentarily dizzy.

I wish he wouldn't watch me as I walk away.

Sirena: si·re·na

1. (n.) a half-fish, half-human creature of the sea
2. (n. VR) a calling that reverberates inside you, impossible to ignore

Chapter 3

THE FIRST TIME I SAW THE mermaids, I was seven and wearing a cast from my chest to the toes on my left foot. They wore tails with fins as delicate as algae, and each time they flipped or twirled, I imagined millions of microbubbles tickling my own skin. I held my breath watching them—at moments from the pure awe of it, at others, out of a desire to be them. They seemed mythical then, like they'd come from some faraway land. Sitting in a hospital-rented wheelchair in the front row of an underwater amphitheater carved out of limestone, I felt, for the first time, that I was in the right place.

It didn't matter that I couldn't move. The surgeons said it would be at least six weeks until they removed my cast, and months more of physical therapy. Unable to see my legs, I felt a kinship with the mermaids. My cast covered my left leg in its entirety and my right down to my knee. It created a dividing line between the upper and lower parts of my body that I could and couldn't use. Like the mermaids, I, too, was a hybrid creature with two halves that didn't match. Until I first encountered them, I'd never considered that this could be beautiful.

"Do they breathe like fish?" Dani asked, loud enough to be heard over the fading finale music. She was sitting between my dad and my mom, and from the end of the row I tried to tune out Mami's sharp whispers as she leaned in to explain the mermaids' secrets to my little sister. I knew—of course I did—but every twenty or thirty seconds, when a mermaid twirled and quickly sipped on an air hose she oh-so-subtly reached for, I'd look away. I wanted to pretend, just a little longer, that it was all real.

There were seven of them, and they were dancing some thirty-four feet underwater, according to the brochure we'd gotten at the entrance. The clear water springs and the limestone caves had been here for millennia, carved by the force of the current. The underground theater we sat in had been built in the late '40s. We watched the mermaids from behind eight large panels of glass the length of a school bus. Instead of a curtain, every once in a while gusts of bubbles would shoot out from below the glass, and suddenly the mermaids would be in a new formation or they'd be holding new props. That day's show was a tribute to Mermaid Cove's seventieth anniversary; with each new song, they'd go through the decades, recreating routines that the mermaids performed as far back as the early '50s. There was a pirate-themed fight, an underwater picnic sketch, and for the very last one, a simple ballet-like dance to classical music. Everything slowed down—the sounds, their movement, my breath.

"¿Por qué esa mueca? You look angry," Mami said. I relaxed my cheeks and forehead and assured her I was fine, though I was so awestruck my face had probably contorted into some expression caught between a sob and a smile. I envied the way gravity seemed like a plaything for them. Their hair jellyfished around their faces, pulsating in slow motion.

When it was over, the four of us waited by the end of the front row, letting everyone else leave before we cleared out. We always did this, because it was easier than having Papi try to push my wheelchair through a moving crowd. "¿Te gustó?" Mami asked.

I nodded. "When can we come back?"

"I don't know," Papi said, and I could already hear the judgment in his voice, threatening to dull the mermaids' sparkle. "A mí me parecieron un poco huachafas."

"Déjala," Mami said. "If she likes them, she likes them. ¿A ti qué te importa?"

But Papi didn't seem to care either way. He was always calling things in the US tacky and cheap, which made no sense because we were always tight on money. He inhaled in the heavy way he did when he wanted to say something but wouldn't, like he was loading up his words for a later moment.

"They're just like la sirena de Huacachina," I said. According to Peruvian legend, a young Inca princess turned into a mermaid centuries ago in the desert oasis now known as Huacachina. I begged Mami to tell me the myth anytime she brushed my hair in front of the mirror. During the weeks I was home recovering after surgery, Mami would help me bathe and dress before braiding my hair. She ended up telling me the story so many times she began playing with it, editing and adding details, each embellishment a new surprise. Over the years it'd become our own secret story, like a family recipe that evolves with each hand that makes it. It changed with our moods and preoccupations. Now different versions of the Huacachina stories are forever intertwined with the surgeries I've had at different ages.

"Sí. Something like that, hijita," Mami said. I was about to tell her what my favorite part was when I heard a boy whine from the row behind us.

"Why'd they get to cut in front of us just because she's in a wheelchair? It's cheating." Instead of looking right at me, the kid bored his eyes into my left foot, where my toes poked out of my cast because no shoe would've been big enough to cover them. Instinctively, I clenched my toes, as if that could hide me from the coldness of his stare.

But neither his parents nor mine said anything. The mom just turned his body away from me by gently redirecting his shoulders. I felt out of place all of a sudden, all right angles and stiffness. I wished I could be underwater, where a simple twirl made all the hardness of the earth disappear.

Mami pushed me into the souvenir shop while Papi and Dani went to get the car. A machine that looked like a jukebox was dispensing wax statues the size of a small doll behind a pane of glass, pressing them together with two hot sheets of metal.

"Would you like one?" the lady at the register asked.

I smiled as Mami gave her a firm *thank you, but no.* The lady turned away, then gasped and clapped her hands together as if something had just occurred to her. "You know, you're our fiftieth customer in the store today. Which means you get a special prize." She took a golden token from the register and pushed it into the machine. Minutes later, the statue of a mermaid lying on top of a rock came out of the slot at the bottom, still warm. The whole ride home, it smelled like wax and blown-out candles, like it was my birthday.

They took off my cast six weeks later exactly. I remember feeling the vibration of the electrical saw, its teeth millimeters from my skin as it sliced through the plaster. It almost tickled, but I was too afraid of the sensation turning into pain to move. When they pulled apart the fractured pieces, all I could do was stare at my leg. It looked like one of those lizards that come out at night, so small and pale its veins show through its skin.

"Her muscles have atrophied, so water exercise would be best for her, to help regain mass," the doctor said, talking, as usual, to my parents, as if I wasn't in the room. "Gravity is weaker in water than on land, so swimming is far more gentle on her joints and hip than other activities."

"Does that mean I can be a mermaid?" It was the first time I actually said it out loud, but they all laughed.

"That park put ideas in her head," Papi said, pointing at

his temple. Making a small loop in the air. Even back then, Papi never missed a chance to remind me I should be focusing on serious things, like school, good grades, and a promising career—all the things my parents came to this country seeking for me and Dani. The only reason we had even gone to Mermaid Cove was because Mami insisted that we also should have a little fun.

The doctor simply reiterated, "Limit strenuous physical activity. Or stick to swimming." Then he rattled off a list of things I shouldn't ever do. Run. Walk long distances. Horseback riding and tap dancing and kickboxing and basically anything that was high impact.

I don't remember that doctor's name anymore. All I know is he's the reason we moved to Palmview Lakes, with its two large pools. My daily ritual. My one escape. The place I go to hear my thoughts and the reason my skin is perpetually pruny and my hair is dry as hay. In the water, chlorine tastes like peace and movement becomes freedom. Nobody notices my limp or scars; nobody stares as I move past them. Gravity is so much kinder here. Water is home.

Anomaly: a·nom·a·ly

1. (n.) something different, abnormal, peculiar, or not easily classified
2. (n. VR) a weak spot, a place that hurts the most

Chapter 4

BECAUSE THERE'S NO SUCH THING as privacy when you live in a two-bedroom apartment with three humans and a beta fish, sometimes Leslie and I hang out in my parents' room when they're at work. I lie on Mami's side of the bed by the window. Leslie lies just off the bottom edge in the middle, her feet still touching the floor. We stare at the ceiling like it's made of clouds.

My parents call her Leslie la atrevida because they think she has a wild streak and it amuses them; she's not *their* daughter, after all. They roll their eyes playfully at her "loud" makeup and purple highlights, or at how she once got caught stealing her mom's car just so she could take it to the car wash and shoot a TikTok video of all the colors of foam. Meanwhile, I'm not allowed to wear red lipstick or foundation, and I still haven't been able to get my driver's license. Los americanos get away with *everything,* my parents will say, then let out a resigned, it-is-what-it-is kind of laugh. I don't think it's funny. Back in seventh grade, they thought it was adorable that Leslie dressed up as Morticia Addams for Halloween, but they forbade me to dress up as Wednesday to match.

"Es que that little girl has such bad manners," Mami said. So I asked for my second choice, an astronaut costume, which she sewed for me in pink because it was the only fabric on sale.

When Leslie and I posed for pictures, I looked like an earless Easter bunny that Morticia was going to hunt. To make matters worse, the temperature that night had dropped below seventy.

"Here, ponte una chompa," Mami said. No one understood what I was as we went door-to-door for candy, because astronauts in space don't wear hand-knit button-up sweaters that look like doilies.

But Leslie loved my costume so much she asked to borrow the suit the next year. And the sweater. When people asked about her costume, she said, "Don't you know it's super cold on the moon?"

I guess she basically *can* get away with anything. Maybe it's because she doesn't care if people laugh at her so long as she beats them to it. I aspire to her level of confidence, but it's harder than she makes it look.

Today it's so hot out Leslie's cheeks are still red from the few minutes it took her to walk over. Dani's in our room doing a workout, and the apartment's quiet except for the pounding of her feet and snippets of sound that escape her headset. We're killing time before Leslie has to pick up her sister, Tanya, from work. Of course I'll be tagging along. Tanya became a mermaid at the Cove last summer, and we've been begging her to let us sneak into a dress rehearsal ever since. She's always said no—something about being the new girl with hardly any pull—but I guess she's feeling more confident this year, because she finally told us we could come. It's lucky timing, too, because there's no way my parents would have given me money for tickets to an actual show; I'm not grounded so much as sentenced to a constant, quiet period of "thinking about what I did" and their passive-aggressive judgments. My nightstand is stacked high with a pile of books Mami checked out for me from the library, practically all of them outdated college exam guides and career assessment workbooks that promise to help me chart a path to a successful career. Then she snuck in a book on abstinence and teen pregnancy, something with a real subtle title like *One Night: A Life of Consequences,* that looks straight out of the 1980s. Leslie laughed so hard at the illustrations of two teens hiding behind a tree as they looked in horror at a pregnancy test that she nearly woke Papi from his post-nightshift nap.

It's not just that I'm pseudo-grounded or that the tickets are expensive, though. It's that Papi's general disapproval of the mermaids, ever since we went that first time, runs deep, and I hate the expression he makes anytime I mention them. Like it pains him. Like it stings to know my passions have nothing to do with his dreams for me. He'd never say that out loud, but I can tell by how he always finds some way to disparage them. He'll call the Cove an overhyped tourist trap, or say that the mermaids have no future in the real world. Mami doesn't agree, but she doesn't bother contradicting him, either. She probably thinks it's just his harmless opinion.

So now I try not to mention Mermaid Cove when my dad's around. The handful of times I've gone to a show with friends, I lied and told my parents I needed money for the movies. Everything else I know about the mermaids is thanks to the pictures and videos they post on social. The fact that we finally got access to a dress rehearsal—with no one else in the darkened theater—feels surreal. The anticipation rolls around inside me like bubbles when you blow into a straw. Leslie, on the other hand, is calling out shapes she sees in the popcorn on the ceiling.

"Look, see that?" She points her arm straight up, but it wobbles as she opens and shuts each eye. "It looks like the profile of a ghost."

"Ghosts have profiles?"

"When they look like a dead guy from the 1800s, they do."

"I don't see it," I tease. Because surprisingly, I do. Leslie's mind works in just the right amount of weird. People at school have always thought she's too dark, even a little snobby, but that's only because they don't understand the humor in her constant, flat-toned sarcasm. By contrast, I find it comforting. So little fazes her, which means she's never judging. She just takes things for what they are, usually with an "oh" or an "all right" that people mistake for lack of interest.

Which makes getting a rise out of her exponentially more fun.

"So Bob had me give the new guy a tour around the neighborhood yesterday."

"The one with the huge moving truck? They had soooo many fake plants in there. I bet their apartment looks like a Rainforest Cafe." She pulls a thick lock of hair down over her nose and starts braiding it.

"I hadn't really noticed the plants. His name's Alex. He's from Houston." I shrug and then add like it's an afterthought, "We ended up hanging out for a while."

Leslie's fingers freeze. She turns her head slowly, owl-eyed. "Do go on."

I press my lips together, suppressing a smile. "He's nice. Kinda cute."

"Ronnie! ¡Qué escándalo!" she whispers in a thick accent. It's been one of Leslie's favorite phrases ever since she heard my mom say it while she watched the evening news, and she relishes any excuse to use it. "What'd you guys do?"

"We just walked around. I took him to the lake."

"This one?" She points out the window in its general direction. "You daredevil. Your parents could have seen you within a ten-foot radius of a boy again."

My stomach twists like a towel being wrung. "They were at work. And it wasn't exactly something I planned."

"More of a heat-of-the-moment thing?" she says, twisting her body in such a way that I know she's playing cheesy, sexy music in her mind.

I tell her to quit it. "He's nice. That's all. I don't want to make a big deal out of it."

"I won't. Just be careful. Your parents even scared *me* that night." Her voice is tender and protective; she sounds ready to jump to my defense at any moment.

"Trust me. I'm not making that mistake again." I roll onto my stomach and prop up on my elbows, picking at a scab on my arm. The thing Leslie doesn't know is my mistake wasn't just getting caught by my parents; it was choosing Jeremy in the first place. I'd never even paid much attention to him before that night, but he's That Guy at our school, the one everyone fixates on, and suddenly, in the hot tub, he was fixated on me.

He was a good kisser. Eager, rushed, like he wanted to drink me in. His hands were all over me, my body suddenly a desirable thing. His touch moved down my back, further and further, until I knew he would've been upset if I told him to stop. So I didn't. Because it would've been impolite. Because I wasn't supposed to be there, making out with a boy in a hot tub, but I wasn't supposed to be desagradable, either. My whole life, it's been this: smile, be agreeable, don't make others uncomfortable, no matter how wrong it feels. With his arms still around me, I tried to put some distance between us, but he steeled his embrace and pulled me back. I probably should have said something.

But maybe not everyone is fluent in body language.

Maybe not everyone is fluent in *my* body's language.

Then Jeremy squeezed my ass. He paused and tilted his head, like he was listening for something. I asked if everything was okay, and he shushed me. Then he squeezed again, alternating butt cheeks.

One of these things is not like the other, he said, over and over again.

More like . . . he sang. Like some messed-up lullaby you taunt children with.

He laughed while I was still in his arms. I told him it wasn't funny.

Oh come on, I'm just teasing. Can't you take a joke?

That's what people like him always say. Like I'm supposed to be fine with being the joke, and take it.

But this was so much worse than kids making fun of my limp, or the fact that my legs are uneven.

This was my skin pressed against his. My body in Jeremy's hands as he felt his way through its asymmetries — the visible and invisible scars of my leg muscles shrinking inside my cast after each surgery, the physical therapy sessions trying to make the strength come back and catch up. My left side may be smaller than my right, but I'd never felt so wholly shrunken as I did in that moment.

And then my parents showed up.

The humiliation comes back, bare and intimate. It makes me want to climb out of myself, leave whatever's left on the floor like a pile of dirty laundry.

Next thing we know, we find you sleeping with him, Mami said. The conviction in her statement haunts me, because I honestly don't know what would've happened next. Had my parents not caught us, would I have stopped him? Would I have wanted to?

"Anyways, I'm done being physical with anyone. For a while," I say, trying to get the taste of that night's memory out of my mouth. The morning after, I told Leslie that all the trouble I got into wasn't even worth it because Jeremy was a sloppy kisser.

A half lie, and I doubt she bought it, because she tilted her head and said, "You know you can tell me anything, right?"

I just nodded and changed the subject.

"You okay?" she singsongs now.

"Yeah. Totally fine. But enough of that. Has Tanya texted yet?" Tanya's supposed to tell us when the troupe is getting into costume so we're there in time to see the dress rehearsal.

Leslie scrolls through her phone and shakes her head. I get up and go through the top drawers of my mom's nightstand for the remote control. My fingers brush a small velvet ring box next to Mami's night cream.

"Oh hey, look."

"What . . . is that?"

"Our baby teeth," I say, sorting through them with one

finger like they're coins in a wallet. They're tiny, not even half the size of a Chiclet, and just as white. "I found them when I was little, and I started crying because I always thought the Ratoncito took them. My parents made up some story about how they bought them off of him after he collected them from me. Like some baby tooth black market."

"Ugh. And I just got stuck with a boring tooth fairy," she says, holding up a molar. "How much did your rat pay?"

"Five bucks a tooth."

"Seriously? That's, like, a hundred and fifty-something dollars a mouth. I only ever got a dollar."

"I guess teeth are the one thing my parents never go cheap on." I dig under the flap of the ring box and pull out a thin gold chain. "She even had this made." A pendant holding my front tooth hangs along the bottom, swinging and twisting in the air.

"How are you not wearing this every day of your life? If I had a tooth necklace, you'd have to rip it off my corpse to get it from me."

"It's my mom's, not mine. It's more of a sentimental thing. She hardly ever wears it." The last time I remember seeing it was the morning of my surgery a few years back. It rested delicately in the gap between her clavicles, like the bones had made a bed for it.

"Can I try it on?"

"Go for it," I say.

She sits up and takes a bunch of selfies with my baby

tooth around her neck, then tags me in one with the caption *Dental Chic*. Just as she leans over to show me, an alert pops up on her screen.

It's Tanya. Finally.

Getting into my tail. Get yours over here!

Formation: for·ma·tion

1. (n.) an arrangement of a body or group of persons in some prescribed manner
2. (n. VR) a shape you were always meant to be

Chapter 5

THE ENTRANCE TO MERMAID COVE IS basically a giant grotto, two arches formed by carefully arranged stones with water streaming through the cracks. The rocks are randomly shaped; some are the size of my head, while others are as tall as a grown man, and small bits of tropical vegetation poke through all the wedges. I used to think the rocks were too much, but over the years I've started noticing how the water running down their surfaces makes them change colors. They look almost gold against the sunlight. I never knew something as still as stone could shimmer with so much motion.

By the time we arrive, the ticket booth is empty, since it's after hours. Leslie jumps over the turnstile, and I sit on top and twist myself over it. Just past the entrance, we arrive at a fountain with a statue of a mermaid in the center—it's the same one I got in wax replica at the souvenir shop all those years ago.

"Can I help you ladies?" A woman in a teal jumpsuit crosses the breezeway with a flashlight and a walkie-talkie at her waist.

"We're just picking up my sister. She's a mermaid," Leslie says.

The woman points to her left, down a concrete pathway with ship rope partitions along the edges. "They're just about to begin the last act. Maybe you'll catch the tail end of practice."

We thank her as we rush toward the theater. I wonder if everyone that works here purposely speaks in mermaid puns, or if it's just an instinct they can't help. When we get to the large double doors, Leslie cracks one open and a slice of cold air blows into our faces.

"Tanya said we should sit in the back row," Leslie whispers. It's like we're arriving late to a movie, our bodies crouched low as we walk down the aisle. Instead of the beam of a projector, though, light splashes across the limestone walls that enclose us as the curtains draw open to reveal the glass and the underwater view of the springs beyond it. A vintage show tune begins playing over the speakers, and a group of five mermaids swim into view in perfect synch.

I inhale and start counting.

One Mississippi.

Two Mississippi.

I get to thirty Mississippi, and I don't even miss the air.

"She looks unreal," Leslie whispers.

But it's the opposite. As Tanya dances in the far left corner of the formation, she moves like she was born in her shimmery pink tail. She does two backflips, her fins gently undulating through the clear water, and then, one by one, each of the mermaids glide across the windows before us. They're naturals.

I exhale and my whole body expands.

"Hallie! Relax your shoulders." A woman sitting in the front row yells into a mic that must be connected to an underwater speaker, because immediately, a blond mermaid drops her shoulders.

"Lila, what's with all the bubbles? And, Tanya! You're off by a half beat. Speed it up."

They scramble like fish in a tank startled by a tap on the glass. They rush back to their places, grab a quick sip of air from the hoses they hold in their hands, and wait for the music to start again.

"Is that . . . Barb?" I ask.

Leslie nods. "The living legend."

I've read all about the troupe's director on the pictures they post on social. She was a mermaid in the 1970s, during Mermaid Cove's biggest slump. Everyone knows that when Disney World opened, this place could barely compete. It's a miracle the shows survived at all. Now they only have daily performances in the summer and on the weekends during the off-season, and they mainly stay afloat by charging admission for the waterslide and renting out the auditorium for events. It's no golden age of the early '60s, but they have a cultish following now. Myself and Leslie included.

"Toes! Chins!" Barb marks the choreography. She has grey hair and thin, leathery skin that looks like it's tan year-round. She wears purple yoga pants with fish-scale patterns that catch the light as she marches out of the theater. I immediately want a pair.

"It's all wrong. Where's the passion? The fantasy?" Her voice fades as Leslie and I are left in the darkened silence. Her words echo, reminding me of what Alex said about this place being manufactured fantasy.

"That can't be it. Are they done?" The theater is freezing. There aren't enough bodies in this space to justify all the AC, so I just sit there, rubbing my arms while my teeth chatter audibly. Through the glass, the mermaids look at each other with the sad eyes of children who just disappointed their mother. A girl in a black sequined top sucks on her air hose while another adjusts her tail. I wonder if the material itches; I've always imagined it'd be like a second skin.

Tanya, having just taken another breath of air, goes up to the glass and cups her face with her hands against it, like she's trying to look through.

"Let's get closer," Leslie says.

I follow her to the front row. We wave at Tanya, though I doubt she can really make us out with the water blurring her vision. Her face is held in a perfect smile, and her hands are Barbie-esque as she uses her arms to stay in place. When she finally joins the other mermaids, they start making quick little gestures at one another, like they have their own language, their own weightless world. They swim out of our view, and I'm left feeling like I'm in an altered reality where everything that's real and beautiful is underwater. All I can do is watch from this dry, heavy place.

"Maybe we should go. It's kind of creepy with no one else around," I say. We're literally about thirty feet underground. The water is so clear that the visibility stretches for miles. Schools of colorless fish swim past and in the distance, and a slow-moving blob of mass that must be a manatee catches my eye. But on this side of the glass, without a show or rehearsal going on, the space feels cold, musty, and abandoned.

"Barb's probably tearing them a new one," Leslie says. "They'll be back."

I try to pass the time by checking my phone, but there's no service.

A few minutes later the music starts and the rehearsal resumes, but this time Tanya's movements seem hesitant and overly measured.

"Is your sister okay?" I whisper to Leslie.

"Can I help you?"

A booming voice startles us. Barb reenters through the same place she left. "This is a private rehearsal. Who are you here with?"

"No one," Leslie says. "We were just leaving."

We start running before she can ask any more questions, all the way to the park's entrance, until I signal for Leslie to slow down.

"Can we just wait for her here?" I say, sitting on the curved bar of a bicycle rack. Just because I can run doesn't mean I should, and besides, I detest doing it because apparently, I run weird—though I had no idea until the day Chelsea Meadows pointed it out to the entire fifth grade during PE.

Leslie nods and goes to grab us a couple of drinks from the vending machine. Now that we're aboveground, all my messages come in at the same time. One's from Mami, reminding me dinner's at six.

And there's two scrolls' worth from Alex. I hadn't expected to be this excited about hearing from him, but my thumbs are sweaty as I hold my phone tight, smiling at all the little notes he left me.

He wants to know if he can book me for another tour.

He asks if I have experience swimming through a pool of packing peanuts, because his new apartment is drowning in them.

On his third message, he sends a selfie. It's just him next to a giant picture of a gator. He has his hand over the gator's head like he's petting it, and he's making a scared face, with his bottom lip turned down.

I think I found your little friend. All grown up?

TEARS, I write. Where the hell'd you find a giant picture of an alligator?

Haven't you heard? They're everywhere here. NBD.

I take about fifteen selfies before settling on one that looks cute enough to send him. It's just me with my hand in my hair, posing like one of the mermaids in a poster behind me.

Guess where I am today?

Hanging out in your natural habitat?

45

Ugh. This guy. This guy's gonna make me fall for him, isn't he?

I dim my screen because I don't have a clever answer for him yet. There's always all this pressure around the first few texts. Like you're trying to sound effortlessly fascinating, but casual, so you keep things light and talk about nothing. Except it has to sound like interesting nothing. Witty-banter nothing. Anything-to-feed-the-novelty-of-whatever-this-is nothing.

When Leslie gets back, she's carrying two Coke Zeros and wearing a secretive grin on her face.

"You won't believe what I just found out." She does a little leap and lands on one leg as she hands me a can.

"What?"

"Tanya just texted me. She has to stay late, so she's going to get a ride with someone else, but . . ." Her eyes are practically shimmering. I know she's stretching the moment for dramatic effect, waiting for me to play along.

"And?"

"They're holding. Auditions. For new mermaids." She punctuates each pause with a flick of her wrists.

"You're kidding!"

"Nope," she says, making a *pop* sound.

"Did Tanya say that?"

"Yep. She said that's why Barb was so pissed at rehearsals today. One of the mermaids got injured yesterday, so now their formation is completely off. They need to replace her asap."

This is such a huge deal. Mermaid Cove auditions almost *never* happen. They hold them whenever there's a need for new people, but it's not exactly a high turnover job. In all the years I've been following them, they've held auditions three times. I've never been old enough to be eligible, though, and even if my parents had miraculously decided to let me go for it, we barely got our social security cards and visas sorted out—for real, finally—a few weeks ago. Mami cried that day by the mailbox. She said, *So many things are possible now.* Then she placed all the paperwork in the fireproof lockbox where she keeps our important documents.

Now, out of nowhere, I'm old enough and eligible to be a mermaid.

"So . . . you're going to try out, right?"

And my parents are still my parents.

I have to grip the bar I'm sitting on because suddenly everything feels unsteady. "But what about our Epic Pre-Senior Year Plans?" I ask. Leslie's come up with a million ways for us to spend the next couple of months, and they all involve different flavors of nothing.

She lets out a high-pitched scoff. "Our summer of loitering? I just said that so you wouldn't feel bad about not getting a job. Just because I plan on working solely on my tan doesn't mean you have to."

"When are the tryouts?"

"Next week."

"That soon?!"

"They're in a crunch, I guess. I don't get it. I thought you'd be ecstatic."

"I am." I start walking back to her car. The thing I never told Leslie is how my parents reacted when I told them Tanya was becoming a mermaid the summer between her junior and senior years of college. Even though our town is full of people who know people who once were or who are mermaids, none of us actually knew one. People come from all over the world to become mermaids; they're as mythical here as they are in the stories.

That girl has no ambition. She's throwing away her future on a childish dream, Papi said. To him, the only acceptable ways for a young person to spend their summer involve prepping for the "real" world. Which is why I spent the summer before junior year taking an SAT course he worked months of extra shifts to pay for. And why this summer was supposed to be all about me getting a job or an internship that would look good on my college applications.

Emphasis on *supposed to.* Thanks to our good old trusty Immigration Services Agency and a filing error that had Mami on edge for months, our green cards got delayed yet again. By the time they finally sorted it out, it was too late; all the good internships and summer jobs were taken. I've sent out a few applications since then, though. There was an opening for a part-time lifeguard at the Y and an internship at the Florida Aquarium, where I would've gotten to help rescued sea animals who are victims to our polluted waters and awful, inconsiderate boaters. But I applied and got no response. It's like I've been cursed by the paperwork gods—everything I send goes straight into a dark abyss.

"So you're trying out, right?" Leslie says again as she catches up with me.

I'm so upset to have this thrown at me. "How am I supposed to figure this out in a week?"

"Figure what out?"

"Nothing. Everything."

We get into the car, and Leslie starts pulling out of the parking lot. I cross my arms and stare out the window, completely aware that she's stealing glances at me as she drives.

I think of the stacks of books on my nightstand, how they tower over me every night as I fall asleep, reminding me that none of my dreams are good enough to justify all my parents' sacrifices. They want me focused on *goals instead of boys,* or whatever they imagine should be *the most important thing in my life* right now. Mami's latest piece of vague advice, after I complained about all my job inquiries going unanswered, is to stop waiting.

"Ponte las pilas," she said as she handed me a load of laundry to fold. "Make it so no one can ignore you."

Somehow I doubt mermaiding is what she had in mind.

"What about Barb?" I don't know why I even ask.

"What about her?" Leslie says.

"You said so yourself. She's a total sea bitch. A, quote, 'washed-up former fish with a superiority complex.'"

"Who you'd die to work with."

"How many spots are there?" I ask. "If it's only one, then you should be the one who auditions."

"Verónica," she says, each syllable deadpan, like she's already bored of my excuses. "You know that's not my thing. Watching their videos on repeat, yes. Swimming all day, no. That's your department."

I let out a sigh that sounds more like an exasperated grunt.

"Fine. I'll think about it," I say, just to get Leslie to shut up. I don't think I've ever both wanted and dreaded something so badly. It's like someone just wrapped all my dreams into a giant ball and threw it at my chest, but it's full of broken glass when I catch it. No matter what I do, this will hurt.

We pass a picture of the original mermaids as we exit, and I try to actually imagine myself in their place. They have such bright, carefree faces. Light skin, light eyes, light hair, and these perfectly symmetrical bodies. I have exactly none of those qualities. Zero.

"You really think I'd make it?" I say.

"Do you even have to ask?"

"I'm not ready."

"You were born ready."

"I was born a lot of things."

"Ronnie. You've got this. You've wanted it forever."

I can't argue with that. But what if want is not enough?

"My parents would kill me if they found out," I say.

"They're at work all day. What's the worst that could happen?"

Sometimes Leslie just doesn't get it. She doesn't know what it's like to have parents who constantly remind you, either in words or by actions, that the endless hard work they endure in this country is all so you can have a better life than they did. That as a result, subconsciously you're always measuring, comparing, asking, am I doing enough to justify what they gave up to come here? You carry all their dreams into your future, which is somehow also theirs, wrapped up in their past and present. You fear making mistakes. You dread coming up short of their expectations. And you can think of nothing worse than disappointing them, because in this family, the opposite of pride isn't shame.

It's guilt.

The unbearable regret of knowing it's your fault that their sacrifice wasn't worth it.

Dysplasia: dys·pla·sia

1. (n.) abnormal growth or development
2. (n. VR) the state of being displaced, inside and outside of your body

Chapter 6

MY WHOLE LIFE THEY'VE EXPLAINED IT to me like I'm a child.

Make a fist with one hand and cover it with the other.

Pretend paper just beat rock.

This is a normal, healthy hip in its socket, doctors say.

Now move the fist out slowly, toward the edge of the hand that covers it, until it's barely hanging on by what looks like some miracle of gravity.

This is my hip.

Not normal.

Not healthy.

Practically unhinged.

Except not at all like a rock in a game of rock-paper-scissors, because that rock is supposed to be strong and my bone is more like limestone, fragile and freckled with holes.

The way they talk about it, sometimes I don't know how I'm still standing.

How I'm literally standing is off. Chueca. Crooked. I've never liked the word in either language. In Spanish, it's a *tsk* on your tongue, something to hide in shame. How dare my body not grow in a straight line? And why should it matter, anyway, when so many things in nature—rivers and trees and shorelines and mountains—are free to be imperfect?

No one calls a flower chueca as it bends its way toward the sky.

Then there's the English. Crooked cops, crooked bones, crooked politicians, crooked systems. My body gets lumped in with all of them like it's morally wrong.

Sometimes they've called it dislocated, except fixing it isn't as simple as snapping it back into place. The more technical term sounds like something you'd name a continent: Dysplasia, like a floating mass of land with no home.

And yes, it's the thing that dogs get. Leslie's mini pinscher has dysplasia on both hips. He's had almost as many surgeries as I've had—four to my maybe five or six. It's hard to tell, because a few of them happened when I was a baby, and my parents are never specific about how many. When I ask they just say "a series," like it's a nameless TV show they never want to rewatch.

"How many seasons?" I asked once. They didn't laugh, and I resorted to calling them the Lost Peru Surgery Series. The ones that happened before we moved to Central Florida when I was three. The ones that, like everything else about my birthplace, I can never remember.

But back to Leslie's dog. His name is Jester, and he always smells like toe and swamp water and when Leslie first learned that I have the same hip condition as him, she just shrugged and said, "Oh. Okay." She didn't do that crinkly thing with her nose that people do when they find out. She didn't say *I thought it was only in dogs.* She didn't stare at my legs, or try so hard *not* to stare that it's essentially the same thing. She didn't call my scars ugly like the first boy I ever liked did.

Leslie's my only friend who's stuck around through the thick of it. She's seen me just come out of surgery, with the anesthesia smell still in my hair and lungs. Every time I've been in casts and wheelchairs and crutches, she hasn't disappeared for several weeks until I can hang out at places convenient to her again. She's the only person who's ever treated my surgeries as the least interesting thing about me.

We pull up to the parking spot in front of my apartment. It's usually empty because we used to have two cars, but shortly after my last surgery, my parents sold one. Papi insisted it had nothing to do with the hospital bills, just that it made no sense to have the added car payment when Mami's job at the smoothie shop is within walking distance. I don't buy it, though. It's been three and a half years, and nearly every time I stop by our mailbox, there's a bill from the hospital or the anesthesiologist or my orthopedist, and it makes me feel like my surgery splintered off into a bunch of mini procedures, each of them costing us an arm and a leg.

Which is a terrible expression, now that I think of it.

"Promise you'll think about the tryouts. I bet Tanya can help you train," Leslie says.

"Okay. All right," I say, my voice teetering on the edge of annoyed. I get out and hop over the yellow parking block in front of our spot. It's marked RESERVED in black stenciled letters, except someone messed it up and spelled it *resvered*. Those three misplaced letters are the bane of Mami's existence; when we first moved in, she said of course it'd be us, one of the few Latinx families in this entire apartment complex, with a parking spot that makes us look like we don't speak proper English.

Mami's really big on us speaking proper English. And Spanish. She's always saying we need to show people we belong here, but not so much that we become gringas. To her, that means we shouldn't call attention to ourselves. We should blend in but also remain connected to our roots. It doesn't make any sense. Sometimes I feel like being bicultural means having to be perfect for two groups of people instead of simply being accepted as part of both.

Inside our apartment, Mami's making dinner while my sister sets the table. It smells like cilantro, onions, and chicken, which can only mean she's made my favorite, arroz con pollo. It sounds basic, but the whole dish is simmered in herbs until every grain of rice turns green. I feel bad for people who think cilantro tastes like soap, especially if they're Peruvian. We put that shit in everything.

"Here," Mami says, handing me a wooden bowl. "La ensalada."

"Good evening to you, too," I say.

"Very funny. You're late. And you know it's the one who arrives who says hello."

"Yeah, Vero," Dani says. "Who do you think you are, coming in here como si fueras un caballo?" She raises her arm dramatically and accentuates each vowel in her best imitation of our mom as a telenovela star. Mami's always calling our friends "rude as horses," barging in without so much as a hello. Dani's impression is on point, but instead of cracking a smile, I just focus on chopping the tomatoes.

"What did you and Leslie do today?" Mami asks. Since Papi's not around, I tell her we stopped by Tanya's rehearsal. Her face lights up, eyes full of curiosity, as she says "¿Viste a su hermana nadar?"

I nod apprehensively, wondering if this is a trick question. It's been a while since Mami's smiled at me like we share something in common. Most of the time when I catch her glancing at me, it's like she's looking at a dead plant, a mixture of sadness and hopelessness wrestling across her face.

"¿Y?" she says, egging me on with a gentle tap of a wooden spoon against my shoulder. "How was it?"

"It was amazing. We caught part of their routine, and Tanya was in full costume: mermaid tail, makeup, everything."

"Full nothing. Those girls go around media-calatas." My father walks into our conversation with the same ease he walks into the room—like it belongs to him. Just like that, Mami clears her throat and the aura of disapproval is back.

"They're in bikini tops and a tail, Papi. If anything, they're half *covered,* not half naked," Dani says. I stay quiet because it's pointless; he's always finding new ways to criticize the mermaids, though this particular line feels different.

He sits on the couch and turns on the TV. In our apartment, the living room and dining room are one large room, and the kitchen has a hole in the wall, like a wide-open mouth that connects one space to the other. The fragmented sounds of commercials, novelas, and news reports come in and out as he starts flipping through the channels.

"Doesn't matter. You know what they say about sirenas, don't you? They lure men into the ocean. Seduce them in the water. It's no way for a young girl to behave." His eyes land pointedly on me, and there it is. He's not just talking about the mermaids after all. Like everything else he says lately, it's another veiled attempt to remind me of my misadventures in the hot tub with Jeremy. Like I could ever truly forget.

If Dani catches it, though, she doesn't let on. Her face goes blank and her voice floods with sarcasm as she says, "You know they're not actually real, right?"

"Realmente ridículas." He chuckles lightly at his own little joke, but I don't join him. He may think he's making fun of the mermaids, but it feels like he's laughing at me.

Dani starts folding napkins into triangles. "They're artists, Papi. I heard they choreograph all their own routines, right, Vero?"

I let the silverware clang loudly as I set the table. I no longer like where she's going with this. "What's your point?"

She gives me a mischievous grin and whispers, "Leslie texted me."

I give her my most threatening death stare. I'm not ready to broach the subject of the auditions with my parents, but apparently she and Leslie have decided I have no say in the matter at all. Dani just continues blabbering as we sit down to eat. "Not just anyone can become a mermaid. They're super skilled and disciplined."

Now Papi's getting annoyed; I can tell because he starts stabbing his food and chewing with his mouth open. I wish Dani would just drop this and leave me out of it.

"What kind of skills and discipline does it take to hold your breath and splash around all day?"

"Edgar, no seas vulgar," Mami says, though she means his table manners, not how condescending he's being toward female athletes. There are lines we don't cross in my family, but most of them involve appearances instead of actual respect.

"I splash around every day," I say. "Isn't that why we moved here?"

So much for dropping the subject.

"That's different. Those are medical purposes." He groans as he adjusts in his chair, super exaggerated, like his bones are cracking one by one.

"I think I'd make a good mermaid," I say under my breath.

"¿Qué dijiste?" Papi asks.

"She says she'd make a good mermaid," Dani says.

"Ay, Vero, no empieces," Mami says.

I turn my head to give Dani an angry stare. *I'm* not the one who started anything.

"Enough of this. You need to be focused on getting a real job. One that'll stand out to colleges."

I'm about to retort that mermaiding would definitely stand out when Papi flicks his wrist and says, "Plus, no self-respecting daughter of mine is going to splash around in a pool, half naked"—he looks down his nose right at me, as if it's a name he's calling me—"for money. Punto."

So that's that. The real truth comes out. Papi thinks me being a mermaid would be equivalent to me selling my body. But I know he's implying a different word, a word so ugly it makes me see red. So much for respect. So much for men who treat women and girls right because they have wives and daughters. It all goes out the window the second we try doing something with our bodies that doesn't have their stamp of approval.

"It's not a pool. It's a freshwater spring," I say. Papi glares at me. Mami drops her fork on her plate.

"Vero. Really?" Dani whispers.

Because, I know, it was a pointless excuse to get the last word in. But I couldn't help it.

We keep quiet for much of our dinner, but then our upstairs neighbors start shouting and it sounds like someone's walking around in heels and rearranging furniture. They moved in three months ago, and it's been nothing but random noises at all hours.

"I've asked them twice, nicely," Mami says. "I even made them alfajores last time. That woman looked at them and said no thanks. That she works in fitness."

"That's probably what she's doing," Dani says. "Shooting videos."

"Videos? This is getting ridiculous." Mami is firmly in the social-media-is-going-to-rot-our-brains camp. She and Papi share a Facebook account, and even then, they only check it once a month to see pictures of our tíos and primos in Peru. Dani and I don't bother arguing with Mami, because it means she and Papi don't poke around our profiles like some of our friends' parents do. It's the one thing in our lives our parents aren't super strict about, but it still doesn't make up for our ridiculously early curfew, the fact that we're not allowed to go to sleepovers, or how hypervigilant they are about our clothes and makeup.

"She's not going to stop making noise," I say. "We might as well just move. We can get an A3, like Leslie. They're really spacious. And not that much more expensive than what we pay now."

"Oh? And how do you know that?" Papi asks.

"The blueprints are framed in the leasing office. I see them every month when Mami sends me to drop off the check." Palmview Lakes has A1 and A2 models, which are both two-bedroom apartments with different square footage. But the A3 is a town house with three bedrooms and a second story, with the master bedroom downstairs.

We live in the A1 model. The smallest and cheapest.

My parents couldn't look less interested, but as usual, I keep going. "I don't know a single other senior who still shares a bedroom with their little sister. And now that Dani's going to be a freshman . . . we'll be at each others' throats."

Dani scoffs, but I know she's not really offended. We've been plotting ways to get our own rooms for years.

"Ay, qué lindo. What I wouldn't give to see my sister even *one* day." We groan in unison. Mami never misses a chance to guilt-trip Dani and me by mentioning how much she misses our Tía Betty back in Peru.

"We can't afford it," Papi says. "If we move, the new management will make us upgrade. They're renovating every unit with new leases. And those townhomes have stairs."

I wish he'd just left it at *we're poor.*

"I can do stairs."

"I know, hijita," Mami says. "But what about next time?"

Next time.

Sometimes I think my hip is like a ticking bomb inside my body, each surgery a failed attempt to disarm it. I thought surgeons' jobs were to fix things, not open you up and cross their fingers that your body will "cooperate" with their procedure. Twice now, they've drilled a giant screw into my femur, left it in for a couple of years, and then operated again to take it out. The idea was to make the head of my bone align properly in its joint, but it didn't work so great the first time, and the jury's still out on the second time. Four surgeries later, I'm tired of all the do-overs. This *has* to be the one that takes, and I'm pretty sure it has, because I've had three and a half years of regular, uneventful checkups. Last time I went in, my doctor said my hip looked like it was doing nicely, and as long as I'm not in any significant pain, he didn't anticipate more surgeries in my near future.

It's not exactly the kind of concrete reassurance I was looking for. How much pain is enough to be significant? How close is enough for the future to be near? I hope it's years, maybe even decades, before I see another operating room again. But my parents act like *near future* could pretty much be tomorrow. I wish they could have more faith in me. I wish I could prove them wrong.

"Next time could be years from now. I'll probably have moved out by then."

The same amused kind of doubt comes over my parents' faces, and maybe I'm being paranoid, but I swear I see a glimmer of something unspoken pass between their eyes.

"En serio, I'd manage. I do fine with stairs." I wonder how many times I have to say it for them to believe me.

The thing is, my parents wouldn't understand. Day to day, I actually *do* do fine with stairs, by my standards and not theirs. Maybe not go-up-eight-stories-in-a-row fine or wear-heels-up-and-down-the-stairs fine, but I can climb a flight without any really big issues, and really, what more do they want? Mami and Papi swear they know what's best for me, but how can they? My body has all these quirks and conditions no one understands but me.

Correction: no one *tries* to understand. Because as much as people say they want to accommodate me (at restaurants or stores or school), they rarely listen to what I really want; they just assume they know what I need. They say they want me to feel *comfortable*—not happy, or fully supported—just fine, satisfied enough that I'm not in any pain. Which feels like a low bar to me. Like maybe it's more about their comfort than mine. Like maybe what they're really saying is: What do we have to do to make you not complain?

"Pásame la sal," Papi says, raising his chin and eyebrows toward the salt—a clear indication that he's moved on from this topic of conversation. I say nothing as I pass him the tiny silver shaker that's been in our family for generations. The herbs and ají in my chicken go bland as I contemplate how unfair it all is.

People act surprised by what I can do and surprised by what I can't, as if I'm supposed to exist in this narrow, static margin in between. But my body is a fluid thing. Sometimes it's complicated and inconsistent, but it makes sense because it's mine. My choices. My comfort. My decisions.

If only.

Memory: me·mo·ry
1. (n.) the process by which the mind stores and remembers information
2. (n. VR) a record in the mind that becomes the language of the body

Chapter 7

AN ANNOYINGLY ADORABLE THING about my sister is that she cartwheels everywhere she goes. It's like the invention of walking was not enough for her. We'll be on our way somewhere, and after an arbitrary number of steps, she'll decide, *Let me try this with my hands instead of my feet,* and suddenly her head's replaced by her legs whizzing through the air like turbines.

"So let me get this straight." Her feet swing past me in a perfect curve. "They're holding auditions for your dream job, and you're just like, no thanks."

"I'm not saying no. I'm just saying . . . I don't know."

We're headed toward the pool, where Leslie and Alex are already waiting for us. Right before we left, I made Dani swear not to make a big deal out of the auditions or the fact that I've been talking to Alex, but judging by the way she steps off the sidewalk and cartwheels three times straight from one curb to the other, I'm not so sure she'll keep her promise.

"Okayyyy." She brushes the dirt from the pavement off her palms. She doesn't even seem slightly out of breath. This shouldn't be surprising, since Dani's always been, by default, the athletic one in the family. It's an easy title to earn, considering her competition. "So I guess you have, like, better things to do this summer?" she yells.

I cross the street to catch up to her, uncomfortable with the idea of our conversation being so out in the open. "Maybe I do."

"Like what?"

"Seriously? Please don't turn into one of those people, Dani."

"One of what people?"

"Our parents. All our friends' parents. Our neighbors. Everything's all about plans with them. Everything has to be calculated, and practical, and responsible. Like nothing I want to do with my life is good enough. They're all, *Oh, well, Benjamin's taking an internship at a law firm this summer,* and *Julie is going to be a camp counselor.* It's all so boring."

"They're just making small talk."

"*Very* small talk. You're lucky they're not obsessed with what *you're* doing this summer."

"You honestly think . . . You know what? Never mind. Stop trying to change the subject. I'm just trying to look out for you."

When I don't say anything, she slows down so that I'm a few steps ahead of her.

"Don't do that," I say.

"Do what?"

"You know what." I can feel her gaze, observing my gait. It's a habit of Mami's she's picked up: watching me walk. The two of them keep an eye on my body like it's the weather and they're trying to get the forecast. Sometimes, without my even noticing, my limp will be super obvious because I've been walking longer than usual. Other times, my hip becomes stiff and hurts for no apparent reason, and I know I must look like the Tin Man in *The Wizard of Oz* when he's searching for his squirt can of oil. But it's never anything out of the ordinary, never enough to make my family or the doctors worry. I wish instead of trying to gauge from my limp, they'd just ask me outright how I'm feeling. Mami does it because she's always worried about money, always calculating what we can and can't afford. But what's Dani's excuse?

"I'm fine! I swear. I have no pain. Except maybe . . . in my neck?" I place my hand on my shoulder and make a circle with my head. She leans in to get a look, and just as she does, I add, "Oh wait. No, it's just you. You're the pain."

"L. O. L. That's super lame."

"Dani!"

"Shit. Sorry, I forget sometimes."

I can't hear that word without my blood boiling. When did a word that describes a person who limps become synonymous with boring and bad and uncool? People can say they're two different things, but I know language doesn't evolve by accident.

When I was recovering from my surgery when I was eleven, my teacher had me read *David Copperfield*. Her name was Pat, and she came to our house three times a week, and Mami would make her tea while she and I sat at the dining room table, going over fractions and word problems and short stories—whatever my classes at school were doing, except tailored to me, one-on-one.

In the book, there's a character who's writing his own dictionary, so Pat made me start writing my own. I'd never thought about the dictionary being written before. In my mind it was just something that had always existed, like the Bible or the map of the world that hangs in our bedroom. But it turns out words don't just have meaning, they're given meaning. It turns out we define things by how we see them. By how we feel about them.

I kept going with the dictionary, even after my homeschooling ended. I write an established definition on top, and then I write my own version as the second one, with my initials right next to it: VR. It's kind of an on-and-off thing; I only add to it when I think of a word that intrigues me. Words I love or words I long to redefine. But I haven't written an entry for *lame* yet. Maybe there are some words that are too far gone. Past redeeming or reclaiming, all they do is speak in daggers. This one just gets tossed around like it's nothing, always followed by a laugh. It's hard not take it personally. If it were up to the rest of the world, would the synonym of *lame* just be my name?

"Must be nice to forget," I say.

"Vero. You know I didn't mean it like that."

I shake my head. "Whatever, it's fine."

Which it's obviously not.

Dani keeps quiet until we arrive at the clubhouse, then makes a dash for the vending machines by the water fountain. They still have handwritten OUT OF ORDER signs taped across the front, but Dani ignores them and holds her eye up to the coin slot as if it were a peephole in a door.

"I knew it. Check this out."

Inside the opening, dozens of coins are piled one on top of the other, stuck on their way down the chute.

"What's your point? We can't get to them."

"One sec."

She rips two strands of a palm leaf out of a plant by the tennis courts. They're sturdy enough for her to clasp together like tweezers, and she slides them through the slot with surgeonlike precision.

"Who taught you this?"

"No one," she says, a little too quickly.

I'm about to repeat the question when we hear the faintest jingle of change. Several quarters, then two dimes, and a bunch of nickels fall into her open palm.

It's pretty ingenious. Dani and I don't exactly have an allowance; we just ask our parents for money when we want it,

68

but it always comes with twenty questions: ¿Para qué? ¿Y por qué? ¿Y con quién? So we try to stretch every dollar down to the last penny.

"You little thief," I say.

"It's not stealing if it's just going back into the machine." She races up the stairs toward the gym, and I go after her. I may not be able to cartwheel for miles, but my legs are still longer than hers and I can sprint pretty fast if I feel like it.

"You still upset at me?" she asks when we get to the top.

"What do you think?" I say, popping open a can of iced tea.

It's impossible to stay mad at Dani for long.

Downstairs by the pool entrance, there's a giant sign at the gate that says:

NO FOOD OR DRINKS.
NO UNATTENDED CHILDREN.
NO SMOKING.
NO LIFEGUARD ON DUTY.
SWIM AT YOUR OWN RISK.

On the other side of the gate, I see Leslie lying on one of many pink-and-yellow-striped loungers, and sitting right next to her is Alex. He's got his elbows on his knees and his chin on his hands as they talk, but he sits up and smiles when he sees me.

"Oh good, you two already met," I say, happy to skip any awkward introductions.

"Bob came over and did the thing," Alex says. "He seems very devoted to being my official welcome committee."

"He wishes he was an official many things," I say.

"And we were totally talking about you, in case you were wondering," Leslie says, dipping her sunglasses at me.

"I'd expect nothing less." I glare at her playfully and grab the lounger next to Alex. "Anyways, sorry we're late. Dani took forever to shave her legs."

"Vero!"

"What? It's true."

Dani turned fourteen a few weeks ago, which means my parents finally let her start shaving her legs—a whole year before they ever let me do it. Even then, Mami only allowed my shins, as if my calves were miraculously hairless. The next day on the bus ride to school, the boy across the aisle couldn't stop making fun of the vertical line of hair that ran from behind my ankles up to the back of my knees. I took a picture of my calf and sent it to my mom. *It's bad enough kids stare at my scar, now I have to worry about this?* That did the trick. Guilt trips are powerful motivators in my family, and I learned from the very best: Mami and el niño Jesusito. You try stepping slightly out of line with your mom's disappointed voice in your head saying, *What would baby Jesus want you to do?* at any tiny, insignificant little thing. The only way to turn it off is to turn it around on them.

After that, my parents changed their shaving policy, then, apparently, changed it once again for Dani. She has so much to thank me for, she doesn't even know. Still, she's been waiting so long for this rite of passage that she treats it like a sacred ritual. It takes an utterly unreasonable amount of time.

"Ooh la la," Leslie says. "Dani's fresh and sexy calves have officially arrived!"

"Shut. Up." She tosses her towel at Leslie's face. Alex looks amused but doesn't say anything as he leans in toward my ear. "I'm guessing this is an inside joke?" he whispers.

I nod, letting my ear brush up against his lips. Nothing about our conversation really needs to be kept a secret, but there's something so delicious about being close to him.

"My mom won't let my sister shave past her knees," I whisper back. "Not till she's seventeen."

"Ah. I see."

"It's so boys won't be encouraged to let their hands wander," I say out loud, wiggling my fingers over the air above his legs.

Dani shoots me her most vicious STFU look as Alex tries to suppress a laugh.

"I don't know. I wouldn't let it stop me. As long as you were fine with it, of course."

Well. This just got intense real fast. The other day, I wasn't sure if Alex was flirting with me, but now it's undeniable. I flip my hair over my left temple and catch sight of the hot tub in our periphery. That night in the hot tub,

Jeremy flirted with quiet, pointed looks and barely spoke to me. And it worked and it was fun until it translated to my silence. He was so quick to assume my saying nothing meant I was fine that I felt like saying anything to contradict him would be . . . impolite. It sounds ridiculous, the more I think about it. We're taught that being rude is *the* worst possible thing a girl can be, but what about guys like Jeremy? Manners were the last thing on his mind that night in the hot tub. No *pleases* and *thank-yous* there. Not even an *I'm sorry for ruining your night*. For ruining my nights, and days. All these random moments when I just run over and over it in my mind.

I clear my throat. I just want to stop thinking about it, but my parents' voices are practically filling up the pool right now, telling me they better never catch me like that in the water again. *Good girls don't put themselves in the kinds of positions where boys can take advantage of them.*

It's why I could never tell my parents what happened. They'd probably say it was my fault.

But this moment with Alex feels so different. Unlike Jeremy, Alex is direct. Fresco, as my dad would call him, except that would make him too direct, almost shameless, whereas . . . this. Is a conversation. No hidden meanings in the unspoken. No second-guessing his words or mine, for that matter.

He's actually waiting for me to respond to what he just said about wandering hands.

It feels nice. New.

"I would be very fine with it," I say.

He smiles and starts emptying the pockets of his swim trucks, pulling out his keys and a bit of change, and a couple of sticks of gum. He pops one, and says, "Want some?"

His words come out minty and dry, the flavor so fresh it's aseptic. I almost choke on the familiarity of the scent. I thought only anesthesia smelled this way, but here it is flooding the air between us. It makes my lungs grow cold. It makes me feel like I'm drowning.

"No thanks, I'm good." Without thinking, I've placed the bag over my left hip to block Alex's view of it. "Hey, so, unrelated but not really, is that I have some scars from these surgeries I had on my hip, but it's fine now, and I just wanted you to know in case you were ever wondering." The words tumble out in one breath as I poke around my belongings to avoid looking at him. When I finally set the bag down, my heart's at attention in my throat, waiting for him to respond. To stare, to laugh, to anything.

He only looks into my eyes and says, "Okay. Thanks for telling me."

And it's weird, because it's just one sentence. But no one's ever expressed gratitude for me sharing this small part of me. They've just always asked, as if I owed them an explanation. Or assumed they knew my story.

We lie back side by side in our loungers, our hands almost touching in the space between them like a nearly finished bridge. I feel every nerve on my left pinkie start to tingle, relishing the nearness of his aura. When I close my eyes, the silhouette of the sun glows through, a pink neon ball that flutters and flashes, turning blue and green and back to pink.

"Hey." Alex sits up and tugs gently at my arm. "Do you want to go in the water with me?"

It's sweet the way he says it, like he's asking me out on a date. He even wads up his gum in its leftover wrapper, like it's a meal that he doesn't want to chew in the water.

We slip into the pool slowly, his stomach contracting at the sudden coolness of the water. I submerge myself without hesitation and come up, miming like I'm going to splash him. He starts to back away but then he jumps in after me, and soon I'm swimming to the deep end, betting him he can't catch me. His hand only grazes my shoulder when we stop at the pool's edge to catch our breath. It's a light, soft tap, but it feels like a wave coming over me.

"So this is what Florida people do for fun?" he finally says.

"Basically. Yeah."

I push myself off the wall, and he does the same. We don't move fast or make much of a splash, we just allow ourselves to kind of float back and forth.

"You know you never answered my question the other day."

"Which one?"

"About booking you for the full Verónica tour."

I let out a light laugh. "That's because there's not much to show. There's a few touristy spots . . ."

"Not those. I was thinking, what about more of your favorite random places around town? I want to see our home the way you see it."

Our home. "And how's that?"

"Like it's a part of you. Like you have history here."

My heart. I thought hearts skipping a beat was a metaphor, and a cheesy one at that . . . but mine actually pauses a second, as if trying to synch up with his. No one's ever looked at this place and seen my stories in it. They've never even called it mine. I feel like Alex just drew me onto a map, saw me as part of the landscape instead of an outside object. Like I'm a point with actual coordinates.

"All my favorites involve water," I finally say.

"That's fine. I like swimming with you."

I dip my burning cheeks into the water. I feel like I could swim with him all day. Like I could do it all summer. Maybe that will be the new plan. Maybe I'll show him my favorite places and we'll swim until our fingertips turn soft as clay. Until we melt into each other, waiting for the sun to make us solid again.

Suffocate: suf·fo·cate

1. (v.) to deprive of oxygen by force
2. (v. VR) to take the life out of someone with too much pressure

Chapter 8

WE EVENTUALLY END UP BACK in the deep end, except this time we hold still. We draw close. We're out in the open and yet completely submerged. The ripples our bodies form in the water pulse away from us and then contract.

Alex holds on to one side of the metal ladder while I hook my arm around the other. My heart and breath race, and I know it's not from the leisurely, quiet swim we just took around the pool. It's like we've disappeared into our own universe, eyes locked, two bodies floating inevitably close, caught in each other's gravity. I close my eyes inches away from his lips.

"Verónica!"

My entire body freezes.

"Qué. Haces. Aquí."

I look up to see my father's dark, fuming figure tower

ing over us against the baby blue sky. It's impossible to see his face, but it's unnecessary—his look is one that's buried in my memory. It surfaces like a rubber ball popping out of the water.

"Sal de ahí. Now." He glares at Alex as he says this one word, making clear that not only does he speak English, he barks it.

Immediately, I pull myself out of the pool like he commanded.

"Out like this. In front of everyone." He gestures at the space around us, spanning the pool deck with one arm. I look around. It's just Leslie and Dani. It's just kissing. Not even, thanks to him.

It was almost kissing.

But I know my father doesn't see it this way.

"Who's *this* now?" he says, as if catching me with boys in water is a common occurrence.

"This is Alex. He's just moved here, and I was only—"

"Making him feel welcome?"

I feel the bridge of my nose burn from the buildup of anger. Everything that only seconds ago felt warm and alive feels like it's turning to rot inside of me. I want to yell, *What are you implying?* but I already know the answer.

Alex starts to say hello, but Papi cuts him off and turns to me.

"I don't have time for this. Get your things. We'll talk about this on the way to the hospital."

"The hospital?"

"You have your checkup today. Your mother thought it was tomorrow."

I start toweling off so vigorously my skin aches. Of course my checkup would be today. Of course it'd interrupt anything good in my life.

"¿Qué pasó? We called you and Danitza thousands of times," Papi adds.

Dani and Leslie have already packed up all our things. They know as well as I do how much trouble I'm in. Everything with him is extremes. A few missed calls become a thousand. An almost kiss becomes a sin. When I was eight and drew a picture of a naked man and woman out of pure curiosity, my father told me good daughters don't do that. Then my mom pulled me aside and said, *Do you know what promiscua means?* It means a girl that is easy but ends up having a hard life. A girl who gives her body to others but can never have it back for herself.

They laid the shame on me super thick. It's messed up, considering I was just a kid, but even though I know this on an intellectual level, it doesn't stop me from feeling afraid of my body and all the things it craves.

"Excuse me, Mr. Rentería?" Alex attempts to introduce himself as he wraps a towel around his waist. He extends his right hand, but my father lets it hang midair. "I just want to say, Verónica and I . . . we weren't doing anything wrong."

"No no no no no." My father waves his hands over his

face and starts laughing. Actually laughing. Then he turns to my sister and says, "¿Y tú? Where were you when all this was happening? Maybe we should stop paying for your phones since neither one of you ever picks up!"

A weak gasp escapes Dani. It's not fair that he's bringing her into this, but my father rarely sees us as two people. We've always shared the same room, the same clothes, the same rewards and punishments.

"I'm so sorry," I mouth to her as we gather our stuff. I'm so mortified I'm afraid to even look at Alex, even more afraid my dad will only make the situation worse if I do. Leslie signals for me to go and winks as if she'll take care of it. If anyone can explain my parents' constant and complete overreactions to any little thing they deem inappropriate, it's her.

We follow Papi out the gate. He already has the car running by the curb of the poolhouse, with Mami waiting in the passenger's seat. She steps out to push the seat forward so Dani and I can squeeze into the back.

"Here," she says, handing me a change of clothes. "There's no time for you to shower. Qué vergüenza." To Mami, there's nothing more humiliating than me not being squeaky clean in my gown when the doctor examines me. Nothing except maybe what my father just saw in the pool.

Minutes pass, and I'm shocked he doesn't recount what just happened. Maybe I've finally done it, embarrassed him to the point he can't even bring himself to tell my mother. There are only two other times in my life he's been this ashamed of me. That Night, of course, that night that's kept me perpetually in hot water—and the one time I finally broke down crying before one of my surgeries. I was twelve, and my father wanted me to be brave. I was so tired, I just couldn't.

I ended up doing something I'd never done before: I yelled at him to leave me alone. To allow me my tears for once. To not dismiss all the times I never cried because of the one time I finally had to.

He was so taken aback he began pacing around the hospital room. It took him forever to process what I'd just said. As his face went from angry to sad, I wondered if he was about to cry. But he just took my hand, kissed it, and said, "I'm sorry, hijita. You're right. I'm very sorry. Cry if you need to. I'm here."

That was the only time I've ever gotten to see past my father's shell to the softness he guards inside. Mami says he was never taught how to love another way.

Tú sabes cómo son los hombres, is what she always says. Which is such a ridiculous excuse for pardoning boys' and men's behavior. I'm glad Dani and I never had a brother or else he'd get away with murder. If I were just a boy, floating toward a girl in a pool, would my father still call me promiscuous?

We've been in the car for nearly twenty minutes of silence, and the hospital is another forty minutes away. Dani takes a hairbrush out of her tote bag and gestures for me to skooch closer to her. Her hands weave my hair into a loose braid, tying the ends with a yellow scrunchie.

"Done," she says, showing her work to my mom and dad in the rearview mirror. With that simple word, she's made the atmosphere all around us feel lighter. In our most heightened moments, Dani knows how to carry us back to ourselves again.

"When you see Dr. Brown, wish him a belated happy birthday," Mami says.

I don't know how she keeps track of all these things — my orthopedist's birthday, his wife's, the names of his sons and daughters. I'd think it was cute and thoughtful if it didn't feel like an attempt to prove something. Look how nice we can be. Look how human.

I shift myself back toward the window and accidentally kick something tucked beneath my mom's seat. It's a large manila folder where she keeps all my medical records and X-rays. No doubt Dr. Brown's office has backups, but Mami insists on having hard copies of every bit of paperwork. She's like this with all our immigration forms, too. Vigilant down to the last checkbox.

I don't know what else to do with myself, so I start rummaging through the folder.

"Just keep everything in order, Vero," Mami says. The way her head is tilted toward the window, I can tell she's dozing off.

The stack of yellowed papers I've seen countless times is about an inch and a half's worth of doctors' notes, pre-

and post-operation reports, and the occasional Get Well Soon card that my mom sprinkled in for sentimental value. Below that are several films of X-rays, folded over to fit into the envelope, but not enough to leave a crease.

Dani slips one out from the top of my lap. We're driving on the Florida Turnpike, and as she holds it up to the window to let the light through, passengers in the next lane turn their heads, curious to see what she's seeing.

"It's so cool," she says, taking in the lower half of my skeleton. "It's wild to think that we can take pictures of bones."

Mine look, on the one half, just like any other skeleton would look. One long golf club of a femur connected to a pelvis and a knee.

It's when you look to the left that everything gets discombobulated. Nothing's level with its counterpart. The ball of my hip looks like a worn-down eraser at the top of a pencil. The bone is marked with the outline of two large screws that were drilled into it and then extracted three and a half years ago.

"Here, put it back," I tell her. She's fascinated by my images because she's never had to get an X-ray of her own. I start wedging it back into the folder and notice a small postcard at the bottom. It's a black-and-white photograph of the mermaids sitting on a rock, juxtaposed next to a recreation of the same shot with the troupe from all those years ago when we visited. They all wave at the camera, and the words say *Tail us Old as Time. Since 1949.*

"Mami? You kept this?" I didn't know she had hidden mementoes of that day, same as I do.

She looks it over, confused. "Oh. Mira. I used it to write notes about your post-op medications."

When she hands it back to me, I see the flip side is full of her hurried writing. The postcard was nothing more than scrap paper.

"Do you think mermaids would have leg bones beneath their tails?" Dani asks. "Or maybe they'd look more like fish? That wouldn't make as much sense, though. Because their skeletons would be so brittle from the top down. And so strong from the top up." She holds her hands at her waist to demonstrate, as if these are perfectly serious factors to take under consideration. I've never thought of a mermaid's body as an either/or. It's always been their hybridity and fluidity that speaks to me. That they're not just half fish, half human; they're beautifully, completely whole.

"I think . . . you have this whole conversation covered on your own," I say.

"I'm just thinking out loud."

"Think a little less loudly, please," Papi says. For now, at least, it seems he's back to his usual teasing self. You'd think humiliating me in front of my friends and crush is just another Tuesday for him.

As we get off on the exit marked Shands Hospital and approach the main road that runs past the university, Papi points out all the buildings he usually does. The law school, where he got his first on-campus job as a security officer. The stadium, where he got us all discounted tickets to go to Gator Growl when Dani and I were five and eight.

"Quirks of the job, no?" he says proudly.

"Edgar, it's perks," Mami says, proving that she can correct his English in her sleep.

Even though I'm still mad at him, I can't help laughing along with Dani.

"Ya, ya," he says.

"Not so fun now, is it?" Dani relishes the chance to make fun of him the way he makes fun of our flawed Spanish.

"I like this drive better when it's just me."

Papi's one of the university's security managers now, but he mostly works at their pharmacy program's campus, which is closer to home. He claims that the free volleyball games and Gator gear are the best parts of the job, but I know he took it for the health plan. It's not the same insurance that faculty and administrators get because the university outsources their security to the company Papi works for. But he's convinced that being a subcontractor will eventually get him an in, and then maybe, *maybe,* we'll get the tuition discounts for employees' children, even though my counselors are positive I could get a scholarship to most of Florida's public universities. But it's more than the money; my parents would have a heart attack if I ever went to one that was too far from home. I once floated the idea of going to a West Coast school to Mami, saying it'd be nice to study marine biology in the Pacific. She took in this loud, dramatic gasp that made a piece of her spit go down the wrong tube, so she started choking and I had to bring her water, and it all ended with her saying, *See? Me vas a matar.*

So, yeah. Nothing puts a damper on your hopes and dreams like your mom saying it would literally kill her.

"Okay, we're here. Go. We'll find parking while you change. Dani, go with your sister to find a bathroom," Mami says. As if I could possibly get lost here.

Dani and I rush through the main entrance and the lobby toward the elevators. Up to the third floor. Dr. Brown's office is in the pediatric wing, so everywhere we go, the walls are plastered with illustrations of animals and plants and giant Band-Aids. The bathroom has a stepping stool for kids to reach the sink. Fitting, since my parents insist on treating me like a child. Sometimes I think the only reason they still bring me here is to remind me that they're the ones making big decisions about my body. Not me.

I go into one of the stalls and start undressing.

"It's so pointless," I mumble. "The second I get in there, I'm going to have to put on one of those paper gowns anyways."

Dani's standing on the other side of the door, holding my bag for me.

"Your phone's buzzing."

I zip up the blue-and-yellow colorblock sundress Mami

packed for me in a hurry. It's cute, but it's the kind of thing I'd wear to church, not to see the doctor.

I open the door just in time to catch Dani rummaging through my bag for my phone. "Give me that."

"Two minutes before we're late," she says. We make a dash for the doctor's office, and I sign myself in at the receptionist's window. Dani takes a seat in the waiting room, pretending to flip through old copies of *Cosmo* before picking up a *Highlights*.

"What? These things never get old."

I laugh because I, too, want to know what Goofus and Gallant have been up to. But first I check my phone.

There's two new messages. One from Alex:

Sorry if I got you in trouble with your dad. Everything ok with the doctor?

I fire off a bunch of quick replies.

It's fine.

It's a regular semiannual thing.

SO not a big deal.

My parents almost forgot about it.

The second message is from Leslie:

Don't kill me but I asked Tanya if she'd train you and she said yes.

All the blood rushes to my face.

Are you serious right now?!

Is that an angry question or an excited one? she responds, using a couple emojis as if it were multiple choice.

Before I have a chance to reply, my parents enter the waiting room, looking like they just ran a marathon to get here.

"Verónica Rentería?" a young woman calls out. "We're ready for you."

Replace: re·place

1. (v.) to put something new in place of some-thing old
2. (v. VR) a painful process of taking something out of its home

Chapter 9

IT'S NOT ACTUALLY TRUE THAT THE doctor will see me now. I've been through this enough times to know the drill. Dani stays behind in the waiting room while my parents and I head to the examining room. I change into a gown behind an accordion partition, take off my shoes, and step onto one of those scales that measures both my weight and height at the same time. I'm four pounds heavier than last time. I wonder if Mami will check the chart. She never comments on my weight, but sometimes she pinches me lightly under the arm when I'm eating bread and says, Ten cuidado. Like gaining a few pounds is a sharp turn up ahead on the highway, a dangerous thing I should avoid. She says she does it out of love, that Abuela used to do the same to her when she was young. It makes me sad for all of us, all our bodies made to feel less than for decades, for yet another reason that feels arbitrary.

The nurse takes me down the hall to radiology, where I stand up against a wall while a technician positions the X-ray machine. It shines a square-shaped beam over my pelvic area.

I prefer this method to the other one, which requires me to lie on a cold metal bed while they take the X-rays horizontally. The last time they took them that way was because I'd just had my cast removed. I couldn't stand on my own because my muscles were atrophied, and my left leg was still bent at the knee in the same shape it'd held for two months. Not that it mattered to the technician. Without even a warning, she pushed down on my knee so my leg was flat against the steel surface. The pain was instant and all-consuming, like a rod being rammed into my foot and torso.

To this day, I don't know how I didn't scream. Maybe I was just used to it by then, this idea that pain is meant to be endured quietly.

It doesn't scare me now, though. I'm actually kind of bored more than anything else. The room and the equipment and the gowns are all a shiny white, making the space feel sterile and empty, but also incredibly ordinary.

"You good there?" Today's technician has a gentle touch and an ID card hanging from her collar that says MISHKA RAO. She makes microadjustments to my posture, her fingers reminding me of how Mami dabs cream on her face every night.

"How's that?" she asks again. I nod, trying my best not to move otherwise.

Her coat collar is lined with enamel pins, mostly of cute

89

animals and bone jokes like IT'S GOING TIBIA OKAY. A light-blue one that looks like a butterfly catches my eye, and I realize it's actually a set of fins. MAKE WAVES is written beneath it in bubble letters, and next to that pin there's one of a mermaid inside a clam with the words SHELLF CARE.

"I like your pins," I say.

She looks down at them and smiles. "Thanks. Bring your hip just a smidge-bit toward me?"

It's always these tiny moves that surprise me. A twist of the hip. A tilt of my foot. I never feel that my natural stance is off until someone starts realigning me. At rest, everything is slightly turned out. If my feet were a clock, the short limb would be pointing at eleven, the longer one perfectly upright. It makes sense because I was born at eleven at night: proof, as Mami says, that my body carries all my stories.

Mishka shuffles over to her station behind the glass partition that protects her from being exposed to radiation. The machine hums on like it's a waking monster, then it gives off two quick clicks.

"Just one more to be sure," Mishka shouts.

Soon I'm back in the examination room with my parents, waiting for the doctor to see me. He'll do what he always does: pull my X-ray up on the screen so he can annotate the degrees of scoliosis that my hip displacement is causing in my spine. Point out the cartilage in my hip socket, how it's wearing thin, but as long as I'm not in pain, it's fine. He'll tell me how much the arthritis in my hip has progressed since last time, which I'm guessing is not a lot, because for years it's been happening slowly. It makes it sound like I have a bunch of different conditions, but they all spring from dysplasia. They all have one root.

I start to pace the cold room in my socks.

"You okay, hijita?" Mami asks.

"I'm fine. Just want to get this over with."

Dr. Brown enters the room with a big shuffle of papers announcing him. "Okay!" he says, as if he's continuing a conversation instead of starting one. "How's my favorite Peruvian patient?"

I fight the urge to roll my eyes because my parents are practically gushing. It's obvious that to them it's flattering, to be seen as this one thing. Dr. Brown has been calling me his favorite Peruvian patient since I was ten, when I first visited him and handed him a small silver llama, a gift Papi insisted on. In all fairness, it still rests on the shelf in his office, a fact they're pretty proud of, and I sincerely doubt he has many other patients from Peru, or anywhere south of the equator, for that matter. It's not that Dr. Brown is the *absolute* worst, but he's more like that tiresome uncle that's constantly saying well-meaning but cringe-worthy things. My parents would kill me if I ever called him on it. Heaven forbid we offend el Doctor.

"She's been limping more," Mami says.

I shoot her a look.

"What? I notice these things. Maybe because you and Leslie spend all day walking around the complex now that it's summer?"

"And what's wrong with that?"

"Nothing. I'm just telling him, that's all."

"Any pain?" he asks.

"Nope." He looks at me skeptically. "Not more than usual," I add. "It's on and off. And random."

"Have you been feeling the rain?"

"Sometimes." I used to think this meant I could magically predict when it was coming. It wasn't until my joint started getting stiff and hesitant before a storm that I understood. When the air gets humid and the pressure drops, I feel it in my bones. "It's just a tightness," I add.

"Painful?"

I shrug. It's not like I keep a journal of it. When I feel fine, it's hard to remember how often I don't. And when I don't . . . I wish I could just forget about it.

Dr. Brown does his thing as he talks, checking the reflexes on my knees by using his finger like a tiny hammer, then placing his hands on my shoulder so that I lie flat on the bed. He pushes on my foot, bending my leg at the knee toward my chest. A bone cracks softly inside me. I wonder if he heard it.

"How's that feel?"

"Fine."

Checking the rotation, he turns my leg in and out, like it's a door with a squeaky hinge. Even though Dr. Brown doesn't say anything, I can tell he's hyperfocused by the way he sighs through his nose. The room is so quiet, the only sounds are the paper crinkling beneath me and his breathing. He scribbles a few notes in my chart, then opens the door and steps out into the hallway. "Walk for me? Just relaxed. Normal."

I go in a straight line to the end of the hall and back, letting my spine, shoulders, and steps fall into whatever place feels right. Letting go of the constant, nearly unconscious effort it takes to keep my body well aligned means I'm probably not straight at all. Probably one shoulder is higher than the other and my gait is an offbeat rhythm. If I were a machine, these would be my default settings. My home screen. My normal.

"So, let's have a look." The monitor against the wall lights up as he loads my X-rays onto the screen. One is from today and one is from six months ago, and I can tell he's comparing them. I try to see what he sees, but all I notice is how the left femur looks cloudier, like dense cotton candy. "Looks like some of your necrosis here has progressed!" he says, as if he's talking about muffins that have just browned.

"What? Wait. Necro—as in death?" I say.

"Of the bone tissue, yes. Like we discussed last time."

Not with me. I look to my parents, but they won't meet my eyes.

"We hadn't thought to mention it to Verónica . . ." Papi's voice is low and raspy, and he has to clear his throat to get the words out. "Not until it was cause for concern."

"Oh," Dr. Brown says, suddenly slow and cautious, as if he's trying to back out of a tight spot. "Well, either way, I'd like to take more images. To get a clearer idea of how far along it is."

Mami places her hand on my elbow, barely touching me, but I snap myself out of her grasp. "You didn't tell me that my bone tissue was dying?"

"It's actually very common. The bone doesn't get enough blood circulation in a dislocated hip like yours," Dr. Brown says. "Sometimes it's a result of an open reduction surgery, like those we've performed. Sometimes it just happens in arthritic hips. We don't know exactly what causes it. Or how fast it progresses."

"Pero, hijita, if you say you haven't been in pain . . ." Mami says, letting the sentence fade.

I brush my hands through my hair and squeeze my scalp, the crown of my head. Thoughts of lies and dead tissue and the dry, lifeless bones swirl through my mind. My toes turn cold all of a sudden, and a numbness creeps from my neck down to my shoulders. I try to think if I missed something. Have I been in more significant pain than usual?

What is *significant*?

What is the *usual*?

"I want to monitor it," he says to my parents.

"Should we discuss it more in your office?" Papi says.

"No. I'm not twelve anymore. I'm seventeen. I want to know."

They look to Dr. Brown instead of me. Whatever he says goes.

He scribbles something in my file and clicks his pen shut. "It'll be important for Verónica to be involved in this. After all, she's the one who can truly tell us how she's feeling."

What I feel is confused and betrayed. What I feel is a knot in my throat.

"If it causes you pain in your groin or when you put weight on it, it could mean it's progressing. Degenerating . . ."

He makes me sound like an object powering down.

"If that's the case, we'd want to discuss options. Therapy, surgery, arthroplasty . . ."

"Arthroplasty," I repeat.

"Hip replacement," he says back.

"Of course, Doctor." My father's voice sounds miles away.

"Yes, when?" Mami says.

They're talking like I'm not here.

"Wait. No. I don't get it. I thought this was just a checkup."

"It is," Dr. Brown says. "And we're getting ahead of ourselves. I want to do an MRI first. To see where things are at. We'll have a better idea of next steps from there."

Things. Steps.

"We knew this was a possibility, Vero."

We.

"A replacement could be very good for you."

Good.

I don't even know who's saying what anymore.

All I know is that I want them to stop.

"When's the MRI?" I ask.

He says we'll figure that out with scheduling. He shakes my hand good-bye, and the three of them step outside while I get dressed.

Everything is happening so fast.

Everything is taking forever.

At the front desk, my parents sign a bunch of papers and then the receptionist smiles at me, her hands dancing across her keyboard.

"Let's see . . . yes, here we are!" From the tone of her voice you'd think she just found buried treasure. "Looks like the next opening for an MRI is August tenth."

Mami looks disappointed. "That's almost two months from now. There's nothing sooner?"

The receptionist tells her the best they can do is put me on a wait list in case someone else cancels. "It's unlikely, but you never know," she adds cheerfully.

"One can only hope," Mami says, in the stiff, formal way she talks when she's trying to impress strangers. As we leave the office, the word *hope* loops around in my mind, over and over, until it gets caught in a spiral, out of my reach and devoid of all meaning.

Left: left

1. (n.) the side of a body or thing that is to the west when one is facing north
2. (n. VR) the side of my body that has never felt right

Chapter 10

MOST PEOPLE DON'T KNOW THAT THE original Little Mermaid story—the one by Hans Christian Andersen written in eighteen thirty-whatever—is actually full of the pain and heartbreak of wanting something so bad and being destined to never have it.

There's no redheaded Ariel and her happily ever after. The Little Mermaid gives up her voice for the chance to walk on the earth and find true love, but what they don't say in the Disney version is that *each time her foot touched the floor, it seemed as if she trod on sharp knives.*

I've read it more times than I can count. I've memorized entire lines, sketched her image on notebooks and receipts and napkins. What I can never forget is that not only did the mermaids have no legs, they lacked even the words for them.

They couldn't name the things they didn't know. To

them, normal was only the things they'd lived. I guess it's easy to assume everyone's like you, unless you're different. Unless your whole life, you've wanted to be like everyone else.

In the story, the little mermaid's tail, considered so beautiful among her own, *is thought on earth to be quite ugly; they do not know any better, and they think it necessary to have two stout props, which they call legs, in order to be handsome.* She wants to belong on land so badly, she covets a pair of legs more than any other treasure.

I felt her longing when she looked at people's legs. There's something stunning about legs that for the most part goes unnoticed. Like how, when they're the same length, they can glide someone across a room, make it so their heads are held high and graceful.

Sometimes I catch myself staring at them as people walk. Envying their ordinariness. The way they move over the earth so flawlessly.

It doesn't help that when we cross the hospital lobby, I see it in people's eyes. I used to think their eyes followed me for some flattering reason until I realized I cause them discomfort. I make them see things they'd rather ignore. My limp is a glitch in their otherwise idyllic worldview, a disturbing reflection of themselves.

People ask me all the time, *What's wrong? Why are you limping?* They hope I just sprained an ankle because if something is wrong, then eventually it can be made be right.

But as we get into the car, I feel like nothing will be right. How can it, when there are parts of me slowly dying?

"I'm sorry, Vero." Dani squeezes my hand, but I can't look at her right now. In the elevator, Mami told her what Dr. Brown said, so now she repeats one of my mom's favorite phrases. "But nothing's certain yet, right?"

"Of course not," Mami says. "Dr. Brown says you'll probably need a hip replacement, but it varies for every patient. It could be next year. Maybe five years, when you're done with college. Maybe even after that. You have to think positive." She reaches behind the seat and slaps my knee twice, light and eager, as if she's offered some big solution. I know Mami means well, but thinking positive isn't going to change the blood flow in my bones.

"When did he say that?" I ask.

"When I spoke to him."

"Behind my back?"

"While you were changing. Not behind your back."

"But you knew, Vero. Remember?" Papi says. "Dr. Brown's always said a replacement was a possibility."

"When I was forty! And not because my bone was dying!" I lean forward so fast my seat belt snaps me back.

"No. Nos hables. Así," Mami says.

But how else am I supposed to talk to them if I want to get the truth?

Once, years ago, my parents told me I'd need a hip replacement someday. They said it was so far into the future I shouldn't bother worrying about it, like it was a meteor soaring billions of miles away.

Now it's closing in on me, crashing into my atmosphere.

I should've known better. I should've been prepared for this.

But it'd gotten so easy lately, to ignore the knowing. To settle into the comfort of thinking I'd left that part of my life behind. The last time I had surgery was three and a half years ago; I hadn't even started high school yet. The ones before that came in much quicker succession. Jumping from one to the next didn't give me enough time to get acquainted with any other reality.

That younger version of myself seems so far removed from me. Far enough to let me think I could outrun what's been waiting for me all along.

I feel so naive. It was foolish to think anything was ever in my hands in the first place.

"Don't cry," Dani whispers, but my father hears her and gives a concerned glance in my direction. I lean toward the window to block his view of me. I won't give him or Mami the satisfaction of thinking they can console me with their empty words and eyes full of pity.

"Don't worry. I wouldn't dream of it," I say.

Mermaids have no tears, and therefore they suffer more.

Trámite: trá·mi·te

1. (n.) a procedure or process, a transaction
2. (n. VR) the hopeless process of being caught in a never-ending mistake

Chapter 11

IF WE HAD THE BIGGER APARTMENT, I'd stomp up the stairs and make my way up to my room. Slam the door behind me so my parents and my sister would hear me loud and clear: *Don't even try me now. Just leave me the fuck alone.*

But when we finally get home from the hospital, I barely get in three steps across the living room before Mami tells us dinner's in twenty minutes.

"I'm not hungry," I say.

"I didn't ask if you were hungry," Mami says, a giggle at the edge of her voice. "Whose turn is whose today?"

"I set the table yesterday," Dani says. She's already standing at our bedroom door, one arm leaning against the threshold. "But, like, we can switch for today . . ."

I must really look destroyed for her to offer this small kindness. I want to squeeze her and say thank you, but I'm worried all the volatile emotions I've been trying to hold in the whole ride home will explode if I do.

"No, no, nada de switching ni que switching," Mami interjects. "It becomes impossible to keep track when you two start changing things up like that."

"Are you serious? What difference does it make?" All I want to do is lie down and be more than three feet away from her and my dad for five minutes.

"Don't talk back to your mother," Papi yells from his room. I hate that our place is so tiny, anyone can hear anyone from one end to the other.

"Oh, so *he* gets to lie down and rest for a few minutes, but I can't catch a break?"

"He? Excuse me?" Mami hates it when I refer to her and Papi as just pronouns. She says it's disrespectful to not use someone's name because then you're talking like they're not even there.

I wish I wasn't here, but apparently if the dinner table doesn't get set right this instant, all the order in the world will collapse.

I try to get it done fast. I move the plant from the center of our glass dinner table and place it on the living room coffee table. I put out four placemats and fold the napkins into triangles before bringing out the silverware and plates.

"Don't forget bowls for the soup this time. I made caldo de pavo," Mami says.

"I know. I have eyes, you know." On the top of the stove

there's a pan full of turkey bones reheating in their own broth. One of the thighs sticks out of the liquid, the lifeless marrow dry from the fog of its own steam.

"Oye. ¿Qué te pasa?"

"Nothing. I'm fine."

"You better be by the time we all sit down to eat. I don't care if you're hungry or not. You know we sit down as a family together." She pats her palms dry on her apron, then tucks one of my loose tendrils behind my ear. "It's going to be fine," she whispers. "We've been through this before."

"*We* is a lot of people."

Mami's curved lips drop like a pencil snapped in half. Maybe it's not fair that I used this phrase against her. The way she usually says it, it's a cute joke, a gentle jab when someone's included themselves in a situation that's not at all about them.

"*We* have always gotten through it together, as a family."

I nod, careful not to contradict her or agree.

I get what she's saying. What she wants to say.

But it's not her or Papi's or Dani's skin they cut into. Not her bone being drilled and excavated and replaced. Not her body that carries the scars.

"I'm tired of getting through it," I say. "I have plans, you know. Getting a hip replacement senior year isn't exactly on my to-do list."

"You're jumping to conclusions, hijita. And you talk like this is the end of the world. What have we always told you? There's nothing you can't do. You can't let this define you."

Let it? It's not like I have control over this. I'm not the one *letting* cells in my bones disintegrate and fade to nothingness. By the time we sit down to eat, it's all I can think about. All the secrets they've kept. All the things they know about my body that I don't. Even they can't control what's happening to it, though God knows they've spent all my life trying.

"You should have told me. About the necrosis."

Papi sighs but doesn't look up from his plate. "I'm sorry, Vero. But we were just trying to protect you."

"A lot of good that did." The words barrel out of my mouth. Papi slams his palm against the table, and Mami just wipes at her mouth with her napkin like it's paint she's trying to scrub off.

They scowl and throw all the usual rhetorical questions at me—the *who do you think you are*'s and *what is wrong with you*'s and *is this how you treat your own parents, after everything we've done for you*'s—before telling me to go to my room, that they can't bear to look at me. That they don't know when I became such an insolent, disrespectful child.

It's a relief, honestly, and even they let out a sigh as I march the few steps it takes to get from the table to my room.

The silence settles and their forks start clattering again, and all I hear is my father say, "Okay, bueno, Dani, ¿cómo te fue hoy día?"

My sister answers flatly, "Fine."

I take a hot shower to drown them out.

It's after dinner when I'm done, and in our bedroom, Dani is at our desk, headphones on as she watches a livestream of a couple of skateboarders and distractedly sprinkles food into our betta fish, Fuego's, bowl. My sister can't even sit still when she's sitting still—everything is about movement with her, bodies through the air, bodies in motion. During the school year, she's always involved in the season's sport: volleyball in the fall, basketball in the spring. Sometimes she'll mix it up and do cheerleading and baseball instead. I know it's the one thing that kills her about summer break. When there's no school, there's no sports, because my parents can't afford club sports during the off season, with all their dues and the uniforms team members have to pay for out of their own pockets. The way she complains about it lately, though, it's like she can't imagine a more pathetic reality.

Like maybe she's afraid of being even a little bit like me.

I'd never really thought about that until now. I'd always just assumed that nature made us this way, polar opposites.

But maybe it's on purpose. A choice at least one of us has.

The music from her headphones creeps into the room's silence, static noise that's impossible to ignore.

"Dani." She doesn't hear me. "Dani. DANI!"

She startles. "What?"

"Nothing, just . . . It's a lot louder than you think, you know?"

She sighs and puts the headphones back on, but doesn't unpause the video. I wrap my hair in a towel and collapse onto my bed, closing my eyes in search of solitude. Everything in here is not mine but ours: the desk, the bathroom, the closet, the computer. We share everything, half and half, like Mami always says. Everything equal.

There's a rap on our door. Before Dani or I can say anything, it swings open and there's Papi, stepping into our room.

"I don't know why you bother knocking," I say, "if you're not going to wait till we say 'come in.'"

He signals to Dani that he'd like her chair, and without question she gets up and plops onto her bed. Now I know I'm in trouble, because Papi's not even using words. He closes the door gently behind him and sits, rolling toward me.

"You want more privacy," he says.

"It'd be nice," I say, keeping my voice low.

"To do what with? To go around kissing boys? In public? In the pool?"

A jolt rushes through me. After the doctor's office, this afternoon feels like ages ago, but now I realize Papi's just been waiting, holding it in while his anger multiplied.

"We weren't doing anything wrong," I say.

"Oh no? So I should tell your mom, then? I should call her in here, tell her how I found you? Again?"

"Papi, please."

"It would destroy her, you know that? We didn't raise you this way."

"What way?" I narrow my eyes, looking right into his. Daring him to say it. He presses his lips together, holding the word just past them, until finally he clears his throat and lets all the tight creases in his face deflate.

It's embarrassing to him, talking about this. Everything with Papi's about implications, while Mami's always been the one who is more direct about sex, or at least more direct in shaming us out of it. The first time she dropped me off at a movie with a group of friends that included a boy, she placed her hand on my neck and said, *This is where it starts. Let him touch you here, and he'll touch you anywhere.* I'd never felt so violated. Until Jeremy.

"You know, you're lucky," he says, pausing to nod and flare his nostrils. "You're lucky your mom has enough to worry about, with this news at the doctor and all the trámites she's trying to clear up with immigration right now—"

"What happened with immi—"

"That's not important. But you're lucky I'm not telling her. She has enough to worry about without having to think about you getting yourself pregnant."

"Pregnant! ¿En serio?" It shouldn't surprise me by now, but it's so completely ludicrous, every time. My parents don't so much jump to conclusions about me becoming pregnant one day as much as they perpetually operate under the threat of it. If their dream for me and Dani is for us to get good, respectable jobs, then this is their nightmare: I become promiscua, get pregnant, drop out of school, and throw my life away. It's why they've been telling us we can't "get involved" with boys ever since I told them I held my crush's hand at the playground when I was in third grade. They turned a totally innocent thing into something I should be ashamed of. Said I should be "careful" not to stain my reputation. Which is really just a euphemistic way of calling an eight-year-old a slut.

Aw. Qué nice.

"How is it that you always assume the worst? I would never—"

"Don't start, Verónica. I didn't come here to be lied to. You think I was born yesterday? Piénsalo bien next time. Think about what you're doing to this family when you act like that. In public, in private. You can ruin your life and ours, and for what?"

"It's not like that," I say.

"I know what I saw, hija."

But he doesn't. He doesn't know anything.

Star: star

1. (n.) a natural luminous body visible in the sky, especially at night
2. (n. VR) a natural luminous body that died a long time ago, suddenly being seen

Chapter 12

I WAIT UNTIL EVERYONE'S ASLEEP TO sneak out of the house through the sliding glass door in our living room. It leads to the lanai, which is full of Mami's plants and a wicker bench that leaves painful dents up and down your thighs if you sit on it longer than a few minutes. Our baby fig tree blocks the door to the side of the porch, and even though it's not more than a few feet tall, its ceramic pot is filled to the brim with soil. It's almost too heavy to move quietly. The plant makes a light scraping sound as I pull it a few inches across the cement. I hold still, listening for any indication that I stirred my parents or Dani awake.

When none comes, I dash across the grass behind our building, my feet bare and my flip-flops in hand. I just need to be alone, for real. And there's only one place I can do that.

When Palmview Lakes was built in the 1970s, they put

in a pool and a gym by the tennis courts, and then, I guess maybe as an afterthought, they built a racquetball court all the way over by the mailboxes, a good five-minute walk away.

None of the facilities look like they've been updated much since then, but at least the gym has equipment from this century, and the tennis courts got a new paint job last summer. The racquetball court, though, is just four cement walls with no roof. It's a rectangle with a door on one side and when you walk in and look up, it's like a giant window to the sky.

In the corner near the entrance, someone scribbled a message on the floor before the cement dried: *Merle and Gus, August 4, 1978.* Sometimes when I come here I make up stories about who they were. The construction guys, which is an easy one, just wanting to leave their mark on something instead of letting the bosses take all the credit. Or maybe two teens in love, who found a place where they could finally steal moments together without others watching and judging them, claiming this spot as their own.

Tonight it's a full moon, and the space feels like a cup with all its light pouring in. I slide my back against the wall until I'm sitting next to the inscription. I massage the *8* and feel its edges scrape against my fingertips. If I focus enough on just that, I can empty myself of the day's contents—the way my father's words left me feeling like a tainted body, the way Dr. Brown held my leg in his hands like it was an inanimate thing. If everything inside me is out of alignment, then it means I was born displaced. I wonder if I'd have fit in better if we'd just stayed in Lima, if I'd spent my childhood seeing doctors that didn't look at me like I was a foreign specimen, fascinating only because I was from another country. I wonder how much more of me they would've seen if this one part didn't make everything else invisible. Here, it seems everyone gets to be whole but me. They get to be seen for who they are, not for what they aren't. They get to be defined by the things they do instead of the things they don't. Meanwhile, I get split into all these little pieces: Peruvian. Disabled. Immigrant. Fragmented as if I couldn't possibly be everything all at once, and more.

I sit with my legs stretched out in front of me and take out my phone to scroll through Mermaid Cove's timeline. This year is their eightieth anniversary—ten years since the first time we visited them, for their seventieth—and they've been posting vintage videos, then having the new mermaids reenact the routines through the ages, just like they did a decade ago. I prefer the old ones, though. Maybe it's the black-and-white footage or the graininess of the film, but there's a magic in them that isn't easily recaptured.

Still, I would've liked the chance to try.

I play the one in which a mermaid isn't actually dressed like a mermaid at all. She's just in a one-piece bathing suit, the kind that looks like shorts on the bottom, with a sweetheart neckline up top. She and a guy in swim trunks stretch a checker-patterned blanket across the floor of the springs for an underwater picnic. Fish swim all around them as they take dinnerware out of a basket and set up a small radio. Then they take a sip of air and start dancing, joining hands and flipping in tandem, graceful circles, until you realize they're slowly spiraling across the water toward the surface, like a pair of ballet dancers exiting the stage.

It's entrancing. They float between worlds. Every motion is a smooth glide, carried by a soft, even rhythm. No hiccups. Nothing off-kilter or out of balance. They're home under the water but breathing the same air we breathe on land. Magical creatures that we imagined into being, into existence, into place. No matter how many times I see them, their performance pulls me under its spell.

Heyyyy

A notification from Alex pops up across the video. Spell officially broken.

Was just thinking of you

I smile. New spell commencing.

Any particular reason? I write.

Just that the moon is huge right now. And I was thinking it must look nice by the lake.

Very subtle hint.

You like?

Yes. Nicely done.

So you'll meet me there?

I have a better idea. Here's the next spot on our tour. I send him a ping to my location.

He arrives a lot sooner than I expected, which means he probably ran. When he walks through the door, I can tell he's out of breath but he's trying to pretend he's not. It's kind of sweet.

"Is this, like . . . a fort or something?"

I laugh and extend my hand to him so he can help me up. When he does, he swoops me seamlessly into a hug, and though his skin is dewy, the fabric of his shirt is cool. I press my palm to his chest.

"You've never seen a racquetball court?"

"Not like this one."

"Okay, that tracks."

"You come here a lot?"

I nod.

"What do you usually do?"

"Nothing. Except get away from everything."

His hand slides slowly down my arm, his fingertips pausing at my wrist, the place where my veins meet just beneath my skin, blue like several rivers pouring from my heart. He taps against my pulse, light and timid, as if knocking on a door he's afraid won't be answered. I slide my hands into his, and even though it's just our fingers intertwining, it feels like my whole body is wrapped in his.

We walk down the length of the court and then across. A quiet evening stroll in an enclosed, endless place.

"What's wrong? You seem sad."

I'm surprised he noticed. I was trying to do my most romantic breathing-in-his-scent, and instead he picked up on this. The melancholy must be sticking to me, emanating. I take a step back.

"It's just my parents. They're bent on making my life hell."

"Did they ground you?" His forehead creases with concern.

"I wish." If only it were so simple. All my life, I've marveled at how my white friends' parents ground them on such certain terms. Everything is outlined, defined, on a specific timeline with a specific punishment. Two weeks without a phone. No going out for ten days. My parents have never actually done any of that. When they're upset with me, their torment is more psychological, a quiet, general sense of repression. A steady drip, drip, drip of guilt that eventually suffocates me in shame. It has no solid beginning or end.

"They're being assholes," I explain. "That's why I came here. Just to have my own space for once."

"I get that."

"What about you? Is your mom super strict but super vague about what you can or can't do with *your* body?"

Oh God. I can't believe I phrased it like that. I watch his lips curl as he tries to figure out how to answer, and to clarify, I quickly add, "I mean, like, controlling. About where you go and who you spend time with."

"Oh." A sound like a tiny motorboat escapes his lips. "Not so much that. My mom's just obsessed with how I'm feeling all the time. What I'm thinking. To be honest, lately I'm more worried about making things hard for her than I am about her making things hard for me."

I don't know how to answer that. On the one hand, it seems kind of him, but then it makes me uncomfortable, because it makes me have to think of how today might've been hard on my parents. And I don't want to go there. Not yet, anyway. Because did they ever bother going there for me?

"And what about your dad?"

He shrugs. "All he ever does is text me links to articles about looking on the bright side and meditating and whatever self-care meme he found going viral that day. It's like he wants to make sure I'm okay but can't bring himself to actually ask me."

"And are you?"

"Am I what?"

"Okay?"

He looks up at the sky, deep in thought. I take in how the moonlight accentuates his nose, the way it curls up a little, and his lips press together as if he were nibbling them.

"Most of the time, yeah," he finally says. "I mean, moving here was the last thing I wanted, you know? But then my mom kept saying it was time for us to come home, even though it's not *my* home. I'm not the one who was born here. I know she grew up here, but she never really talked about it, aside from saying it was a place she needed to get away from."

"Did she ever tell you why?"

He shakes his head. I know how he feels. My parents are always talking about how great things were back in Peru but never actually explaining what made us leave. Just that things got hard. Too uncertain. That life would be more promising here in the US.

"But then for the most part . . . It hasn't turned out as

horrible as I thought, you know?" He wedges his fingers between mine and squeezes. I cover our hands with my other and slide to the ground so we're both sitting.

"I'm glad things are non-horrible," I say, placing my head on his shoulder.

He chuckles. "Yeah. Me too."

In our silence, it dawns on me that Alex and I just had our first non-nothing conversation. Real talk about real things, small parts of ourselves that we're trusting with one another. It makes me want to contribute something of my own.

"So I didn't really answer your question earlier."

"Which one?"

"What I usually do when I come here." I take out my phone and open up another mermaid video. This one isn't from the archives; it's footage from last season's opening show.

"It's kind of an obsession of mine," I admit.

He places his hand on my phone. "*This* is what you were talking about? This is awesome. It looks nothing like I imagined it. Oh God, I'm so sorry for making fun of it the other day. I must've come off like such an ass."

"I mean . . . wait, what did you think it looked like?"

"I don't know . . . maybe those fluffy mascot costumes?"

"In the water?"

"I don't know! My brain doesn't always make sense, okay?"

"I can believe that," I say, nudging him with my elbow.

We watch a few more videos, and I tell him all I know about the mermaids. Most of them are either my age or in college, and they work part-time at the Cove except during the summer, when they do shows daily instead of Thursday through Sunday because it's the heavy tourist season.

All the mermaids have mythical origin stories that they've posted about on social. Mermaid Lila is originally from the ocean, but she followed her friends the manatees into the river and decided she liked the fresh, clear water. Tanya lives in an underwater cave with her sisters, Mermaids Hallie and Val, with their pet fish and turtles. There's even a guy, Geoff, who always plays a prince or love interest in their routines, and though he's never played an actual mermaid, he has a really big online following. Last week, someone posted the most beautiful photoshopped images and illustrations of him in a tail.

"Of course, it went viral with the fandom," I say, just as a new video begins autoplaying. They must've uploaded it earlier because it's one I haven't seen before: a couple of mermaid flips and then a text overlay announcing the upcoming auditions.

"Are you auditioning?" Alex asks. Like it's not even a big deal. Like there's no reason in the world I shouldn't. I wonder what version of reality he imagines we're actually living in. I want to live in it too.

"Come with me," I say, getting up and extending my hand to him. We start walking so fast we're eventually in a light jog, and I lead him through the side of the leasing office building toward the back entrance to the pool.

"Isn't it clo—"

"Shhhh," I say, bringing my finger to my lips. I step out of my flip-flops and motion for him to take off his, then stretch my arm over the gate to open the latch. It's only about as high as my shoulder, and to my relief, it doesn't creak as I swing it open. All the lounge chairs are piled on top of one another under the tiki huts, and the round patio tables have their chairs stacked upside down on their tops. The hot tub is completely covered, which makes it blend into the deck like it's not even there. It's weird to see the pool with no lights on, but the darkness keeps us from being visible.

We tiptoe to the edge of the deep end, and I take off my shirt and shorts. I'm wearing a dark blue bra and matching underwear, the same set that Mami picked out for me to wear earlier to Dr. Brown's. It's definitely not how she ever intended me to use it, but I don't care about any of that right now. Alex strips down to his shorts and rubs his arms as if he's cold, and even though the air is warm, I get it, because suddenly we're both vulnerable, nearly naked, with so little to hide from one another. It's terrifying and thrilling, like a chosen dare.

The water feels perfect as we step in, the temperature welcoming our bodies as if we were always meant to be here.

"It's no lake in the moonlight, but it's close enough," I whisper.

"Close is good," Alex says. We let our bodies float face-up along the water's surface, holding hands like otters. From this angle the sky floods my vision, dotted with more stars than I've ever seen in my life. It feels infinite and intimate, like a ceiling I could reach up and touch.

"Did you know we have star matter in our bodies?" Alex asks.

"Shut up. Like how?"

"I'm serious. I read about it online. Half the calcium in our universe is from these calcium-rich supernovae. The stars lost all this mass at the end of their lives, and when they died and exploded, all that calcium ended up here. So it's in us now. All the calcium in our teeth and bones."

I stare up at the splotchy sky and imagine my femur shriveling up like a beached starfish. This afternoon I looked necrosis up on my phone and learned that it becomes arthritis. My aging bone. Freckled like the limestone beneath the mermaids' springs. All its holes, piercing in all its light.

"We were once dying stars," I say.

He squeezes my hand, and we lie still and silent. If a star can die millions of years ago and still illuminate our bodies, then maybe nothing is final. Maybe the water we're barely stirring is a mirror to the sky, and we're just caught in their two reflections, being created over and over again.

"I like that. Their end was only our beginning."

I slip out of his grasp by doing a backflip into the deep end. I let the air leave my body, let it make me weightless so I sink easily to the very bottom. When I open my eyes, Alex's blurry silhouette is inching toward me. His shadow crosses the pool's wall, and I push off the floor to meet him, shooting through the space between us soundlessly. He starts rising toward the surface, and I meet him there. Half underwater, half above, our heads barely poke over the water's crest. I take a breath. A deep one, like when I'm about to jump into the sea, knowing I won't want to come up for air.

That's exactly what our kiss is like.

Pretend: pre·tend
1. (v.) to give a false appearance of being
2. (v. VR) to make believe you inhabit another place, another being, that feels truer

Chapter 13

IN THE MORNING I FINALLY TEXT Leslie back.

Tell Tanya I can start training today if she's around.

Still in bed, I stare at the screen, anticipating her response. Probably a string of questions about what happened, what made me change my mind. The truth is I'm not sure. Even if by some miracle I got in, my parents would never let me become a mermaid. But it's like all those out-of-state colleges I know I won't apply to: a part of me just wants to know if I'd get accepted. If it wasn't for my parents, or my doctor or this maybe-future hip replacement, could I really do it? I need to know, on my own terms. I need to at least try.

Leslie sends me the gif of Ariel rising atop a rock as the ocean splashes in triumph behind her. You next week!!

I flip over and set my phone back on my nightstand. The teal sequin-covered pillow that normally sits on my bed is face-down on the floor, and I consider tossing it across the room at Dani. She's such a deep sleeper, she needs to be shaken awake. No amount of shouting will do.

But I want her to come with me to the pool today. Somehow knowing she and Leslie will be there makes it feel more real, like I won't be able to back out of it. All my life, I've kept the things I've loved a secret. While most little girls were playing pretend with their dolls and stuffed animals, I used to line up no more than two in a "classroom" and point silently at an invisible chalkboard as I made believe I was their teacher. That way, if my parents or Dani came in, it was easy to act like I was doing something else. The same for when I went through my cheerleading phase, and my doctor phase. There's something about giving myself over to things that are not real that's always left me feeling utterly embarrassed. Exposed. Like if I pretend to be something I'm not, everyone will see right through me.

But this is different. Becoming a mermaid isn't about pretending to be something I'm not. It's about being who I really am.

I get up and give Dani's shoulder a couple of shakes. "Dani. Dormilona. Despiértate."

She swats my hand away, groaning like a tiny Frankenstein monster. God, she really is a sleepyhead.

"Daniiiii . . . we have to get to the pool! Leslie's sister said she'll teach me all her turns and flips and pretty mermaid shit!"

Her head pops up, her upper body propped on her elbows. "You're doing it?"

"I'm doing it."

From the way she smiles, I can tell she's about to burst, but she holds back and looks at me skeptically. "What made you change your mind? Does this have something to do with where you went last night?"

"What? I didn't go anywhere last night."

"Don't lie. I heard you sneak out."

"To the lanai? That's not exactly *out*, Dani." I hate lying to her, but I want to keep last night with Alex to myself.

"Fine, whatever." She sits up and gasps in excitement. "Does this mean I can do your makeup for the auditions?"

"Yes, okay."

"And I can decorate your bathing suit?"

"What?"

"For good luck. Just a small charm."

Dani embroiders all her sports bras with a tag or saying that becomes like a good luck charm for her team. It's totally one of those superstitious things, and it changes with each season and sport.

"Yes, of course, whatever you want. But do me a favor. Don't mention the hip replacement thing to Leslie or Tanya."

"Ugh, fine. Everything is secrets with you." She goes into the bathroom and grabs two of my bathing suit tops from the towel rack where we leave them to dry. "Which one will you wear to the auditions, so I can work my magic on it?"

"*This* is what you're worried about?" What I wouldn't give to trade concerns with Dani on any given day.

"I'm serious. You need to bring good energy. Pick one."

The blue top on the left is what I was wearing yesterday, when Papi caught Alex and me doing literally nothing more than looking longingly into each other's eyes, so now it feels like it's bad luck. The purple one on the right is what I was wearing the day Alex and I met.

"The purple," I say. "We should probably burn the other one. But we gotta go. Now."

We have a super-quick breakfast—yogurt, granola, and leftover fruit that Mami brought home from her last shift at the smoothie bar. I grab an oversized straw bag from my closet and stuff it with a couple of towels, my phone, my wallet, my journal so I can take notes on whatever Tanya tells me, a few pens, and a hairbrush. The bag is dyed blue in ombre shades that look like pool water, which feels fitting.

Tanya has to be at work in an hour, and her schedule is so busy, she won't have much time to train me before the auditions next Friday. That means I have exactly one week to prepare. Instead of the usual route, we cut behind buildings H and I, through the grassy, hilly area that we're supposed to stay out of because it slopes too sharply toward the lake. Dani does her usual flips and I break into a light jog, ignoring the steepness of the hill or the way my joints feel stiff, like they've rusted shut. None of that will matter once I'm in the water. I push through by imagining it all being washed away.

But when we finally arrive at the pool, there's a printout taped to the usual entry sign. I resist the urge to rip it off the gate and crumple it into a tight ball as I read:

OUT OF SERVICE.
POOLS CLOSED FOR MAINTENANCE
UNTIL MONDAY.
STAY COOL,
MANAGEMENT.

Physical: phys·i·cal

1.   (n.) a medical examination to determine a person's fitness
2.   (n. VR) the worst type of test in all existence

Chapter 14

"WAIT, WHAT? THAT'S IMPOSSIBLE." I set my bag on a bench outside the tennis courts and go looking for someone, anyone, from the leasing department. It's not long before I run into Bob. He's pulled up to the curb by the back entrance of the pool, talking to a petite white woman standing beside his golf cart. They stop their conversation mid-sentence when they see me approach.

"Hey, Verónica! What's cooking?" Bob wipes his forehead sweat with a hand towel. "Aside from us in this weather, of course."

"Why's the pool closed?" I ask, ignoring his attempt at humor.

"Oh, that? It's for maintenance."

"I gathered as much from the sign. By why now? No one even sent out an email."

"We sure did," the woman says. "I saw to it myself. Unless

our new address is going to spam? Shoot." She starts mumbling as she goes through her phone. With her face turned down, I notice the slope between her cheekbones and her nose. I can't help feeling like I've seen it before.

"Oh. I'm sorry," I say. "Are you . . . ?"

"Where are my manners?" Bob says. "Verónica, meet Palmview Lakes' new manager, Alice Morales."

Alice? As in . . . ?

"Alex's mom," Bob adds. "Ma'am, this is Verónica, the nice young lady who showed Alex around the other day."

She shakes my hand just as a breeze passes between us, blowing up her silky long-sleeve blouse like a balloon. "Oh yes, he mentioned you." Her tone is light but flat, so I can't tell if she means this in an approving way, or in a who-is-this-random-girl-who-hung-out-with-my-son kind of way.

"Thanks." I don't know why I said that. I decide to focus on the more urgent matter at hand. "You all were saying? About the pool?"

"Oh. That." Bob shifts in his seat and signals for me to come closer. "The problem is, the brake pumps broke this morning. Turns out there's been a leak in the kiddie pool's foundation, and with the water level going down, the pump broke. So they gotta fix it."

"But that's the kiddie pool. Why shut down both of them?"

"Well, it's called efficiency. Alice suggested upgrading all the locks and security while they're at it."

Great. The one time management finally figures out how to make themselves useful.

"But then we can't use the pool," I say.

"It's just for a few days," she says. "The new security system is for the best. We've had some reports of kids sneaking in for some night swims after hours. We can't be held liable for whatever might happen. Make sense?"

I feel my face turn warm, and I have to immediately look down at the cart's wheels to avoid their eyes. Alex's mom is nearly impossible to read; I can't figure out if she knows about last night or if she's just doing her job. She could be speaking in generalities—we're not the only ones who have ever snuck into the pool at night. And we were so quiet. Not a single neighbor turned on a light or came out on their balcony to shush us, the way so many of them did the night of the last-day-of-school party. This can't possibly be our fault. But maybe someone called the office on us. Worse, maybe Alex's mom saw him come home soaking wet, and this is her first official act as property manager. My mind starts spinning down a rabbit hole, the way it always does when I get an inkling of suspicion that I'm in trouble.

"It'll be okay, promise." Alice smiles, and I can really see the resemblance, though her complexion is lighter and her hair curlier than Alex's. "They'll be up and running full of water again by Monday."

That'll be too late. I can't afford to lose three whole days of training. My phone buzzes, and it's Leslie telling me what I already know.

Dude, the pool has no water.

"I have to go. It was nice to meet you," I say, though I can't decide if it really was.

When I get back to the entrance, they're all standing there—Dani, Leslie, and Tanya—looking like they just showed up to a sold-out show. Tanya's in jean shorts and a loose-fitting Mermaid Cove T-shirt. The neckline has been cut so that it hangs over one shoulder, and she's scrunched up the rest of the fabric in a knot over her left hip. She's tall—probably a good eight inches taller than me—with light brown hair full of blond highlights that rests on the crown of her head in a messy bun. Nothing about Tanya looks put together, and yet she manages to look perfectly summery.

"What if we go to the community pool?" I say, pulling up the information on my phone. "It opens at noon."

"I have to be at work at noon," Tanya says. "As it is, I probably only have, like, forty-five minutes tops to help you out today. I can try to move some things around next week, though."

"It's fine. I don't want you having to go out of your way," I mumble. This is starting to feel like more trouble than it's worth. I stare at the sunken, half-empty concrete box that is now our pool. They've drained it so fast, the only water left is a giant puddle that is quickly collecting mosquitoes in what used to be the deep end. If that's not a sign that I'm just wasting my time with these auditions, I don't know what is. Maybe this is the universe's way of protecting me from disappointment.

The way my parents are always trying to do the same.

"What if we just use the gym?" I say. "Go over some general moves and pointers." The gym is my least favorite place in our whole complex. It's bad enough that there are weight machines everywhere with nothing but sub par illustrations teaching you how to use them, but then they had to add mirrors everywhere, so people can actually see how *not* strong and sleek they look. Still, it's not like we have any other option, and everyone else agrees.

As soon as we get inside, Dani grabs a yoga mat and goes into a handstand, her feet resting against the mirror on the walls like it's a vertical bed.

"Actually, that's not a bad idea," Tanya says, grabbing a couple more mats.

"The handstand?" Leslie asks.

"The mats. Some light stretching first." She sits on the floor with her legs open and her toes pointed, then slowly moves her torso toward the floor, as if she's folding herself in half.

I hate this part. I'm in PE at school all over again. I mimic Tanya's movements, but I'm not nearly as flexible, so my chest just kind of hovers in the space in front of me. After a few seconds, she switches to a butterfly, bringing the soles of her feet together so her knees jut out like wings. I opt to just bring in my right foot and leave my left leg straight. A butterfly is simply not in my range of motion; it's right up there with sitting cross-legged. Anytime I try, I end up falling back on the floor, like a beetle with its legs caught in the air.

"Is there, like, a routine the mermaids have to do? To stretch?" I ask.

"Not really. It's not like in a ballet studio or anything, if that's what you mean."

Which is a relief. I used to beg my parents to let me take ballet classes, but they couldn't afford it. Then when I was fourteen, I found out about a free "master class" being offered, one time only, at a local studio, and I guess they ran out of excuses not to take me. I still have nightmares about the way the ballerinas looked at my leotard from Walmart. The instructor's cold, piercing fingers as she tapped my hips and said my turn out was *never going to cut it in the ballet world.*

All the other girls' hips rotated so far out, they looked ready to snap, and yet mine have never gone more than forty degrees. You'd think, for a hip that's ready to pop out of its socket, it'd be more flexible. But that would make too much sense.

"So I'm thinking I can help you with arms, and then some moves they'll probably have you try. In the water, of course."

I nod and catch Leslie sliding her body into one of the weight machines and beginning to film us. I shoot her an inquisitive look.

"Relax. I'm taking notes for you. I'm not posting or anything."

Tanya sits on her knees and starts doing what looks like a breaststroke. "You're a swimmer, right?"

"I swim," I say.

"She's a swimmer," Dani and Tanya say in unison.

"Okay. Sorry." I don't see the point of getting into semantics here.

"So you're probably used to swimming like this. Like you're pushing the water away."

I move my arms the way she's doing, in big circles with my palms facing away from me.

"Mermaid arms are the opposite, though. Mermaid arms are like . . . imagining you're hugging the water." She flips her palms. "And no stiff hands. Swimmer hands are like fins, but mermaids hold them a little loose, graceful. Like you want to let the water slip through a little. Barb is a huge stickler for hands."

I try to do what she's doing, but it doesn't feel natural. It's like having to unlearn everything my body thinks it knows.

She demonstrates a couple more moves for me. The pike, which is basically a yoga boat pose, with the legs straight in the air at an angle, is how they expect us to do an underwater flip. The legs are still, and the thrust is all in the arms.

"But gracefully. None of this," she says, flailing about.

Dani laughs from her handstand corner, even though she's moved on to doing crunches while she watches us work. "Vero never looks like that," she says. "She's too shy to admit it, but she's been practicing the Mermaid Cove routines from the YouTube videos for, like, forever."

"Is that true?" Tanya asks.

I nod. "But there's a bunch of stuff you can't pick up on from the videos. I've been doing arms all wrong. And the hands . . ." I let my voice trail off, and Tanya continues giving me pointers.

With every formation she arranges her body into, I feel more and more like one of those long balloons that a clown twists into animals and hats, except my limbs can't help untwisting. I wobble anytime we're on one leg, my tendons screaming inside my skin. Soon it's almost time for her to get going, and I'm sweating and out of breath.

"Okay, last one." She bends her left leg so her foot nearly touches her butt, then grabs at the ankle with the same hand. As she leans forward, Tanya swoops her other arm over her head and arches her back until her toes are practically touching her messy bun. All while balancing on her right leg.

It looks effortless when she does it. I mimic her, turning my torso into a C. I'm so deep in focus that when I feel a light tap at my forehead, I'm surprised to realize it's my toes. My body's a closed circle. A giant O. Which is probably what my mouth looks like too.

"Whoa. You're, like, really good at that," Tanya says.

Dani sits up from across the room and gasps. Leslie snaps a picture. I let go and stand on both legs.

"I've tried it in the water before. Just not like this."

Tanya looks at me like I'm a mystery unraveling before her. It may not make sense to her—I definitely struggled with some of the other moves—but my body's just random. Good at some things, not so great at others, and it can change at a moment's notice, depending on the weather or how I'm feeling. It has its own set of rules, its own language only I know. Which version of me will show up to auditions next week? That's the big unknown.

"Just keep it up. You'll do great," Tanya says.

"Honestly? You're not just saying that?"

She starts digging through her purse for her keys and tells me not to worry. "Yes. And so you know, there's also a swim test. But I've heard you're an expert at that." She gives me an encouraging smile, but I can't help wondering if it's coated with pity. Maybe she's afraid to tell me the truth, that I'm not actually cut out for this. Maybe I'm just setting myself up to be humiliated.

Leslie takes a few steps toward me, back to filming on her phone. In the mirror, I can see myself on her screen, how she's zooming in on my face.

"What's wrong?" She tucks her phone into her back pocket.

"Nothing. I'm just . . . super nervous all of a sudden." I sit on the mat with my legs stretched before me, trying to make my toes line up exactly side by side. It's this thing I do some-times; I like to pretend they match.

"What? Why?" Dani shuffles toward me on her knees, and the bounce makes her voice shake as she moves.

I look around the room, at all the metal and reflections. Parts of it feel familiar because it's the same kind of equip-ment my physical therapists have used for all my post-op re-hab sessions.

For medical purposes.

"I'm not . . . I'm not a *physical* person."

Dani and Leslie look at each other like they're trying to

figure out who'll speak first. Finally my sister nudges me in the shoulder. Soft. Then harder. Hard.

"What the hell was that for?"

She pushes me again, smiling as she squeezes my arms like I'm a cantaloupe in the produce section. "What do you think?"

Leslie pats my skull. "Seems pretty solid to me. A little thickheaded, actually."

"But ripe. Ready," Dani adds.

I wave them off me. "Oh my God, seriously?"

Leslie stifles a laugh.

"You are *so* a physical person," Dani says. "You're taking up space. You're made of all this matter. What more proof do you need than that?"

Foreign: for·eign

1. (adj.) describing a body or object that is introduced from the outside; alien

2. (adj. VR) a meaningless word because outside is relative

Chapter 15

AT THE FAR EAST END of our apartment complex, there's a stretch of ten-foot brick wall separating our buildings from the big houses on the other side. The wall and the houses didn't always used to be there. When we were eight and my family had just moved here, it was just a wooded area, and Leslie and I would wander into it and find random things like an empty whiskey bottle, a lone gardening glove, rusty tin boxes. Then it got barricaded off, and for years there was a sign that said COMING SOON: TESORO RIDGE.

Which translates to Treasure Ridge, but you wouldn't know it's a Spanish word by the way the locals say it. It irks me every time I see it, because I can't even count how many times people have told my parents to speak English here, only to turn around and use our words to name their fancy homes, like they can claim any language they want as their own.

But apparently that's where Dani's friend lives, and Dani's friend has a pool. After we left the gym, she had the brilliant idea to ask him if we could use it, and now we're all headed there in Alex's mom's car. His house is close enough to be walking distance, but the wall is so tall that we can't just climb over it. We have to drive all the way around, to the security gate that's on the other side.

I turn to face Dani and Leslie in the backseat. "Who's your friend again?"

"Jason Parker. He was my lab partner in science this year. He's really sweet."

"For a Ridge Rat?" Leslie says.

"Don't start. We don't have to go if you're going to give him shit," Dani says.

"Ooh." Leslie grins, and her eyes seem to sparkle. "I like testy Dani. Do you have a thing for him?" she loud-whispers.

"Stop," Dani says.

"What's a Ridge Rat?" Alex asks, interjecting before Leslie can continue her teasing.

"Nothing. It's just what people call the spoiled rich kids at our school," I say. "Most of them live at Tesoro."

"Yeah, but they looove coming over to Palmview Lakes for our parties," Leslie says. "Ruin our place so they don't have to ruin their own."

I feel my neck tense. I wonder if she's not just thinking about the shaving cream fight or all the stains they left scattered around the pool deck, but about what happened after.

"It's really cool of your friend to let us come over." I

place my hand on Alex's thigh, and he does the same, our arms crisscrossing over the center console. I'm wearing shorts and an old T-shirt over my bathing suit, so when he begins rubbing my skin with his thumb, it's like every nerve in my body becomes hyperaware of his touch. Somehow, though his hand is nearly big enough to cover my whole thigh, he manages to stay completely clear of my scar without even looking.

Dani's phone buzzes. "Jason says we can either go to the pool at their rec center or we can use the one at his house."

"Wow, so many options," Leslie says sarcastically.

"The one at his house is fine," I say.

Dani nods. "Less people. This way it's just us." She gives Alex the security code that Jason texted her when we pull up to the gate. Leslie raises her eyebrows, feigning like she's impressed.

"Look at that. Super high-tech. I guess that means they don't need to have a Bob driving around in his golf cart for security, like we do."

"Is that what Bob does?" Alex asks. "I was wondering what his job is."

"Well, technically, it's security," I say. "But he has his nose in a little bit of everything."

"I bet you that people here have their own golf carts they drive around pointlessly," Leslie says, pulling a fun-size bag of potato chips out of her purse.

"You brought snacks," I say flatly.

"Of course. We're on a field trip."

"Don't ever change," I say. The things my best friend gets a kick out of never cease to amaze me.

When we arrive at Jason's, the house is exactly as I'd pictured it, with a stone exterior accentuated by neatly laid palms and several tropical flower bushes. We don't even go inside, because there's a side entrance that leads straight to the pool. Jason meets us by the open gate, standing barefoot in the grass. He's tall and thin, and with his swim trunks already soaking wet, he reminds me of what Mami would call un trapo mojado, left out to dry in the sun. But from the way Dani smiles when he opens his arms to hug her, I can tell this Jason's exactly her type.

"This place is wild," Alex says under his breath.

It really is. The whole back wall of the pool is lined with waterfalls that jet out of smooth black stones. Dani makes introductions, and Jason offers us our choice of flavored water from the spritzer machine on the poolside bar and tells us to sit on whichever lounge chair we'd like.

"There's extra towels in the cabana if you need," he says.

Alex puts his hand on the small of my back. "The cabana? Is this for real?" I recognize the awe in his voice, like he just stepped into another world. I felt it too, the first time I came to one of these houses for Lola Griffin's party in seventh grade. It was like being in a hotel, every need and comfort accounted for. Lola's parents went all-out with the unicorn theme, down to the last napkin and cupcake, and after that, Lola molded her obsession into an entire personality, talking about how unicorns were so *on brand* for her, colorful and mystical and a total rare catch. All year long, people would bring her unicorn candy, stickers, and balloons at random moments, just because it made them "think of her."

It was so shallow and overdone, which is why I confide only in my closest friends about my mermaid wishes.

Jason dives headfirst into the pool and swims up to the edge right by my feet. "So Danitza said you're auditioning at Mermaid Cove next week."

"Dani!" So much for it being a secret.

"It's not like he's going to tell our parents, Vero. Relax."

I stretch my towel over a chair by the deep end, sandwiched between Leslie and Alex on either side. They've both already stripped down to their suits, while I'm still in my shorts and flip-flops.

Dani takes a few steps back and makes a run for it into the pool, her body clenched together in the air. She hits the water like a bomb, causing a massive splash that practically soaks me from the waist down, then pops her head up a few seconds later.

"Now are you coming in?" she yells.

"In a minute!" I pull up the video Leslie shot of Tanya and me at the gym, making note of which moves I'll want to run through. Sitting on the lounger with my legs straight in front of me, I try to touch my toes, then stretch my shoulders by swinging my arms in big circles.

"Do you need help with anything?" Alex looks like he's itching to get in the water, but instead he squats down next to me.

I shake my head. "Go. I'll be right there."

He dives in with his hands over his head and his body straight and sharp as a pencil—effortlessly smooth. Out of the corner of my eye, I see Leslie's jaw drop and then she turns to gauge my reaction. We both know that my first celebrity crush was a US Olympic diver.

"Don't even start," I say to her under my breath.

She lets out a groan that is also part squeal. "He's just . . . so dreamy for you," she whispers. I smile but otherwise try not to react. I don't want to get too excited too soon about things with Alex. Even though the way his shoulders shimmer as he tosses around a Frisbee with Jason is making it near impossible.

I jump in and swim the length of the pool four times while skimming the floor, all in one breath. It's my favorite thing to do when I first get in; it makes everything go quiet as I put distance between myself and the water's surface. I take a breath and go again, only this time I practice the mermaid arms that Tanya showed me in the gym. The movement makes me feel stiff and ungraceful; it's going to take some practice and getting used to.

When I come up, Leslie's still lying out on the lounger. I know without even asking that she's not planning on swimming. Leslie doesn't like getting her hair wet, or her makeup wet, or anything wet, for that matter. She is, as she says, a land animal, destined for leisurely perching. Sometimes I can't think of a single thing we have in common except our friendship. Which is plenty.

"A girl could get used to this," she says. "We should definitely come back."

So we do. The whole week, we come back every day during the same two-hour window, like clockwork. Alex and Dani give me my space while I practice my moves and swim times, and Leslie plays the routines for me on her phone, writing down the choreography in my journal so I can put them all together in the water.

Dani was right; Jason's super sweet and actually seems pretty excited for me and my auditions. The nice thing about his pool is that it's ten feet deep instead of six like the one at Palmview Lakes, which means when I practice twirling up toward the surface, I get in more than two pike turns. It's all starting to feel more like body memory, like I know all these motions by heart. Even in moments when I feel stiff and my groin starts to ache as I walk the stepping-stone-lined path along the side of the house, it all fades once I'm in the water. By Thursday, which is when Tanya said she can give me another training session, I'm actually feeling like I could have a chance at making mermaid.

We sit on our towels in the grass facing each other, Tanya pulling on my arms to help me stretch. I let myself imagine that we're already coworkers and this is how we warm up when we're out of the water.

"So how do you feel about everything?" she asks.

"Excited, nervous. I'm just glad I have this last chance to go over it all with you, before tomorrow."

Tanya smiles and jerks her head toward Leslie, who's hovering over us, filming on her phone. "Judging from what your documentarian here has shown me, I'm pretty sure you're already in great shape, but I'm glad to help if it makes you feel better."

I'm about to head into the water when Leslie switches off her phone and her face drops. "I thought your sister said Jason's last name was Parker?"

"Yeah. So?"

"So why's *he* here?" she says, lowering her glasses and looking at something past my shoulder.

I turn around. Immediately, I feel dizzy, as if I got up too soon, even though I'm still sitting on the grass, clutching its blades. I roll up my towel and start buttoning up my shorts, my fingers shaking from rage. "We have to go," I say to Leslie under my breath. "Please, let's just go."

Boundary: boun·dar·y

1. (n.) a dividing line that marks the limits of a place or object
2. (n. VR) a sacred, invisible line meant to keep a person safe

Chapter 16

JEREMY BRADLEY STANDS WITH ONE HAND on his hip and a can of beer in the other. "Bro. You didn't tell me you were having a party," he says, smiling until his eyes land on mine. I don't blink. I feel my breath catch in my throat.

"Oh hey. Verónica. Who're your friends?" he says, gesturing at Alex, Tanya, and Dani.

"Ugh. Who invited him?" Leslie says. Her voice shrinks to a whisper as she adds, "Ronnie, you okay?"

I don't respond to either one of them. I feel like my whole body has turned to stone. He's acting like nothing ever happened between us. This boy whose words are engraved in the folds of my memory and around all those corners in my mind I'm afraid to turn.

Is he pretending, or does he really not remember? Did it never occur to him he might've done something wrong?

How can a person who's cut you so deep come away completely unscathed?

Since I say nothing, Jason pulls himself out of the pool and makes introductions. "Jeremy, this is everyone. Everyone, this is my stepbrother, Jeremy."

Through what feels like a long tunnel, they go around exchanging *hey*'s and *hi*'s while I finish gathering my things. I try to pretend he's not here, but I can feel Jeremy's eyes watching me. They're part of the problem, part of why I didn't get out of the hot tub that night, when everyone else left. He has these crystal-like eyes. Ojos claritos, like Mami says about all the love interests in her telenovelas. As if there were something inherently sweet and innocent about them, just because they're light. Not dark or brown like mine.

And I fell for it. Crossed the water into his arms because everyone else seemed to want to, because how could I resist this guy who, if you looked up *all-American* in the dictionary, you'd find his face there? Synonyms: *gorgeous, handsome, classically beautiful.* Except who got to write that entry? Not me.

Now, as I can't help sneaking a few glances his way just so I know where he's at and what he's doing, his features seem wolflike. Sharp and predatory. Not blue like the sky but blue like a corpse, all the life gone cold and stiff inside of it. He smiles and I remember his laugh, how it pierced all my defenses. Seeing him for the first time since that night is like having a scar reopened. I hadn't realized it ran so deep.

Somehow, even though it's impossible and completely unfair, everyone looks so comfortable. Dani's splashing around playing basketball with the stepbrothers, who seem more interested in covering her than they do in getting the ball. Alex has climbed onto a giant swan-shaped float. Tanya's still stretching as if we could actually go on practicing as planned. All I can do is stand by the edge of the pool with my arms crossed and wave Alex over. It takes him forever to row through the water with his arms.

"What's wrong?" he says once he reaches us.

"I just don't feel well. Can you take us home?" I give an apologetic glance to Tanya, who tells me not to worry.

Maybe it's the acoustics of the water or the walls, but from across the pool, Dani hears us. "But we just got here." She stops treading water and sets her feet down, standing still in the shallow end.

"And now we're leaving," I reply, pleading at her with my eyes.

Something in her expression hardens. "You go on without me. I'll stay here with Jason."

"How will you get home?" I ask.

"I can *walk*."

The way she says it sinks me. Like she's not Dani at all, but just another kid trying to hit me where they know it'll hurt. A twinge of regret sweeps her face, and I look away, scared to call more attention to myself than she already has.

"Fine," I say. "Do whatever you want."

⁓

She stays because she can, because Dani has always known how to use her stubbornness and her wants as a threat, anytime she doesn't get her way. When we were little, she used to throw the most massive tantrums at Publix if my parents denied her a sugary cereal or a candy bar, which was often. Mami always knew how to handle her, though. She'd tell me to stay behind and watch the cart; then she'd carry Dani out of the store, screaming and wailing, and lock her in our car like a dog while we quickly paid for our groceries. That didn't last long. One day a customer came into the store claiming there was an abandoned child in the parking lot and that the manager should call child services. I've never seen Mami turn so pale so fast. It was like watching Papi's coffee every morning when she poured the milk in, all its dark coloring diluted by a few violent swirls. We rushed through the sliding doors and straight into the car, peeling out of the lot like we'd robbed the place, even though we'd left all that week's food in the cart. She went off about nosy Americans, how what's wrong with this country is that parents can't even discipline their children without someone calling it abuse, and that's why they're so spoiled and disrespectful; they think freedom means doing whatever they want, without consequence or responsibility. Then she said, *That doesn't apply to us, of course,* and the whole ride home, she yelled at us about rules. Rules we have to follow if we want to stay in this country and not be sent home. Rules we have to think about even if other kids our ages don't, because they were born with permissions we have to earn. *Rules to prove we belong here,* Mami said, the most important being we don't draw unnecessary attention. Not from cops, not from government officials, not from teachers, not even from our own parents.

That day we learned something I'd suspected all along. We needed to be good to stay here. Good students. Good daughters. Maybe eventually good citizens. Even after we got our green cards, the rules didn't magically lift. *Permanent resident aliens is what we are to them,* Mami said. *The permanent part is fragile. Don't give them any excuse to break their promise.*

Dani rarely threw another tantrum after that; she learned to carry it inside her like a quiet, carefully placed bomb. Which is why I didn't press her at Jeremy and Jason's. Between the maybe-surgery and the mermaid auditions, she's armed with two of my biggest secrets. So I left her there. Leslie and Tanya stayed behind. Now it's just Alex and me in another quiet car.

"Does it hurt?" he says after a while. His trunks are drenched, and he's sitting on my towel to keep from soaking the cloth seats. The wind billows in so loud through the half-opened windows that I have to shout just to be heard over it.

"Does what hurt?"

The car slows at a light. His eyes float down to my hand

against my thigh. To my nails digging into skin. I hadn't even noticed I was doing it. Some people bite their nails when they're anxious, just to have somewhere to place their energy. I carve little crescents along the skin surrounding my scars.

"It doesn't. Not the way you'd think," I say.

"Try me."

I'm not sure I can explain, or if I even want to. It doesn't hurt because I don't really feel it. Because the scar has been sealed for three and a half years but the skin around it remains partially numb. When a wound is still healing, touch is a far-away thing. I sense everything around my scar like it's happening to another body, like my skin is as thick as a dictionary rather than sheets of delicate flesh.

"I just . . . lost some of the sensation around this scar. After my last surgery. Not all of it. Just enough that when I touch it, the feeling is kind of dampened. Like it's only at the surface. I know it's weird—"

"No it's not. I get that."

"What do you mean? How?" I wonder what he could possibly know about it.

"It's not the same. Not on my skin. But I know what it's like to feel removed from a part of yourself. Like it's out of reach, and even when you try to touch it, it's like you come up against glass. And you're numb in the places that hurt."

"That's exactly it," I say, struck by his words and where they might be coming from.

"It feels like watching things from underwater."

"Underwater," I repeat. To me, that's the one place that's

always felt safe. I'd never considered that it might be because of the distance, the millions of molecules cushioning me from all the things that brought me pain. "So how do you get through it?"

"I manage. It's one of the reasons my mom and I moved here. She thought we could both use a fresh start after she and my dad split and he moved back to Mexico."

"I didn't know he moved away. I'm sorry."

"It's okay." He turns into our complex and slows down to let a duck and her ducklings wobble across the street toward the canal. "They were never really good together. And I always felt caught between them yet somehow also torn in two. Like I had to choose one or the other. My mom's side or my dad's side. My therapist thinks that's why I'm not good with confrontation. I just kind of detach. Sometimes I don't even notice it."

I think back to the first time I saw him, closing his eyes by the pool. Twenty-four hours straight of driving cross country, away from a life that fell apart through no fault of his own. He was so tired that day, and sometimes, though our newness feels light and intoxicating all at once, it's still there, in his eyes. I wish I knew how to help. The only therapist I've ever seen is a physical one, and things were always formulaic in our sessions: everything broken down into targeted exercises, sets of reps, to regain strength and muscle mass. Progress we could chart and literal steps I took as I recovered. But I don't know what it takes to heal emotions. What it looks like to love a heart that's hurting. I have so many questions.

So many things I want know about Alex, but only if he wants to tell me. So instead of asking, I explain about Jeremy. What he did, and why I needed to leave. Why I couldn't even talk to him or look at him. Even though I don't go into every humiliating little detail, it feels good to say some of this out loud. Something about this boy—with his gentle eyes and the knowing way he listens—feels safe.

"He wasn't going to stop. And just as I was trying to push him away, my parents walked in. And now they assume the worst of me."

"That's . . . horrible," he says when I'm done. "I'm sorry he did that to you. And that's not fair of your parents. It's not your fault he totally violated your boundaries."

My mind gets stuck on that word: *violated*. For weeks I've tried to convince myself it could have been worse, it wasn't that bad. His hands went places I didn't want and then they stopped. But not of his own accord. And not because I stopped them. Sometimes I wonder if Jeremy made fun of my body to remind me that his was stronger. To make me feel powerless against him.

But *violate*? In Spanish, *violar* is a word I learned young, a word that Mami said meant *the worst thing a man can do to a woman* after we heard it on the news. In English, there's this whole range, and I don't know where that night falls within it.

So I haven't wanted to use that word. I wish I could not even go near it. It's always spoken with the implication that people just let things happen to them. Even though it's right there in Mami's definition: subject, verb, object.

I hate that Jeremy made me the object.

He did that, though. Not me.

"Are you sure you're okay?" Alex says.

"I will be, I think. It just hurts that it's not even a thought in his mind. For me, that night made my life hell. But it was like any other party to him."

"Blades have a handle."

"What?"

"Nothing. It's just something my therapist says. Not everyone that hurts us hurts themselves doing it. Blades have a handle. Get it?"

"Oh. I hadn't thought of it like that." It's an interesting metaphor. I push a couple more half moons into my thigh as I turn it over in my mind.

"Shit. That's probably really insensitive of me," Alex says. "I'm so sorry."

"What? Why?"

"Well . . . because." His eyes point at my hand again. "It was meant to be figurative. Not, like, a literal blade that someone uses to actually cut—"

An unexpected giggle bubbles up inside of me. I shake my head and smile at him. "I know how a metaphor works. And it's fine. Really. Actually I'd prefer we not make a big deal out of it."

"I'm sorry. I wasn't trying to. I just wanted to make sure we're okay."

"We'll be okay if you don't treat me different. Not better or worse. Just normal."

"Normal."

"Yeah."

"I hate that word. I don't even know what it means." He pulls into the covered parking spot in front of his apartment, and the shade rolls over us. I feel like we just crawled into a hole, hidden from the rest of the world.

I rest my head back and let out a sigh. There was a time I thought normal just meant me. It's not like I had any other point of reference. Maybe no kid I knew had hip dysplasia, but I thought we all had something. We were all delicate bodies. Young, growing bodies, new to everything we were learning. Kids fell and broke an arm all the time. They vomited in the middle of homeroom. They needed chunks of metal in their teeth or weekly shots to keep them from sneezing at any bit of dust. The world was not an easy place, and we were all managing in whatever way that looked like. The surgeries, the homeschooling, the scarring and limping, the pain I didn't know to complain about. This was my normal. And I was fine with it. When did my definition of that word begin changing? I make a mental note to work a new entry into my notebook later.

"All I meant was, there are about two hundred and six bones in my body." I reach over the emergency brake between us and take his hand, placing it on my thigh. "This one's important, or I wouldn't have told you about it. But it's not the only part of me that matters."

He nods reassuringly and squeezes my thigh lightly. The edges of his lips twitch, like he's unsure if he should smile.

"What's so funny?" I ask.

"Nothing. It's cheesy, actually." His Adam's apple shifts as he swallows nervously, and he begins tapping his thumb against the steering wheel. "I was thinking of making a joke about wanting to explore the remaining two hundred and five bones in your body, but then I thought, 'Too soon?' and then I thought, 'Perfect timing,' and I'm still not sure, but I've blurted it out to you anyways, so . . ."

I laugh. "Oh my God."

"Now you know how my brilliant mind works."

"I like how it works just fine," I say. Mami told me once, warned me, really, that the average teenage guy thinks of sex six hundred times a day, or something ridiculous like that. I almost countered with *what about the average girl?* At first I thought she was exaggerating, but then again, I know how a person can think about things without really thinking about them. The way all our obsessions and insecurities can sneak in through a back door we didn't know we'd left open, take up permanent residence in every surface, every wall, until it becomes like a heart, always beating, always the surging force behind your brain. What happens when you can't tell your desires from your fears because they live in the same place?

The way Alex's lips stay in a shy smile the entire time he talks is kind of hypnotizing. I can't stop looking at a small, soft crease in the fullest part of them. I imagine them traversing all the curves and dips of my body, leaving invisible tracks that make my skin tremble. But I also can't get Jeremy out of my mind, the memory of his cold touch against me. I close my eyes and will my senses to focus on this moment instead. The warmth of Alex's hand. The lightness of his presence; how he listened, but didn't dwell. Didn't let the hardness of what we said weigh back down on us.

"So, what do you want to do now?" he says.

I know but I'm afraid to say it. Good daughters aren't supposed to crave these things. Good girls aren't supposed to be so direct. But it occurs to me that if we're not, then what is the opposite of speaking our wants?

"Honestly, I just want to kiss you right now," I say.

So we do. And maybe it's because I can still taste the words on my tongue, but it feels good, and different, to have made the first move without shame. I start to lean in closer to him, lifting my butt off the passenger's seat. Everything inside me starts to melt and loosen until his hands slide over my back.

Now they're all I feel. My body keeps going while my mind devotes every ounce of attention to his hands. Hoping they won't move. Willing them to not travel down to my cheeks like Jeremy's did. Begging, *Not this. Not again.* I stop, and before I can say anything, Alex stops too.

"You okay?" he asks. Just like that. Like it's easy.

Maybe it should be. Maybe it is.

"I am. It just really got to me, seeing him. It's still fresh."

"We can just hang out. We don't have to do anything you don't want to," he says.

"Okay." And then we sit, for what feels like an eternity, staring at the dashboard. I'm starting to wonder if I should've never said anything when Alex's whole body shakes, like a chill just ran straight through him.

"Sorry. I'm just . . . freezing. My suit's still soaked." He smiles timidly, and it dawns on me that he's always going to be that person who really listens, no matter what. Even if it means sitting in a cold car while I process everything I'm going through.

"Alex, oh my God. You should change. Since you went, you know, swimming and all. I, on the other hand, am bone dry," I say flatly.

Alex blows air through his lips, trying to hold it together. When he fails not to laugh at my poorly timed bone pun, it makes me laugh too. This afternoon was a total bust, and I've decided we're at the point where it's tragic but kind of funny.

"How was the water today, anyways?"

"It was just okay," he says. "The whole water in a pool thing is highly overrated. Three out of ten, would definitely not splash in again." He leans against the headrest of the driver's seat so our eyes are completely aligned. The moment grows quiet and small.

"I should've stayed," I say. "I should've at least gotten in the water, even for a few minutes. The auditions are tomorrow, and I just missed my last chance to practice."

"You'll be great."

"How can you know that?"

He shrugs sleepily, like it's not even something he has to think about. "Because. What is it they say about mermaids? How they lure people to the sea?"

"That's . . . only one very simplified version of many different mythologies. But I guess. So?"

"So. The first time I saw you, you were swimming. And I couldn't help but come to the pool."

"You said you weren't watching me."

"I wasn't. I was trying not to, anyways. I didn't want to make it weird, but there was just something really peaceful and compelling about you as you moved through the water. I wanted to get closer. My point is, if you ask me, you're already a mermaid. You've been one all along."

Luck: luck

1. (n.) a force that brings fortune or adversity
2. (n. VR) a thing you hardly dare to hope for; a thing you fear wishing away

Chapter 17

ON THE WAY TO THE AUDITIONS I get a text from Alex.

Break a leg.

. . .

No wait. Does that still apply to mermaids?

I'll take it, I write back.

He sends me a meme of a seal waving its fin in the air, then he writes:

Eres una mermaid. Hasta el fin.

In any language, it's the cutest, most encouraging thing a guy's ever said to me.

Bilingual AND on point, I write back, grinning as I add laughing emojis and hearts.

"What's so funny?" Dani says.

I cross my arms and bring my phone under my armpit. "Nothing. Just something Alex said." We're sitting in the backseat of Tanya and Leslie's car while they sit up front.

I'm still upset with Dani about yesterday, but this morning she woke up early just to give me back my purple top. It was adorned with dozens of tiny pearl beads that swirl across the left and climb up the string, forming a gorgeously subtle asymmetric design.

"I'm sorry, okay? Here. It's for good luck," she said. "Like in the story."

I was surprised Dani remembered. In the original folktale, on the day the little mermaid is ready to visit the water's surface, her grandmother puts lilies made of pearls in her hair. Then she *had eight oysters fixed on to the princess's tail to show her high rank.*

"You can come with us," I said. "If you want."

So now I have three groupies. Tanya's shift doesn't start until after the auditions, but she insisted on dropping me off and waiting in the car with Leslie for moral support.

"I wasn't supposed to work until the weekend, but I switched with Ayana, who had to get a tooth filled this week," Tanya explains as she puts on lipstick at a stop sign. "She promised to cover one of my shifts next time."

It's weird to hear her talk about being a mermaid like it's any other job, like she's a server or works at Old Navy. I go through my bag, looking for at least a lip gloss or lip balm.

"Don't be nervous. You look great," Dani says, reading my mind as she hands me a brownish-pink tube. The gloss smells like berries as I apply it.

"That's making me hungry," Leslie says. "We should get smoothies while we wait for the tryouts to be over."

"Not at my mom's," I say.

"What? Why not? We get the discount," Dani says.

"She'll want to know what we're doing today. And why I'm not with you guys."

"There's a juice bar, like, two minutes from the park," Leslie says. "We'll just hang out there while we wait for Verónica to call and tell us she got the part." She sneaks that last bit in there casually. I kick the back of her seat.

"Stop. I don't want to get my hopes up."

"It's not illegal, you know. To want something," she says.

I fidget with my hair to avoid looking at her. Sometimes it feels like it is. Sometimes when I see the way Mami obsesses over the mail, over every form she has to fill out in hopes of getting our papers sorted, it feels like none of the things we want most belong to us. "I know. It's just this thing my parents are always saying. I'd rather celebrate after."

"What are you going to tell them?" Dani says. "When . . . if you make it?"

"I can't even think about that right now. I'll deal with it after. If I even have to."

"Underthinking is better than overthinking," Leslie says. "I approve."

We pull into the Mermaid Cove parking lot, and already I see three other girls walking toward the entrance.

"You've got this," Dani adds.

"The big thing is to relax," Tanya says. "Technique is great and all, but really, they just want to know that you feel comfortable and in control underwater."

I nod and take a deep breath. Everything will be fine once I jump in.

It always is.

It has to be.

Current: cur·rent

1. (n.) the part of a fluid body (such as air or water) moving continuously in a certain direction
2. (n. VR) a moment in the present that will run through my veins forever

Chapter 18

I TRY TO FOCUS ON THE SOUND of the water as I join the small crowd that's already wrapping around the fountain by the entrance. It's two hours before the park opens, but the auditions begin in fifteen minutes. I count maybe forty-five people. Most of them are older than me, probably in their late teens or early twenties.

"Listen up!" A loud, raspy voice cuts through our nervous mumbles. I recognize its source before I see her at the front of the line, yelling into a bullhorn. "I'm Barb, coordinator and choreographer here. As you all know, we are holding emergency auditions today. One of our mermaids broke a leg quite literally, and, well, that's why you're here. To see if you can fill her spot this summer. This is a temp position, with room to grow into a more permanent placement if you're willing to do the work. But before we get started, I want to make something clear. If you thought this was going to be twirls and blowing bubbles, you thought wrong. People all over the world dream about becoming a mermaid, but the reality is it is real, tough work. We're not looking for people who want to splash around all day. We need athletes and performers."

A sharp inhale sends my core toward my spine. Of all the words I would use to describe myself, *athlete* is not one of them. Every PE teacher I've ever had, every student that laughed at the time it took me to finish whatever torture drill we were doing that day—I would've hidden from them all if I could. Not gotten on a stage to perform in front of them. I start shimmying my shoulders and legs. My hip protests, not so much with pain but a general iciness, a reminder that it's not the same as my right hip, my "good" hip, which I never even have to think about.

Barb has us form two lines for registration, and we each get a number they write on our shoulders. The sun barely rose a half hour ago; the sky's still a timid, sleepy blue, and birds chirp passively. I look around and catch a few auditioners yawning, but my nerves have me on high alert.

I couldn't sleep last night, thinking about this swim.

"Forty-three," a girl about my age says once we're both headed inside. She looks longingly at the bright yellow numbers on my shoulder blade. "That's a lucky one."

"How so?"

She's tall and much thinner than I am, and she moves like she's trying to stretch in a new pair of pants. "If you add them up, you get seven. Which is the number of days in one week. And if you subtract them, you either get one or negative one. Either way, you end up with one. Kinda like these auditions will. Lucky."

"Oh." I don't know if that's the word I would use to describe it. *Pressure,* maybe. Or *intense.*

"Are you a swimmer?" the girl asks. "I mean, obviously, right? But do you compete? You look like you compete."

She takes me in, and even though there's no judgment in her eyes—just innocent curiosity—I straighten my spine and roll back my shoulders. I imagine balancing a book on my head, trying to keep my gait natural but not stiff, graceful and even.

"I've swum awhile, but I don't compete." I keep my answer short and to the point. She's nice, but she's also making me anxious. We haven't even jumped in the water yet, and I'm already being observed.

"You should. You have the arms for it. I just . . ." She looks down at her arms with an expression I recognize. Like she can't believe the limbs attached to her body are really hers.

"So!" It takes just one short syllable from Barb to gather us all on the deck. She's standing by the edge of the spring, holding a tablet with a waterproof cover that makes it look twice its size. Next to her, two mermaids that I recognize from the Cove's videos hold whistles between their lips. "You're about to embark on the most important part of the Mermaid Cove audition. The most challenging one. Many of you, I'm sure, have already studied up on what the drill is, but I'll reiterate on the chance a few of you haven't. This is a four-hundred-yard swim. From here to there." She points at a rope floating in the water that looks like it's a football field away. Then she flings her arm in our direction. "And back, twice, is a total of four hundred yards. One hundred yards each time you cross."

Barb pauses, and the sound of wet feet shifting around grows louder. We're all getting restless. We've been stretching this whole time. Now the energy hangs in the air, loaded and poised for movement. Needing to go.

"You'll be swimming with the current one way, against the current the other. You'll be timed. We need to know who can really last out there."

Bodies amble toward the wooden deck that lines the edge of the spring, wanting to get a head start. Barb throws both her hands in the air, still holding the tablet in one.

"Not so fast, little fishies!" Even though she's shouting, there's a softness that creeps into her words. "Safety. Is THE most important thing we care about today, and every day, at Mermaid Cove. Water's dangerous. Every second our mermaids are out there, they're trusting each other with their lives. So we're looking for strong, smart, safe swimmers. Got it?"

She waits for most of us to nod, then steps aside to make room for us to get into the water. The spring is about as wide as a major highway, and at the moment, just as intimidating.

I wait until the last possible second to take off my flip-flops and shorts. But when I jump in, all it feels like is home.

Piercing, thrashing, all-enveloping, home.

I let myself sink. It feels like I've been gone forever. It's everything I imagine the ocean in Peru would be, except the water here is fresh and clear as store-bought ice cubes. I come up and place my goggles over my eyes, spreading out into the starting line.

"Holy . . . I wasn't expecting it to be this cold," the girl from the entrance says. Her teeth chatter as she treads water beside me. I hold my jaw shut tight.

"It's seventy-four degrees," I tell her. All the brochures and Wikipedia entries said so. But I've never been intimidated by the cold. Mami says it's because I'm a child of the Pacific, that even though I might not remember swimming in it, the ocean is in my bones. In Peru, she says, the waters are freezing and the current is so strong, it feels like it'll never let you go. But it's not scary. It's more like a tight embrace, a place that feels safe.

I move my arms and legs in place. I can see my limbs straight through the water, and below them, colorless fish several feet down.

"Ready! On the whistle, you go. One, two . . ."

It takes a couple of seconds. Barb has to nudge one of her assistants. The young woman's chest puffs up and a shrill chirp escapes her.

We start.

Sleight: sleight

1. (n.) deceitful craftiness
2. (n. VR) a necessary lie, a trick performed to survive

Chapter 19

I GO SO FAST IT'S LIKE I'M FLYING. Body stretched long, reaching, I feel my spine expand with every breath, fill with air as it grows lighter, faster, with each stroke. Every inch of pressure in my joints dissipates. The water moves over me, undisrupted, shifting to make perfect space.

I'm halfway through the first lap. Even though everyone spread out at the start, the spring is crowded now, congested with bodies. Some of them pass me. Others lag behind. I focus only on chasing the light dancing in front of me, and soon I'm approaching the rope.

One hundred yards down. Three more to go.

But now that I'm on my way back, the current fights me. It makes each stroke feel half as strong, and all of a sudden, I'm in a slow-motion video, watching the world turn glacial.

I read about this, but the reality is harsh and visceral.

My pacing is off, and my muscles start burning against

the freezing water. They need more oxygen, so I start coming up for air with each stroke.

My body slows to the point I can hear my doubts again.

Was there ever any preparing for this?

The apartment pool I've swum in all these years feels laughable right now.

This water doesn't welcome me.

This water wants me out.

Each second that passes makes my limbs feel like slabs of concrete, one piling over the other.

What ever happened to the weightlessness?

The gentle gravity.

I feel my hip joint creak.

I feel a tension that is not yet pain.

I want to cry. Maybe I am. I start to wonder if I'm still moving or if I'm just thrashing in place. I picture my tears being swallowed by the springs.

All I feel is small. Powerless. Like the current could scatter me to pieces.

Another rope approaches. It's the same place where I started.

I flip again with every bit of force left inside of me.

Everything switches.

Slowly, the current starts carrying me again. It's both a push and an embrace.

After all the fight I gave, this third stretch feels easy.

I feel my heart again, giddy but also terrified.

Because I get it now. The point of this. The whole swim

is just practice until the last lap. The final one will be the hardest. I don't know if I'll have anything left by then. I don't know where I'll pull the energy from. How much more can I give to this dream? What will I empty if I give it all it takes?

My lungs are fire by the time I finish the last lap.

They ravage oxygen to the point I can't control my breath.

"Whoa. You good there?" Someone stretches out a hand by the railing.

I nod and take it. I think?

One of the mermaids, the one who whistled at the start of this, helps me out. I don't have to look at her name tag to know it's Lila, the most senior performer, who's been here almost four years. Lila's family emigrated from Japan, but she was born in our local hospital after her mom's water broke during a visit to the Cove. It's one of those stories that gets told over and over on social, giving her celebrity status among fans. I can't believe I'm actually grabbing Lila's hand. Here. In the flesh. She's wearing a bright pink sports bra, black bikini bottom, and aviator glasses that look like mirrors. When I glance at her, all I see is my reflection, looking every bit as destroyed as I feel.

"Forty-three? Grab a towel and wait over there," she says, pointing at a cluster of five other people by the souvenir shop.

"Did I . . . did I do something wrong?" There's no stopping my teeth from chattering. The water was bitter, but now the wind is downright cruel.

Lila smiles like it's an odd thing to ask, and then her eyes shift to the left. I follow them and scan the landscape. There are people still in the water, slowly making their way back. Some of them don't even move, they just float face-up, surrendered.

I gasp.

"Don't be surprised. It usually goes like this. We start out with, like, fifty, and by the end, it's just a handful of you all that go to the next round. Over there—" She points again. "Just dry off a bit, and we'll be right there."

I make my way toward the wooden bench where we all left our towels and flip-flops. Even though I could barely move from exhaustion a few seconds ago, a jolt of giddy energy runs through me, feeling like it could burst. I can't believe I actually made it through the first part of auditions. In my mind, I'm doing cartwheels à la Dani, I'm doing Leslie's celebratory body rolls as I walk across the deck.

"Um, forty-three?" Lila calls after me. "Are you *limping*?"

I stop mid-stride. Something inside my chest plummets, landing in my gut.

The way she said that word . . . It's like concern bordering on disgust. It's always hard to tell which one.

She rushes over. "Are you injured?" she says in a whisper.

Shaking my head, I put on the face I always do. A casual smile that says everything is fine. Nothing to see here.

But the answers I normally give will only spark more questions.

I was born with a hip problem, but I'm fine now.

We'll need to see your medical records.

It's just that the cold makes my joints stiff.

Then maybe you shouldn't be swimming in these waters.

It's none of your business.

(The one answer I wish I could give.)

"Oh. That. My legs are, like, half an inch uneven," I sputter. "I don't even realize when I'm doing it."

At the moment, all of these things are true. But they don't seem to satisfy her, or the little crease dipping her forehead into a frown.

"But no one will know once I have a tail on, right?" I say it like it's a punch line. Like if I can make her laugh, she'll be more comfortable.

"I wasn't concerned about—it's fine," she says, nodding again in the direction of the other auditioners. "I'll be right over."

I start looking for my sandals by the wooden bench. My hands are shaking, and I have to clutch at the towel over my shoulder to make them stop. There's a small mountain of flip-flops where we all just tossed them aside before jumping in. Sorting through them, I feel like I'm back in third grade assembly, on the days they'd bring out the mats and Coach would tell us to take off our shoes.

I always hated it. Back then, my doctors still insisted I wear a lift. It looked like a half-inch-thick wedge of cheese, and every morning I'd slip it into the heel of whichever shoe I was going to wear. It was fine there, hidden, until the moment I had to slip off my shoes and walk them to the pile.

I was terrified the lift would pop out and give me away. So I'd make a point to take off my shoes and hold them vertically, letting the lift slip into the toe area unseen. Just a sleight of hand. A small maneuver.

I find my sandals, but instead of putting them on, I hold them on my left side, pressed against my thigh to cover up my scar as I tiptoe across the deck. Lifting my left foot just a tad higher than my right, I make my steps featherlike. A perfect glide. I've been performing these microgestures so long they're practically instinct.

Measured and embedded.

Written in my body memory.

A choreography of one.

Buoy: bu·oy

1. (v.) to keep afloat
2. (v. VR) to feel your heart sink only to lift up; to rescue

Chapter 20

WHEN LILA FINALLY GATHERS THE TOP swimmers for the second part of today's audition, my suit has practically air-dried under the sun. I passed the time by braiding my hair onto one side, letting it drape like a wet rope over my right shoulder. The repetitive motion calmed me as I tried to push aside all the feelings of unease about my limp. Slowly, inklings of confidence breathed back into place. I checked my reflection in the gift shop's window display and saw the braid's tip curled a little, as if pointing at the beads on my suit. Dani would approve. She'd say I already look the part of mermaid. This dream my parents would say is a delusion, a fantasy that will be insignificant when I'm older.

But right now it's everything.

There are only six of us. I nodded hello when I sat down next to everyone, and we exchanged "where are you from?" stories and anecdotes about what brought us here, but not a single name. There's a white girl in a red and blue polka-dotted one-piece whose grandmother was a mermaid in the '50s. A girl with a Southeast Asian accent and a heart-shaped face who drove down for auditions from Atlanta. A synchronized swimmer from Miami joked it'd be nice to have an air hose for a change while she dances underwater. A Black girl wearing a silky floral sarong wrap is from the next town over; she starts college in the fall and thinks this would be a perfect summer job.

I can't help comparing myself to them, wondering how I'll measure up once we're in the water. The synchronized swimmer, at least, is definitely more experienced, and the girl whose grandma was a mermaid probably knows all their tricks and secrets.

Lila moves us onto a smaller deck near the underwater amphitheater where a baby blue canvas hangs over our heads, shielding us from the sun. She explains that as head mermaid, she'll be leading us through the rest of the auditions by teaching us several choreography combinations. We wait quietly for her to tell us we can jump in.

"This is the part you've probably all been waiting for," Lila says. "The dancing and spinning and mermaiding, am I right? So to start, I'll demonstrate some pike spin and pinwheel combos . . . some of our more basic moves. We'll work on them in the water for a bit, and then Barb will evaluate you each individually from the other side of the glass downstairs."

"Ready?" Lila says. She has a happy casualness to her, like maybe she no longer fully grasps the extraordinariness of this water, this moment. Standing on the deck, I can see straight through to the very bottom of the underwater set. Chunks of logs and patches of moss line the ground, along with fake bits of a shipwreck and pipes that connect to the mermaids' air hoses. To the side there's a giant tube that I've seen online; the mermaids swim through it to enter the stage area, jumping into it from a hole in the floor of their dressing room. Seeing them swim into view out of nowhere gives their performance a certain magic; it's as if they really live and breathe underwater.

Us newbies, though, climb down the stepladder into the water, one by one. There's no telling yet who can hold their breath long enough to swim through the tube, though we'll probably find out soon enough. At least that's one thing I don't have to fret about, given that I swam the length of Jason's pool several times without a problem.

We take the next thirty minutes to learn the combinations that Lila lays out for us. Most of them are things I've done before, not only this past week but in the Palmview Lakes pool. All these years I've just been emulating the choreographies of the clips I catch online. It feels strange to be doing them now, these movements I always did when no one was looking, stretched out in this clear, open water for everyone to see.

Now that it's real, there are all these little details I'd never thought of in the make-believe, clusters of muscles I wasn't aware of at work. We start the combination with a double pike spin into a mermaid crawl, which is basically an underwater flip and a swim with the legs wedged together. Then we come up for air and dip back in, standing straight but letting our bodies float into the deep while we wave at the stage with one arm and smile. It's a test in buoyancy, and it's harder than it looks because it's all about letting out just the right amount of air from your lungs to keep yourself from bobbing up toward the surface. Even though I got to practice in Jason's pool, here I start to sink twice as far, and the pressure feels like a steady hand pushing down on my shoulder as my ears tense, holding a wad of air in each side of my skull. When I smile at the glass, water rushes in through the space between my teeth and my cheeks, and I imagine them ballooning like I'm blowing out a birthday cake. Everything is suspended between a visage of effortlessness and breathlessness. Grace and panic. A bubble half the size of my head escapes my mouth as I look up at the sky and kick my legs furiously to meet it.

"Nicely done," Lila says to no one in particular. We all stare at her, breathing heavily. "When you're down there, don't forget to point your toes. It makes a difference, tail or no tail. Think also of your face — as much as you're exerting yourself physically, a mermaid never lets it show. Always smile. Make it look natural. Your expressions are an essential part of the performance; they tell everyone that you live and breathe underwater, that this is your world, your home." She stretches her arms and runs her fingers along the water's surface, forming two half circles around her torso.

I hadn't noticed it while I was swimming, but now that I'm treading water, Dani's hand-stitched beads pinch lightly at my biceps. With each stroke, they scratch my skin like coarse sand, but when I look down to adjust my top, I see that they're catching the light beautifully.

"Try it again this time, just more relaxed," Lila says.

We practice the spins again, and Lila goes around making minor corrections to everyone's form. I try to shift focus to my whole body and how it's moving, but I can't help noticing how she keeps telling the synchronized swimmer not to hold out her arms so stiff.

"The movement comes from the arms, but it should look effortless," she says. "And don't kick with the legs. Push yourself through the water with your arms and pretend the legs aren't even there."

We shift into bird arabesques, which have always been my favorites. I flip forward, then reverse the motion and go back. I splice my legs so they're each bent at the knee, like the angles of a star.

"No, you see . . . Verónica, come here a sec?"

She's singling me out. She's actually making an example of me in front of everyone. Even in this seventy-four-degree water, my cheeks start to burn.

"Can you do exactly what you did just now? Everyone, watch. Pay attention to her legs." The girls place their goggles back over their eyes and sink into the water. All the gravity around me feels magnified under the intensity of their glares. I dip back in and bring my left toe to my right knee, my right toe toward my arched back. Sunlight and darkness rush through my eyelids as I spin forward twice, then stop the motion to retrace it.

When I'm done, Lila has a stunned look on her face. "That was . . . perfect," she says.

"Really?" I blink away the droplets clinging to my lashes. Everything comes into clearer focus.

"I don't get it," says the girl with the polka dots. "We all did the same thing." She looks at me, surprised, and I know what she's thinking. If this girl—in this body with those scars—can do these things, surely she can too. I may not have been expecting Lila to call my arabesque perfect, but I knew I could do it. I know the limits and possibilities of my body as if there were a manual written in my bones.

"You almost did the same thing, but not quite," Lila says. "Your arms looked really good. But the legs . . ." She turns her attention back to me. "Your lines looked beautiful under there, Verónica. Tight and controlled but also natural."

Her words echo in my mind. I can't believe they're for me. Tight. Controlled. Beautiful. Natural.

Lines.

Legs.

Mine.

They create a rhythm I keep as we continue the combination. Pike spin, mermaid crawl, bird arabesque into a leg lift.

"Don't turn the hips out," Lila calls out. "You want the audience to see the angles."

She's speaking the language of my body. Finally. Someone is singing it with me.

Possible: pos·si·ble

1. (adj.) within someone's (or something's) capacity or ability
2. (adj. VR) spanning both every dream and every nightmare that can ever come true

Chapter 21

I FIND DANI AND LESLIE LYING out on the hood of the car in the parking lot. Tanya headed into the dressing room to prepare for today's show a while ago, so now it's just the two of them. Dani's got her sunglasses on while Leslie's wearing a scrunched-up T-shirt over her head to block out the sun.

Neither of them hear me coming because I'm still stunned in a foggy silence. I feel like I'm sleepwalking and this moment will soon be a vague memory. My shadow hovers just a few feet ahead of me on the pavement, and it's only when it creeps up over Dani's and Leslie's heads that they stir back to life.

A squeal like a dog toy dying escapes Leslie while Dani just screams "¡Carajo!" in a way that would make even our father blush.

"What the hell, Vero? I thought it was a cougar or something attacking us," she says.

"A cougar?"

"Didn't you see the video of that cougar that attacked a baby alligator in some guy's backyard?"

Dani's always DMing me videos I never have time to watch. Mostly it's a bunch of Florida Man memes or Only in Florida jokes that get on my nerves because they're not the only things that are true about us. I think she secretly hopes to shoot one of her own someday, but so far, our lives aren't that extraordinary.

"Sooo?" Leslie slides off the car till we're practically nose to nose.

I tilt my head so I can see Dani behind her. "They . . . they let me in."

They're on me so fast I almost fall straight to the ground. Dani's squeals are at full dolphin level, and even Leslie starts jumping up and down until we're forming a tiny huddle of hype.

"I knew it! I totally knew it!" Dani says.

"Tell me everything. Including who you beat for the spot and how," Leslie says.

It's hard for me to match their glee. In my mind this moment was unreal and magical, and now that it's here, I feel far away from it. I'm scared its sweetness will fade away, like cotton candy on my tongue, the second I try to enjoy it.

"They did a whole sit-down interview with me," I say.

"After we were done with the swimming part. It was weird. Barb had a stapler with mermaid stickers on it?" I try to focus on the little details. "And anyways, they said they saw something special in me. That I was mermaid material."

"And *anyways*?" Dani says.

"Oh yeah, no big deal," Leslie says, getting into the car. "Seriously, what are you on right now? Did the water pressure get to you? You're now a mermaid, but it's just another Friday."

"I'm not yet, though." There it is. I've said the hard part out loud. After Barb and Lila told me I'd made it and handed me a bunch of paperwork that I'd need to complete before my first shift, I thanked them and asked if I could have a day or two to think about it. They looked at me like I'd sprouted an extra head, but they said of course. Then they added that I should be grateful and ecstatic, that not just anyone gets accepted and I was lucky to have been chosen.

"I don't get it," Leslie says. "Is there, like, a probation period?"

"I just have a lot to think about. I didn't think I'd actually make it," I say. In my wildest dreams, I never got this far. Even if I did, I skipped the parts where I had to deal with real life. I pull the forms they handed me out of my tote. They're tucked safely in a purple folder with the park's logo in the center. The liability form will need to be signed by my parents, since I'm not eighteen. The payroll sheet asks for my social security card, which is literally locked away in a fireproof box in Mami's side of the closet. If by some miracle I make this all work, there's still my MRI to worry about. The perhaps-maybe-possible hip replacement in my near future that is maybe possibly closer than anticipated. It feels like everything I want is right before me, but being kept at arm's length. Like the first time I tried to kiss Alex before my father stopped us. All these almosts.

"I can't believe this is happening," I mumble, covering my mouth with both hands.

"Nooope. No getting all Miss America on us," Leslie says. She reaches into the backseat and grabs a plastic bag with pink palm trees on it. Dani does the same. I recognize the logo—it's from a kiosk just outside Macy's at the mall, the one that sells beach-themed home decor in every iteration imaginable.

"You went shopping?"

"We couldn't just sit here all day," Dani says.

"This is because you're on fire," Leslie says matter-of-factly, holding out a candle shaped like a fish tail.

"And this is for our room." Dani pulls a small plank of wood out of her bag. It's cream-colored, and there's a picture of a bed with a fin sticking out of one end of the comforter. It says SHHH . . . MERMAIDS SLEEP HERE. "We can put it on our door."

"You bought these not even knowing if I'd make it?"

"We kept the receipts," Leslie teases.

"We knew you'd make it," Dani says emphatically.

I smile and say thanks, though I know the gifts will be a secret, things I tuck under a pillow or into a shoebox in the back of a shelf. "They're perfect." Already, I treasure these little tourist trap goods the same way I did my waxy mermaid statue. Maybe this is just the universe's way of bringing that moment full circle. Of giving me what's really mine. Maybe it's okay to pretend, just for a little while, that this is really possible.

"Have you told Alex yet?" Leslie asks.

"I was waiting to tell him in person," I say, checking my phone. When I left the Cove, I sent him a text asking if he wanted to meet at our spot, but so far he hasn't answered.

We get on the highway with the windows down for the hell of it, just to feel the wind tearing through our hair. I recount the full choreography they had us do, trying my best to recreate the arms portion in the passenger's seat. I tell them how my goggles slipped off my face halfway through my first spin, and how I kept going like it hadn't happened. It made everything, including Barb on the other side of the glass, go out of focus.

"I could barely see her. She was just this blob of a silhouette, watching me."

"She obviously liked what she saw," Leslie says.

I hold my hands out and stare at my palms. "Do you know what they call this?"

Dani leans toward me, trying to see what I see. "What?"

"Mermaid hands!"

Now we're squealing all over again, blasting the radio as we pull into Palmview Lakes. Leslie grins at me wider than the Cheshire Cat. "Congratulations . . . Mermaid Verónica."

And I know. It sounds cheesy. But also, so sincere. That's what I've always loved the most about Mermaid Cove. No one's trying to pretend they don't know real from fantasy. They're just choosing to believe anyways.

Fragment: frag·ment

1. (v.) to break up or apart into pieces
2. (v. VR) to splinter into so many pieces you no longer know what's whole

Chapter 22

TO BELIEVE A BIG LIE, YOU have to believe enough of the smaller ones. It wouldn't work, for example, to tell Mami and Papi that I found a summer job at a law firm, or a doctor's office, or some other respectable place that would be a dream for them, because it'd reek of fakeness and force me to make up too many details that I'd inevitably forget or mess up. I explain this to Dani as we walk home from Leslie's and try to concoct a plan so I can actually become a mermaid.

"You start from the truth and work your way back. Break it up into pieces, little by little. Just enough to satisfy them," I say.

She goes into a cartwheel just as I'm trying to meet her eyes to see if she's listening. When she comes back up, I think I catch her sighing and shaking her head, but it's so slight I figure she's just out of breath or tired. I keep thinking out loud. "So if I'm going to be a mermaid at Mermaid Cove, maybe I just tweak the parts that they don't like. Like I'll tell them I got a job there, but in their marketing or accounting department, something boring like that. Something that would be 'good life skills' on my college applications, you know?"

Dani doesn't agree or disagree with me; she just stares blankly while I walk through my thoughts. Lately all my parents seem to care about is this MRI. I'm pretty sure they're hoping I'll need to have surgery this summer, before senior year starts, so that none of it interferes with school. Last night when I went into their bedroom to say good night, I saw them scribbling on Papi's desk calendar, counting dates in July and August. I recognized their math, the calculations of *if I have surgery by x and it takes y weeks to recover, then it'll all be over by z.*

It's all well and predictable except they forget to account for some tiny details. Like *if I need surgery by x, it means y thousand cells in bone have died, and my pain will have been multiplied by z.* Contrary to what they probably believe, I like my body parts where they are just fine. I'm in no rush to replace and fix things, like a Band-Aid you just rip off quickly to get it over with. But there's no getting over it. One day they'll take the dying bone I've always lived with and replace it with a ghost of itself, a foreign object my body's meant to welcome as its own. What if it doesn't? What if the new joint doesn't fit in any better than the old? What if I have to relearn to walk in it? What if its rhythm is one I can't recognize, a language I can't even speak? What if replacement doesn't fix displacement, and this is how I was always meant to be?

But all I could ask my parents was what they were doing. Papi flipped the giant calendar pages back and forth and said, "We're just trying to prepare for every possibility, that's all."

Which is what I'm doing now too. Preparing for all my possibilities.

"I think that could work. Are you listening, Dani? I'm the new accounting intern at Mermaid Cove, okay? They won't be thrilled, but maybe they won't say no. And that way Tanya and I can ride to work together and it won't be like I'm lying."

She claps her palms together, brushing off the dirt and grass they accumulated from all her flips. "If you say so."

"What is that supposed to mean?"

"Nothing. You're just . . . You're too good at that sometimes."

"Too good at what?"

"Lying."

I ignore the cynicism in her voice, the way the joy and pride of only a few moments ago has slipped out of it. Dani was supposed to be celebrating with me, and now that she's not, the afterglow of this morning starts to feel underwhelming. "Don't act surprised. You knew I'd have to keep it a secret." I nudge her elbow playfully.

"I knew the auditions were a secret. I didn't think you'd keep it up all summer. You know *the rules* of the house," she hisses, same way Papi says those words whenever he's warning us out of trouble.

I roll my eyes. The rules are super vague and unspoken, but the gist of them is this: No lying. No promiscuity. No calling attention to ourselves, ever. By their standards, I'm breaking all of them. By mine, I'm just trying to live my life.

"First of all, we live in an apartment, not a house," I scoff. "How's that for lying? And second of all . . . what choice do I have, Dani?"

"I don't know. It just feels . . . unnecessarily complicated."

Story of my life, I want to say. I can't believe she's only figuring this out now, and only when it requires her to keep a damn secret for once.

"Sorry to inconvenience you."

"You know it's not that."

But I don't.

"I just hate lying to them," she says. "Or not telling them things. It's more trouble than it's worth."

"More trouble," I repeat. Dani swears her life is so hard, while I could only wish to have problems like hers, keeping my secrets instead of having to live with them.

"You should be thanking me," I say.

"What is that supposed to mean?"

I let out a sigh. She'd never admit that she learned all the best lies from me.

If it weren't for me bending the truth sometimes, just slightly, the way water bends the light, Dani and I would barely have a social life. We would never get to hang out with a guy if we didn't tell our parents that a bunch of friends were coming along. We'd never get to go to any parties if we didn't swear up and down that we were only playing board games at someone's house. And Alex would just be a neighbor I stare at sometimes instead of a guy whose touch for once feels safe.

And sure, sometimes it backfires. Maybe if I'd stayed home, I wouldn't have gone into the hot tub with Jeremy that night, and he wouldn't have made fun of me while we made out, and I'd have nothing to regret, ever. Just fears and wants that never materialize one way or the other.

"You don't know how good you have it sometimes," I say. "It's not like you'd be the one getting in trouble anyways. I'm the one risking everything."

She narrows her eyes at me like she's thinking real hard about saying something, but nothing comes out. No point in arguing when I'm right.

If it weren't for me bending the truth a little, I'd have no life that's mine, no mistakes to claim as my own to learn from, just commandments we're expected to follow without question, rules that teach me nothing about myself at all.

Listen: lis·ten

1. (v.) to hear with thoughtful attention
2. (v. VR) to intimately understand a person's words and silences

Chapter 23

DANI WAS RIGHT ABOUT ONE THING. It would be nice to celebrate. When we get back to our apartment, it's empty, so I text Alex again to ask where he's at, and I hop in the shower. By the time I get out, I see he's pinged me his location.

No *how did it go?* or *did you make it?* I scroll through our previous texts, all these cute and encouraging messages about my auditions this morning and then . . . nothing. Did he just forget? I'm annoyed that he's not even a little curious.

Be there in 15, I text back.

I put on a cotton romper Mami just finished sewing for me. It's white with '80s-style confetti, and it has a triangle cutout the size of my hand above the belly button. I'm still surprised Mami didn't object when I picked out the sewing pattern at Michaels, though she did lower the hem of the shorts without my asking. Instead of blow-drying my hair, I comb it and ruffle it with my fingers. It makes me feel cute and messy in a beachy kind of way. Like Tanya looks permanently.

"Where are you going?" Dani asks when I step into the living room. She must've changed into yoga pants and a sports bra while I was in the shower, and she's already pulling up a workout video on her phone.

"Why do you need to know?"

She looks away, disinterested.

The funny thing is, I don't technically know where I'm going. Alex's location isn't one I recognize, though when I pull it up in my maps, it shows it's only an eight-minute walk. Clearly it's someplace in our apartment complex. But not one of the lakes. Or the pool or racquetball court. I wonder if it's his place. He keeps saying it's a mess because they haven't finished unpacking yet or else he'd invite me over. So far he hasn't, and I can't figure out if that makes me anxious or relieved. Sometimes I picture us alone in his room, and a soft, rumbling wave rolls through my body so fast I've actually had to grab at something to keep myself together. Other times I think there's no way my parents wouldn't find out I was fooling around with him, either by an act of God or nature or espionage. Even though I know it makes no sense because they don't know where he lives, the thought of them storming in still scares me to my core.

Are you at the mailboxes? I text.

No answer again. Great.

It turns out he's inside one of the storage units off to the side of the mailboxes. The ones no one ever uses. The leasing office charges extra for these rooms, same as how they do for a covered parking spot or for having a pet. They're about twice the size of a walk-in closet, and I find Alex in the far left corner of one, surrounded by stacks of boxes and loose items like a bike rack and folding chairs.

"You guys actually have one of these? I always figured only rich people pay extra rent for their things."

He doesn't laugh. Or even smile, really. He just stands there with his hands on his waist, biting his lip and staring at the pile of stuff.

"You okay?"

"Hmm? Yeah. Hi."

I make my way through the mini labyrinth and give him a kiss. It's short and sweet, more like a peck, really. Sweat drips down his nose and sticks to my face.

"Have you been here all day?"

He nods and starts heading out to his car, which is parked right outside with the trunk hanging open, packed with more boxes. "Ever since this morning," he says as he grabs another to bring into the storage space. "I don't know what got into my mom. She went into an unpacking fit, talking about how we can't clear our heads without clearing our space." His arm muscles flex, perfectly highlighted by this one streak of sweat that's reflecting sunlight. I smirk and raise my eyebrows at him, but he completely misses it. I'm not sure I've ever seen him this hyperfocused on anything that wasn't me.

"Sounds like we've both had a busy day," I say.

"Mmm-hmm."

Now would be the perfect time for him to ask me about the auditions, but he doesn't. I know I could just tell him, but somehow blurting out "I made mermaid" while he tries to play the world's saddest game of Tetris with his moving boxes wasn't part of my fantasy.

I try to get us talking by asking random questions instead. What'd you do for lunch? Are these your mom's or yours? Aren't you hot in here?

Which, I acknowledge, are all a series of pointless questions that only warrant a one- or two-word response. Which is exactly what I get from him. I start to think maybe I shouldn't have come. I feel like I'm a nuisance just being here.

Finally, when I've run out of ways to ask what's wrong without actually asking him what's wrong, I say, "Do you need any help?"

"I'm fine," he snaps.

My breath catches a little, and for a moment we both stay quiet. We don't actually know how to do this part yet. The not-being-okay. I can't believe we're about to have our first argument and it's going to be in this dank-smelling oven box where unwanted junk comes to die.

"Well, you don't have to be a dick about it," I say.

Nice, Vero. Good first move.

"I'm just . . . having a hard day, okay? And my mom rushed off to work, so now I have to make sense of all this crap we brought from Houston."

194

"Well, I had things to do too. Today was kind of a big deal for me. And you haven't even asked how it went."

"Right. I'm sorry," he says, but it doesn't even sound like he means it. He takes a deep breath, and it sounds like it takes all the effort in the world to say, "How'd it go?"

It feels like a trick question. Like no matter how I answer, I'm not going to get the response I want. "I made it." My voice sounds like it could fit in one of these boxes. "I got in," I say again.

"That's awesome. Congrats."

"Congrats," I repeat. *Congrats* is what you write on someone's post when they reach, like, a thousand followers or whatever. It's not for this.

"Yeah. I'm really happy for you."

But he just keeps standing there, two whole box lengths away from me. In the four minutes it took me to walk here, I'd imagined he'd lift me off the ground and my feet would pop into the air, and he'd be beaming at me in awe.

"You don't seem it," I say. I don't understand how this keeps happening. All the things I want to celebrate are getting dampened and diluted. All the life seeping out of them. "What's going on?"

"Nothing." He turns away and puts his hands on his hips, as if to assess the stacks that surround us. "I'm just tired."

Tired. Like I'm not?

I'm about to tell him he's not the only one with feelings when a rumbling sound startles us both. We turn to find Alex's mom nearly tripping over boxes as she tries to enter the unit.

"Jesus, what a mess," she says. True words in more ways than one.

"I told you," Alex shoots back.

She sighs and shakes her head, then looks at me and smiles. "Hi. Sorry, Verónica, right? I'm so embarrassed you have to see all our . . . chaos." She gestures at the boxes like they're an unkempt home.

"Oh, it's fine. I don't mind," I say.

She stands next to Alex and rubs his upper arm. "See? It's not so bad. We'll get through it."

Which isn't really what I said. At all.

"I promise I'll start going through my share of them later. In the meantime, just see what you want to take and what you want to leave in storage," she says.

"Fine, whatever. I'll try," Alex says, in a way that makes me wonder if they're still talking about boxes. She gives him a peck on the forehead and says she has to get back to the leasing office. When it's just the two of us again, I try to catch Alex's eyes, but it's like he's somewhere else. Not this moment. Or maybe too deep in this moment. Surrounded by boxes he's been overwhelmed by ever since the first day we met. I almost ask if he wants to talk about it, but I think I already know the answer.

So I find a giant, sturdy plastic container and sit on it. Immediately, my body welcomes the support and the muscles in my leg unclench. Sometimes it doesn't register until I'm resting what a constant effort it is to just stand, hold myself together, distribute my weight evenly as I put one foot in front of the other. Or maybe I do notice it but I ignore it, let it settle into my bones like a quiet, overstaying houseguest that doesn't want to disturb me, let alone anyone else. It usually works until it doesn't, until I've been swimming and walking and going going going so much that I make the mistake of stopping, holding still long enough to hear the blood running through my veins again. It's like putting your ear up to a seashell. Some days the waves are what carry me. Some days the waves overtake me. I can never forecast which is which until it's too late.

"I'm tired too," I whisper, but in these tight walls the words travel, and I see Alex nod, just barely, as he seals shut a box labeled *Art Supplies—Alex*. He pulls the packing tape from its roll, and it screams, rips a ragged tear into our silence. Then he presses it down over the seam where the flaps meet, running his hand up and the down the line, over and over, until the gentle shushing of his skin against cardboard fills the air like a balm.

I didn't know he made art. I wonder why he stopped, after all the effort it took to pack it and bring it with him, all these miles he drove himself and his mom to Florida. Outside, the sky has gotten overcast, and it makes the lone light bulb overhead yellow. The day we first met, Alex looked as tired as I feel, but I was too busy worrying about him seeing my scars to really notice. I wanted them to be invisible. I'd never thought how much they'd still hurt when they are.

"I don't know how long this is going to take," he finally says. "You don't have to wait for me if you don't want to."

"I don't mind keeping you company. If you want it."

He nods and goes back to rearranging the boxes. Some are small and heavy-looking, and he stacks them in a corner. Others aren't boxes at all, but random tall shapes covered in bedsheets and twine, and loose pieces of furniture like a single chair, a lamp with no shade, and a nightstand with no drawers. He arranges them so they're facing each other against the wall, a living room comprising orphaned parts. I try to imagine what rooms they once came from, how they got separated from their whole. His house in Texas must've been huge, a life entirely unlike this one. Now we're standing in the remnants, all the things this new life has no room for.

I find a cushion from an abandoned love seat and ask if I can use it.

"Sure." He doesn't ask why I need it or if my joints are okay. But his voice is soft and his eyes stay on me just enough for me to know he'd listen if I wanted to tell him.

I smile and the space between us throbs gently. Finally he comes to my side carrying an open box full of books. They're all arranged with their spines up, most of them containing long, colorful self-help titles including words like *positivity, happiness, healing,* and *mind* that peek through his fingers as he flips the books back and forth in the box. I can tell he's not actually looking for one; he's just keeping his fingers busy while giving me a chance to look inside. Unsure what to make of this library, I ask, "What's this?"

"My parents' failed attempts at helping me cheer up. That's what they called it at first, anyways. They thought I was just being too pessimistic, or choosing not to look on the bright side of things, so they got me all these books. They were trying to help, but it just made me angry. It felt like they weren't listening. They kept asking what they'd done or what had happened to upset me, and they wouldn't believe me when I said nothing. I mean, yeah, I hated all their fighting and it made me sad and scared, but even worse was when things were pretty much fine . . . and I wasn't." He shrugs and closes the flaps on the box. Puts another one on top of it that's full of road maps, though it looks like many of them have been cut to pieces. "It was never any specific thing that made me feel off. I would've liked it to be a specific thing, because then I could point and say, *This, let's fix this.* So they bought all these books and they argued some more because my mom wanted me to see a therapist and my dad was all, *Our boy is not crazy,* like there was nothing more offensive than me needing help. But then I had a really bad depressive episode, even though I didn't know that's what it was at the time. But, like, I could barely get out of bed, and then I'd fall asleep through all my classes and seriously started wishing I'd never been born. So we went on this family vacation that my parents thought would help because I'd always loved road trips, and it did nothing for me. I was just somewhere between the Oklahoma–Texas state line and Madison, Wisconsin. We kept driving through all these towns and we'd go see all these sights and I'd just think, *All of these places look exactly the same to me.* Just buildings and people and things that exist outside of me, that I could never feel a part of. Everything was far away."

He makes a short exhaling sound like he's remembering something funny. The map he's holding now is of Michigan, and there's a part on the flap where the road just ends and there's nothing left but blue water. The lake.

"Numb," I say.

"Yeah. That was, like, two summers ago. When we got back I told them I wanted real help. Not books and happy thoughts and a change of scenery."

"And they listened?"

He nods and the corner of his lip turns up into an almost smile.

"That's when you started seeing your therapist?"

"A psychiatrist, too. I'm on meds and I do regular therapy. First thing my mom did before we even got here was find me new doctors."

"And how's it going?"

"It's going. It doesn't, like, fix things, but it's helped me navigate it. Even when it gets bad, I don't feel powerless, like I could drown in my depression."

I don't know what to say that doesn't sound meaningless. I'm grateful to know this part of him, but also, I'm so impressed he not only told his parents what he needed, but that they didn't turn around and pretend to know what was best for him. Still, it sounds like his parents fought a lot about it.

It sounds like they fought about a lot of things, before. I hope he doesn't blame himself. I hope he knows how glad I am he's here. I place my hand on his as if my touch could say these things for me. But then I second-guess myself.

"I'm sure you've heard this a million times, but I'm glad you asked for help. It takes a lot of strength to do that."

He grins, and it's like all the gravity just escaped his body. "That's what they say, right?"

I'm about to make a sarcastic remark about how, if enough people have said this, then it must make it true, but then I realize something. "You ever notice they only say that about depression and mental health?"

"What do you mean?"

I start thinking through it out loud. "I mean . . . I know it's not the same thing, and it's not the same kind of help, either. But when my parents have asked management for ramps or wider thresholds after my surgeries, or if I take the elevator instead of stairs, no one says it's strong of me to ask for help. It's the same at restaurants or stores. People either assume I'm lazy or we're asking for too much."

He starts packing away the maps and looks up at the ceiling, like he's contemplating what I just said. "Maybe part of it's because there's the whole stigma? Like the way my dad was at first, acting like me being depressed showed weakness."

"Yeah." I straighten my back and circle my head to stretch, mulling it over. In elementary school, there was always a kid or two who'd break an arm and they'd end up wearing a pink or blue or green cast, and everyone would gasp and ask what happened as they signed get well wishes on them. It was so fun and temporary. A broken bone was like a flat tire: a simple problem with a simple solution.

My casts were both off-white, the color of an armpit stain on a T-shirt. No one wrote *Get Well* on them because my doctor said the ink could soften the cast. It's not like I could go to school in a cast anyways; it was so huge and hard for me to get around without someone pushing my wheelchair. But my parents took me to the school holiday recital once. And I remember how my classmates looked at me, how their eyes widened in fear.

"Maybe everyone's just scared," I say. And then I think, *Maybe everyone's just scarred.*

I think of how Alex's parents spent so much time tucking his depression under a rug of platitudes and self-help books before finally getting him real help. How mine never planned a single family outing without checking first if there was a ramp, if there was an elevator, and how it made me want to hide from people. How finally one day Alex just said, *Enough: this is what I need in order to manage.* How I've never stuck up for myself the way my parents or Alex did, because the only time people have told me I'm strong is when I've pushed through pain, kept going, kept myself from causing them any trouble.

"Yeah. That's why mom wanted me to come here today," Alex says. "My new therapist thinks I should try getting back to my art. But I don't know if I'm ready yet."

"Why not?"

"It's just . . . a lot of it reminds me of that road trip. And I don't want to go back there."

"Back?"

"Not literally. Just to feeling depressed again. *Being* depressed. It's kind of weirdly superstitious, right? Like a part of me thinks that if I surround myself with similar things or activities, then I might sink into another episode. But it's so unpredictable, I feel like I can't control it. So I guess I try to control other things instead."

"I don't think it's weird or superstitious," I say. "I think it's natural. I have things that I avoid because they remind me of hard times."

"Yeah? Like what?" He tucks his hands into his pockets, and for a second I regret saying anything. I have to really think it through before answering.

"Don't take this the wrong way. Because there's no way you could've known, okay? But there's this one particular gum. And you happened to be chewing it the other day. And it, like, reminds me of all my surgeries. Because of the smell."

All of a sudden he looks sad. Exactly what I was afraid of.

"Damn. I'm so sorry."

"You don't have to be sorry. It's not your fault it smells like anesthesia."

He grows quiet, looking really intently at the floor. "Can I ask you something?"

I grin nervously. "Maybe."

"What's it like? To be out like that?"

"For surgery?" He nods. "It feels like . . . nothing."

"Nothing?"

"Really, truly nothing. At least when you're asleep, you dream or you kind of remember having slept. But being put under is pure nothingness. It's not like I leave my body. I stop being."

"Wow. I can see how that'd be scary."

I'm about to correct him and say I never described it as scary. But just because I haven't said it doesn't mean it's not true. "It's hard. Knowing they can do all these huge things to me and I don't feel a thing. Which I know is better than the alternative. But still . . ."

"You're not in control."

"Exactly. Like how does your body just . . . stop being yours?"

"Or your mind."

"Damn," I say.

"Yeah."

We sit in the silence for a while, until eventually Alex goes back to sorting through his boxes and I start writing in my journal. When he's done, I get off the cushion I was sitting on and hand it to him. He places it in a laundry basket that houses stacks of old magazines. We stand outside the door, and Alex reaches in to turn off the light.

"Thanks for that."

"I didn't really do anything."

He takes my hand, and without even saying so, we end up at the racquetball court, one concrete room to another.

He drops his head back, his face toward the sky, and lets out a breath.

"So my girlfriend's a mermaid," he says.

It's the first time he's called me either of those things, and they both feel right.

Papeleo: pa·pe·le·o

1.   (n.) paperwork or red tape
2.   (n. VR) a code word for things that cause stress, fear, anxiety

Chapter 24

FOR ME TO START AT MERMAID COVE on Monday, Barb said all she'd need was my social security card and the signed liability forms, just a bunch of paperwork. Her casual words ring in my ears.

All she'd need. Paperwork.

Simple, unless you live in a home where your mother's kept every important document under lock and key, in a blue fireproof metal box, ever since you can remember. If everything else burned, at least we'd have our papers, Mami's always said. I can still see the relief on her face the day our green cards and social security cards arrived just a few weeks ago. The finality with which she locked them away.

It takes me a couple of days to find the right time to approach them about the job. I wait until my parents are lost in a moment, dancing in the kitchen after Papi came up behind her while Mami was finishing the dishes after breakfast. They sway next to the sink, Papi's back curving over her small frame, her dish towel tossed over his shoulder. The song is one of their favorite ballads, Braulio's "En la cárcel de tu piel," a slow, keyboard-filled '80s anthem about being a willing prisoner in a lover's skin. It doesn't sound as creepy in Spanish as it does in English. I sit on the couch and listen to the lyrics as I wait for them to finish. It's not so much about imprisonment as it is about surrender. Trusting someone so much, you let your guard down completely.

I think of Alex. The way our intimacy makes every last nerve and hair against my skin feel safe enough to be touched. Embraced. A warmth tumbles through me like the sweetness of sleep, rolled into a ball that sinks deep. I try to let it settle but then it ricochets, scorching and urgent, until it's back in my stomach, a clenched fist. The guilt of it. The shame. It makes me feel trapped in my own skin.

All I've ever known is papers and permissions and places our bodies can't go, can't move, locks we fear and locks that protect us, metal bars drilled into my bone and casts no one was allowed to sign, so I learned boundaries quick, learned my body was a country left behind, a home I fled until it could be fixed, safe, a place where I could never truly be free, no matter how much I longed to explore it, lose myself in it, let go.

Suelta.

I scoop my arms under my legs, holding them as close as I can to my chest, trying not to look at my parents out of the corner of my eye. They would be happy to know that mine is not a body that can easily let its guard down. The closest I've ever come is in the water. Limbs cushioned by less gravity. Embraced by a numbing cold.

The music stops. They kiss and then Mami goes back to her cleaning while Papi starts checking his phone for messages. They leave for their Sunday shifts in just a few minutes, but I'd rather do this now, fast, when there's not enough time for them to second-guess or ask too many questions.

I get up and stop at the kitchen threshold, leaning my shoulder and the side of my head up against it. The seam of our blue-and-white-striped wallpaper sticks out like the pull tab of a packet of gum. I run my thumb over it, back and forth.

"¿Qué haces?" Mami says.

"Nothing. Just wanted to talk to you guys."

She smiles but doesn't stop wiping the countertop. "Bueno, pues. Talk."

Papi raises his eyes from his phone. "Why do I get the sense that you got yourself into trouble?"

"I didn't do anything! Nothing bad, anyways. I just got a job like you said I should."

So far, not a lie.

"A job? ¿Cómo?" Mami places one hand on her hip like she's contemplating what to do with her arms while she assesses if this is news worth celebrating.

"Tanya put in a good word for me. At her work. They needed interns. In their business department." I let it out in fragments, small grains of rice I add, one at a time, afraid to tip the scales of my dishonesty.

"Tanya? ¿En el sitio de las sirenas?"

All these years, and Papi still calls it the place with all the mermaids. I cross my arms. "Yes, but in their offices. Helping with their accounting and operations."

"So you already interviewed. And you didn't tell us?" Mami says.

I say the only thing I know she'll understand, the reason why she never fills us in on anything important until it's final. "I didn't want to get anyone's hopes up. But it's paid. And they want me to start on Monday."

A gasp brings Mami's hands to her mouth, balled together like a fist. She looks to my father, and the second his face cracks a smile, she says, "¡Ay, hijita! No lo puedo creer."

An unfortunate choice of words, since she really *shouldn't* believe it, but I can't think about that right now.

"And you'll be in the office? Not in the water? Learning about bookkeeping and running a business?" Papi says.

"That's what I said," I say teasingly through a wide smile. His question was so direct that I feel slimy and gross trying to wiggle my way out of answering it. Still, I've gone too far now. There's nothing else for me to do but commit. "You know, all the boring stuff you've always wanted me to learn."

It's only when I roll my eyes that I think they actually buy it. They know me too well. They know I'd rather be swimming with the mermaids than crunching their numbers, and that a job like this would be nothing more than a compromise: me settling just to make them happy.

It hurts how well it works. How easily they believe me.

"¿Y cuánto pagan?" Papi asks.

I tell him my hourly rate, and his eyes glaze toward the ceiling, like he's doing the math in his head. "Well, you're really doing it for the résumé anyway. We'll put it into your savings for college. Any little bit helps."

Mami brings me into a hug, and Papi tells me he's proud of me for letting go of tonterías and fantasías. "It's for the best. You'll see. Real-world experience that will help you all your life."

"Just promise me you'll focus on what's important," Mami says.

I nod and step out of her embrace. "Not a lot of people get this opportunity." Again, not really a lie. "They'll just need my social security card. For payroll and stuff."

Mami hisses like I just dabbed alcohol over an open wound. "Okay. It's fine. I'd just hoped to get this fixed before you needed it."

"Get what fixed?"

She signals for me to follow her into the bedroom, then pulls out the little box with my and Dani's baby teeth in it. All this time, the key to the lockbox was underneath the velvet flap, small as the ones they make for luggage locks or diaries.

From the darkened closet, she starts shouting, "They came in a few weeks ago."

"I remember. I picked them up from the mailbox, re-member?"

"Yes. But what I didn't tell you . . . well. Mira."

When she emerges from the folds of clothes she dug through, she's holding something in each hand. A baby blue and navy card, which she sets down on the comforter, right in front of me. And my name bracelet, which she and Papi had made for me in Lima as a newborn, in her other open palm. It's gold; a delicate chain with a rectangular plate in the center, engraved with Verónica Beatriz in cursive. I haven't worn it in years because it no longer fits me, but seeing it is like unearthing family treasure. Dani has one too, and so do Mami and Papi from when they were babies. I'd always as-sumed they were tucked away in a jewelry box somewhere, not locked and protected in the same place as our papers.

"The names don't match," Mami says wistfully. "They left out your middle name. And the accent in *Verónica*. Af-ter all the back and forth we went through, getting copies of your birth certificate from the Peruvian embassy, getting ev-erything translated. All the papeleo. They don't match," she says again, holding the bracelet up to my social security card.

Verónica Beatriz.

Veronica.

"Mami, it's okay," I say.

"It's not okay. Beatriz means 'blessed.' We gave you this name for a reason. And the accent marks the emphasis. The strength. I've been trying to get it corrected. But everything is so slow with immigration. Any little mistake, they say it's ours, not theirs. Your father thinks I should let it go. It'd be easier, and less expensive. But I just . . . didn't want you to have to pretend to be something on paper that you're not. I was so excited when your cards came in and then I saw yours and it felt like a piece of you was missing. I'm sorry, Vero. I don't mean to make a big deal of it."

She looks at me with a tenderness I haven't seen in her eyes in ages. That's what it feels like, anyways, as if the moment in the hot tub when I stopped being her sweet, blessed daughter was both yesterday and years ago, compressed into one heavy hand against my chest. I think the guilt might drill itself into my bones. This must be what Papi was talking about, that day he caught me with Alex in the pool and told me he wasn't going to tell Mami because she already had too much to worry about with immigration. It was all because of me. All because she wanted my papers to be right. True.

"I'm sorry. I never want to bring you trouble."

"No es nada."

But it's not nothing.

It's so much. Too much.

"We'll get it sorted out. Just, here." She places the card in my hand and the key back in the jewelry box. "Now that you know where the key is, lock it away when you're done with it on Monday. After your first day," she says, full of pride.

"I promise."

Papi comes in to finish getting dressed for work, and soon the two of them are off, having kissed me on the cheek and congratulated me once more. I'm left holding a flimsy card in my hand, this piece of pulp that amounts to everything my parents have worked their whole lives for, all so we could live and work here. Live and work, live andwork, liveandwork. Those three words never spoken separate, as if one cannot breathe without the others. That was always their dream for us. A good, serious job was the safe bet, after everything they gave up to bring us here.

And I'm about to risk it all on this dream. This manufactured fantasy.

I think I might be sick. All my carefully told lies feel like they're coming back up inside of me. I go to my room and take the folder out of my bag. I can rip it to pieces right now. I can take back the story about the internship and lock the card away in its box, and my parents would never have to know that they were right, that all I know how to do is lie, make it so their sacrifices are worth nothing because I will always disappoint them, I will always betray their wishes for my deepest wants, the things I dare to desire.

My pen tap tap taps against the file. I open it and read through it one more time. It's a bunch of legal language about the risks I take becoming a mermaid, how it includes physical injury and even death and drowning. How Mermaid Cove can't be held responsible should any of that happen.

It's standard, like every time I've gone into surgery. A risk people are willing to take. I didn't always know. I thought it was a normal procedure, until the day I went through our old photo albums and found a picture my parents took of us when I was five, the morning before I went in for an operation. In it, I'm smiling. When I asked Papi why he looked so nervous, he said it was because a person could die from anesthesia, and they had made him and Mami sign all these forms saying they acknowledged the risk.

After that, I googled everything I could about anesthesia. Turns out it's the closest a person can come to dying without actually being gone.

It's actually a controlled death.

Not much different from a controlled life.

A risk no matter which you choose.

We were only trying to protect you.

Not a full lie. Not a full truth.

Like when they didn't tell me my bone was dying. What was happening to my body.

I think of Alex. Of Jeremy. The mermaids.

I have secrets to keep too.

I get to the bottom of the form and stop at the part where it says *Parent or Guardian Signature.* I've seen Mami's scribbled name on so many lines and x's over the years, I can picture it perfectly. Still, I practice it, over and over, on a scrap piece of paper until it's on loop in my brain, a mark I don't even have to think about.

I do it quickly. I don't even look once my pen starts its dance.

I am only lying to protect you.

Starstruck: star·struck

1.   (adj.) fascinated or captivated by a celebrity or idol

2.   (adj. VR) fascinated by a light that's starting to glow within

Chapter 25

APPARENTLY, THIS IS WHAT IT'S LIKE to be a new girl. Growing up in a town with only one elementary, middle, and high school spared me the awkward indignity of being put on display, but walking into Mermaid Cove on my first day, I feel it.

The sudden silence. The stares.

I hear an actual gasp when Tanya opens the door to the auditorium and we walk in together, and like something out of a '90s sitcom, a guy in bright yellow bike shorts leans so far back to look at me that he actually falls out of his chair. Two girls helping each other stretch on the floor start giggling while Lila offers the guy her hand and pulls him up on his feet with the same nice-but-I-mean-business attitude she had on the day of the auditions. I know all their names, of course, from following them online. But I can't believe they're about to know mine.

"Sorry. Just excited to see the new fins," he says, like I'm a car or a new set of tires.

I manage to crack a smile, but I'm too shocked to respond. Seeing them all up close and in person instead of on my phone's tiny screen is unreal. I wait for Lila to introduce me.

"Ignore him. He's just jealous he doesn't get to wear a tail," the white girl on the floor says. She's blond with freckles scattered from her nose all the way to her sunburnt shoulders.

"Hallie!" The girl sitting across from her tugs hard at her arms. She's Black and has dark brown skin; her hair is twisted into long plaits that alternate pink and blue. If I'm remembering right, her name is Val and she has a killer arabesque. "You go too far sometimes, you know that?" She widens her eyes, shifting them from Hallie to the guy and back. I look around and realize I'm probably the youngest person here. Everyone looks like they could be in their second or third year of college.

"Okay, okay, that's enough of that," Tanya says. "Everyone, this is Verónica. Our newest addition to the troupe, as I'm sure you already know. Verónica, this is nearly everyone. Barb and Janet are probably busy in the office, but as far as who you'll be dancing with, this is it. You remember Lila—"

"Good to see you again," I say, wiggling my fingers in her direction. My voice comes out croaky, hesitant, and I clear my throat in an attempt to get myself together. Lila gives me a warm smile and gestures at the rest of the group.

"Cirque du Soleil over here is Geoff," she says.

"Hey. I'm actually pretty coordinated underwater. Just never been as good on land," he says, grinning sheepishly. He pulls his hair back into a pony. It's straight and dark brown, parted at the center the way Dani often wears hers. I know from following Geoff's stories that he's part Seminole; he's always posting names of Florida places, like Ocala County and Kissimmee, that are indigenous in origin. I wish my mom could meet him so they could nerd out over precolonial history and etymology. But of course that'll never happen.

"Please. You're amphibiously clumsy," Hallie says to Geoff. Val slaps her lightly on the shoulder as they stand up in unison.

"Aw. You turned an adjective into an adverb just for me?" Geoff says.

"Okay, enough," Lila says. "This is Hallie and Val. They're inseparable."

"Insufferable," Geoff mumbles.

I press my lips together to keep from smiling, but next to me, Tanya snorts and Hallie scoffs. Val, though, looks genuinely hurt. Her eyes drop to the ground and her chest deflates, making her shrink alongside Hallie even though they're both about the same height. I take in the jersey short-sleeved hoodies that they're both wearing over triangle bikini tops and drawstring shorts. It looks like they agreed to wear the same thing but with different color combinations. Leslie and I used to do that all the time when we were in middle school and wanted everyone to know we were BFFs. It's kind of cute that Hallie and Val are still doing this; it makes me feel a little less intimidated about being the youngest.

"We're really glad you're here," Val finally says. "Ever since Jessica broke her leg, none of our routines have been the same."

"Val! We were *managing*," Hallie says, clearly offended for some reason I'm oblivious to. "But yeah. I guess it'll be good to have a full group again. Don't worry if you don't get the hang of things right away, though." She says this as if she's expecting me to fail. "We've all been doing this together a long time. We're here if you need anything. Anything at all."

Right now, all I really want is to know the deal about this Jessica I replaced and how long it'll be before she comes back, but I just tell them all thanks and that I'm excited to be here, even though I couldn't feel more out of place if I tried. They're warming up and marking choreography in various degrees of fashionable swimwear while I'm in a sleeveless olive green shirtdress and yellow flats. It was my attempt at office wear as I got ready for work this morning and my parents insisted on taking pictures before I left. Mami hugged me so tight I worried she'd feel the lining of my bathing suit beneath the dress. Papi pinched my chin and told me to take ten slow breaths if I ever got nervous on the job. Then I left our apartment with a towel to dry my hair, my social security card, and the forms with Mami's forged signature stuffed like contraband in my bag. My entire walk to Leslie and Tanya's, I kept glancing over my shoulder, unable to shake the sense that my parents' eyes were everywhere.

Now I'm waiting for it to feel real instead of simply terrifying. Even though I know I earned my spot and I deserve to be here, a part of me expects it to be to be taken away without a moment's notice. That's how it's always felt with things we want too much. Like even the ground we stand on could just crumble.

Tanya checks the time, and soon the whole group except Lila heads out the exit. Seconds later, they reappear on the other side of the glass, diving into the water and swimming down to grab their air hoses. There's no music yet, and the auditorium lights aren't dimmed, and no one is wearing mermaid tails or costumes, but seeing them start to rehearse takes my breath away. I'm that seven-year-old kid lost in wonder again, dreaming of a day like this one.

I take a few steps forward and press my hand against the glass. "Which number are they rehearsing?" From promo clips they've shared online, I know they have a core set they always do, like the Little Mermaid and the Swimming Through the Decades shows, but none of the moves they're doing look familiar.

"They're doing their own short ones. It's Barb's big idea this year. At the end of each show we'll be doing a choreographer's showcase. It's a chance for each performer to bring their own unique style into it and mix things up around here. God knows we need it."

"What do you mean?"

Lila slips into a pair of flip-flops and flings a towel over her shoulder. "Just, audiences aren't what they used to be. And this place isn't exactly known for adapting to the times." She sweeps one arm out, signaling at the space around us. It hasn't changed since the day I first set foot in it. Same light blue curtain scalloped over the top of the glass. Same silver metal railings along the edge of both aisles that split the auditorium into thirds. The seats are still the plastic flip-back ones that Dani was scared to fall into while I sat in my wheelchair at the end of the row. There are hand-painted signs that say NO FOOD OR DRINK and PLEASE DON'T FEED THE MERMAIDS, and the walls are towering, exposed limestone that seems untouched by time.

"That's part of its charm, though," I say. As we leave the auditorium, we pass a giant mural of the original mermaids from the '40s, and Lila slows down and takes a few steps closer to me.

"You could say that," she whispers. "Or you could say that Barb is so resistant to change that it took her decades to hire a troupe that wasn't only all-white mermaids."

I look at their fresh "all-American" faces smiling down on us. Lila has a point, but I'm surprised she's trusting me enough to say this now, when it's only my first day.

"What took so long?" I ask.

"Beats me. If you ask Barb and Janet, they'll say, 'Mermaids have no race,'" Lila says, rolling her eyes. "And anyways, they blame everything on budget and ticket sales, and whatever audiences want to see. So until we have a budget to renovate, we'll be upgrading our shows with the choreography," she says, speaking at normal volume again. "A couple of different mermaid-produced shorts every few weeks."

"Can any mermaid do one?"

She stops in front of a door that says PERSONNEL ONLY and squints at me. "So long as Barb agrees to it. Why? You thinking of one already?"

"Maybe." I don't know what compels me to say it, considering I don't even have a tail yet. They're tailoring Jessica's costume to my measurements, and Tanya said that can take a few days. I'll be using a simple fabric tail in the meantime.

"Sure," Lila says. "If you're up for it. But first let's take care of the admin stuff with Barb and Janet. Then we can start with the basics. Like teaching you how to breathe."

Air: air

1. (n.) the invisible, odorless, tasteless gases that surround the earth

2. (n. VR) an invisible illusion; a mixture of nothingness that is everything

Chapter 26

"YOU TAKE TWO DEEP BREATHS. One at the start of the tube, another at the end of it, got it?"

I nod into the cold air that's emanating from the pool of water several feet below us. After we left the auditorium, Lila and I dropped off all my paperwork at Janet's in admin, and I asked for copies, like my parents have always insisted. She tucked a copy of my social security card into a file in a metal cabinet that rumbled open and closed like thunder, then she gave me back the original. Now it's wedged in the pages of my notebook in my bag, in a locker with no lock on it, in a dressing room that's covered from floor to ceiling in pale yellow tiles. Lila and I stand in the back corner of the long, narrow space wearing nothing but our bathing suits.

A chill runs through me as I stare down a hole in the floor barely as wide as a doorframe. "Two breaths. Got it."

I count six steps in the ladder attached to the side of the hole before it descends into darkness. The hollow sound of water slapping against cement travels toward us.

"Don't worry. The tube is always intimidating at first," Lila says. She jumps in and pops her head out, slicking hair her back with both hands. "But you get used to it."

I lower myself carefully down the steps. "That's the third time you've said that to me today."

The first was at the start of her showing me around the space, when I caught a glimpse of a dozen or so mermaid tails in the back room, hanging from rows of silver clothing racks. Without someone in them, they looked like lonely halves of abandoned creatures. All the flukes (as they call the fins at the end of the tail) drooped toward the floor like fish hanging from a line.

The second time was when we stood waist deep in the water so she could teach me how to switch my air hose on and off. There's a trick to it with your thumb and forefinger, so I spent the better part of an hour practicing, dipping my head in and out, sipping on bursts of air through a hose as thick as a milkshake straw.

"I didn't know air could have a taste," I said. It was dry and earthy, with hints of clean chemicals, as if someone made it in a lab.

"You get used to it," Lila repeated, pulling the hose all the way out of the water. "But you have to be sure to control it. Use it to maneuver your buoyancy. The more air you have, the more you'll float up. Release bits of it, and you'll float down."

We practiced long enough that she decided I was ready to try it fully submerged. Instead of diving in from the deck like the rest of the group did for rehearsals, Lila brought me to the tube. It's exactly what it sounds like. Beginning in the mermaids' dressing room, it twists into an underwater tunnel leading us into the stage area. I slip a mask on over my eyes and nose and push off the stepladder. The cold engulfs me.

"Don't be nervous. Just follow me, and I'll hand you the hose as soon as we get to the other side," she says.

I fill my lungs and go under, following Lila's small hand-held flashlight. A few strokes in, the tube feels like it's growing narrower the more I swim through it. A wave of panic starts knocking at my insides, like the moment when you've gone down a waterslide and wonder if you'll ever see the other end. It lasts only a millisecond before we turn a corner and a huge circle of greenish light signals the exit point.

Lila hands me the air hose clipped to the side and waits for me to take a breath before doing the same. She signals for me to keep following her into a tank the size of a small car. Inside, it's half filled with water, half filled with air. There's a plank along the bottom where we can both stand. I rise and meet her in the air pocket.

"I didn't know this was here."

"Pretty cool, right? This is where we do costume changes or just wait offstage until it's our turn to go back on again. But here." She hands me an air hose, and I trace its winding path with my eyes, all the way to the bottom of the cave that's lined with pipes, lights, and rows of exhaust holes that release the air curtains. One is pressed against the glass panels, while two others are labeled STAGE LEFT and STAGE RIGHT. In reality there's no stage at all. Our canvas is just a giant, underwater stretch of space in the springs.

The ground is so far below us, I feel like I might fall into its abyss if I stare too long. "It looks a lot deeper than I imagined."

"Are you afraid of heights?" Lila asks.

I think of all the times Leslie and I have climbed out of her second-story bedroom window to sit on the edge of the roof. "Not really."

"Then you'll be fine with depths. Promise. Just take it slow. You don't have to swim too far from the tank at first."

I dip my head into the water to practice. I take four quick breaths from the hose and let them sink into my lungs, waiting until it feels like they've vanished to drink in more. After a few tries, I slip completely out of the tank and do a couple of flips, holding the hose in my left hand while my arms propel me forward. Grasping the hose with only my mouth, I do a few strokes of a mermaid swim. The air feels unreal as it shoots over my tongue and coats my throat. It's a surprise and a relief each time, like getting an extra life in a video game you're sure is about to end.

I lose track of time like this, layering more breath and motion onto each sip of air. It should make no sense; it's not natural for humans to stay under this long, breathe like the water has pockets of oxygen we can pick at any moment. All around me, wildlife meanders undisturbed. A school of white-and-black-striped fish scurry past. A turtle the size of a football helmet, with a shell covered in green moss, pushes itself slowly toward the sun. They move around me as if I'm not even here. As if we're all simply cohabiting.

"So? How did it feel?" Lila's eyes are shimmering with the same curiosity of someone whose friend just got back from a date.

I can't stop smiling, gasping. "It's like a whole other world."

"You were great," she says. "Try it again, but this time I want you to switch your air hose between your hands a bit more. You looked close to getting tangled a couple of times. Just switch hands while you're spinning and maneuver the hose around yourself. If not, you end up looking a hot mess." She demonstrates by twirling into it a few times. "Barb calls it walking the dog."

I try not to laugh. "Walking the—"

"I know. It's corny. But it's like when you're walking a dog on a leash and they move all around you, and the only way to keep from tripping is to keep switching the leash between your hands, or bringing it over and around poles and tree trunks?" She twirls out of the tangle as she speaks.

"I figured as much," I say. My parents have never let me have a dog, but Dani pet-sat around the neighborhood one summer when she was eight, which really meant that I helped her pet-sit. The only animal they've ever allowed in our house is Fuego, and that's only because they think fish are clean. Which is hilarious, given they literally swim in their waste.

"So those are the basics. The rest is just practice. Try going in deeper," Lila says.

We swim down. The water is clear so it hides nothing, but that's also what it reveals: depth swallows light swallows darkness until they're chasing each other across my skin, fluid shapes made from shadow and sun. Each moment under feels brand-new, intoxicating and terrifying in possibility. Anything can happen; I feel like I'm dancing with my own mortality. No matter how many years I've known how to swim, a part of me questions if this will be the moment my body forgets what it is made of and drowns.

I take another breath. It feels like water on my tongue on a hot day.

Lila waves at me to swim up to the surface. When we break through, I can't stop gasping. My body wants to swallow the world whole. My heart pounds against my chest like a long-lost traveler coming home. My lungs fill with wind.

"Small sips," she says. "If the audience sees us gasping for air, then it's like we're no longer real. Everything we do has to look effortless. Even breathing. Does that make sense?"

"Sure. I guess so."

"Just don't let the hose become a crutch."

"But. It's air. It's not a crutch." My words squeak by between breaths.

"You know what I mean. It shouldn't look like you *need* it, you know?"

I glance down, past my bare feet to the very bottom of the springs. My legs float slowly over my line of sight, skewed by the bending of light through water. Chuecas. Uneven. These legs have needed crutches so many times before. Same as I need air in this moment.

Lila clicks her hose on and off, and I hear the air go in and out of it like a vacuum. "It's part of the illusion. The magic. We have to make people believe."

And it's weird, because even though I know she's talking about mermaids and air and the magic of making them seem real, the way she said *crutch* makes me feel like needing one is a bad thing. Like maybe the "magic" isn't just about believing in mermaids; it's about believing people like me don't exist. Like maybe admitting I've needed crutches dispels the myths we want to believe about people.

That we're not perfect. That our bodies have needs. That this doesn't make us any less real. Any less human.

Nickname: nick·name

1. (n.) a usually descriptive name given instead of or in addition to the one belonging to a person, place, or thing

2. (n. VR) a name someone gives you when you've been accepted, when you finally belong

Chapter 27

THE NEXT SEVERAL DAYS ARE like a crash course in everything I need to know about being a mermaid. Not just memorizing the choreography, but perfecting it down to the last breath, and learning how to do my own makeup, how to see without goggles in the water, how to smile for long periods of time without my teeth freezing (there's no trick; you just grin and bear it), and how to pose for pictures with guests while staying in character.

We spend a surprising amount of time out of the water, which is frustrating because it upsets my hip. I try to hide it by pretending to stretch or making hip circles in hopes the motion will melt the discomfort away. By the time we dive in, my body's begging for the water's density, but it's too cold for us to be under longer than thirty minutes or so without getting hypothermia. So we go through the routine on the grass, and then Janet films our underwater run-throughs on her phone and sends the video to our group chat for us to review. We decompress for half an hour in the sauna, and then we practice several more times in the grass, miming the movements mostly for timing and memorization, before getting in the water to do it all over again. It's grueling, but I'm not about to complain. We're constantly in and out of our mermaid tails, and since it's just practice, we all use fabric ones, which are made of the same material as a bathing suit. I'm told my real tail, a silicone one with actual scales and texture, is being altered for me, and even though being the newest mermaid means I'll mostly be in the background, I'm just so happy to swim among them that I don't care how small my part is.

For the twenty-five-minute show that'll be my first, in a few weeks, one piece is the Little Mermaid; another is a jazzy Broadway routine for two that Tanya and Lila choreographed, complete with canes and one-piece tuxedo bathing suits; and the last five minutes are TBD. Turns out, they were going to be a modern dance solo by Jessica, but her fractured leg tossed a wrench in that whole idea. Barb wants us to bring new ideas to her next week, but so far I've been too busy learning the basics to even think about choreographing my own piece.

It doesn't matter, though. I'm learning all these tips and tricks. From Val, how to undulate as I swim with both legs in the tail. From Tanya, that I should never use glitter or any sort of shimmery makeup, because the metal particles stay in the water and can harm the turtles and fish and manatees. From Geoff, that Lila is always the person to ask if you need extra hair ties or safety pins for your costume. And from Hallie, I learn to basically stay out of her way.

There always seems to be an undercurrent of bitterness to even Hallie's kindest words. Like just now, as I was blow-drying my hair in the dressing room so my parents won't know I've been swimming at my new accounting job, she caught my eye in the mirror and said, "Your buoyancy's come a long way since your tryouts. Have you been practicing at home?" No smile or frown while she waited for me to answer, just that kind of cool, expressionless face that makes itself hard to read.

I wait for Alex to pick me up by the fountain. My phone is full of text after text from Leslie, who's been checking in with me nonstop for the last few days, dying to know how it's going. Her latest, since I haven't answered her in twenty minutes, is a gif of Sebastian tapping his claws impatiently against a wooden floor. I forward her the video of today's rehearsal. Two minutes later she texts:

Omg you're amazing

You're not even done watching the whole thing.

I know. But I already know, you know?

I'm off by half a count in the second half. Barb said so.

They've been rehearsing all summer. You're playing catch-up. And doing so brilliantly, I might add.

She DID say my flips were nice today.

See?! She sends me another gif, this time of Lady Gaga applauding me.

I'm scrolling through gifs, trying to find an appropriate one that expresses shy gratitude with a hint of cockiness, when Geoff comes up behind me.

"Nice work today. You seemed comfortable out there."

"Comfortable?"

"Believe me, it's a compliment. Most people look like deer in headlights their whole first week."

"So you've been here a while, I guess?"

"Three seasons. Which practically makes me a veteran. Not a lot of people stay more than one or two."

"Why's that?"

"I don't know. Probably because they have real lives to live. College or trade school or jobs that pay more than what a barista makes. People come for the fantasy and then they get it out of their systems," he says, shrugging and shaking his head like he can't relate.

"And what about you?"

"I'm still . . . holding my breath. Anyways, a bunch of us are getting together at my place later if you want to come. Nothing big, just some drinks and music. Bring some friends."

He's walking away before I can even answer. He has a short, sinewy stride, and when his feet push off the floor, it comes from the balls of his feet and toes. It makes me imagine the soundtrack of his mind is a joyful, whistling tune. By the time he's at his car, he's already texted me the time and address.

I send one more quick message to Leslie as Alex pulls in.

Party tonight at coworker's? You and Alex?

I tuck my phone in my pocket and hear it buzz several times. I don't have to check to know she's in.

⁓

Geoff lives with roommates in a newer apartment complex near the local community college, where he's a sophomore. It's made up of towering, identical white buildings that have terra-cotta tile accents to give it a Spanish villa vibe. He's on the fourth floor, and the stairs are those slatted ones I used to be afraid of falling through when I was little. We take the elevator instead, and I step into his place feeling emotionally unsteady, gripping Alex's hand tight for reassurance. It's one thing for them to be nice and welcoming to me at the Cove, but it feels like this is when I'll know if it's genuine, if I'm really one of them.

Leslie starts chatting people up immediately—extrovert extraordinaire that she is—and soon it's like she's introducing me to them instead of the other way around. Val's in the kitchen in jeans and an off-the-shoulder peasant top, sipping on something in a red Solo cup that smells artificially fruity. She offers us all a beer, and we go into the living room, where Hallie's taking over the speakers so she can show us a new playlist on her phone. Through the sliding glass door off the living room, I spot Lila leaning over the balcony. She's in a backless sundress, and I can see the ridges of her spine, one stacked perfectly straight above the other, as her elbows rest against the railing. A thin stream of smoke rises out of the vape in her hand. It doesn't make sense—lung health is crucial to being a mermaid—but then I remember what Geoff said, that they all have lives they live outside of this. I always thought being a mermaid would be transformative, that it'd change me in some obvious way that even strangers along the street would sense. But so far, not even my parents have caught on. Which is a good thing. I try to ease into this part of the role, the part where I'm just me, at a party with my boyfriend and best friend.

"You came!" Geoff emerges from the hallway holding a set of candles. "I wasn't sure you'd come. I was worried you were already tired of us."

The truth is, I am. Not of them. But my muscles are sore, and my back feels like it needs to be cracked in nine places, and my hip is not in pain so much as whiny, like it just needs to remind me that it exists, pay attention, be aware, and I'm more mentally exhausted from trying to remember if this is normal for me or if it's new, and if it is, is it because of the mermaiding or the necrosis?

"I'm okay. Just trying to get my bearings," I tell him. We sit on the floor around the couch. Alex wraps his legs around me and I use them as an armrest, letting my back sink into his chest, while Leslie sits cross legged next to us.

Val is already tipsy, which is probably why she blurts out, "Be honest. Do my toes look like octopus testicles?"

Leslie almost chokes on her beer.

Hallie yells, "I said tentacles!" Then she squeezes Val's big toe gently and smiles.

Val pouts. "That's even worse."

Pretty soon we're all comparing ourselves to sea animals, and Leslie's tossing out random ones like narwhals and seahorses and urchins, and we all come to the conclusion that Lila and Tanya would be seahorses because, being the oldest, they're like our den mothers, and they put up with all our shit the way a male seahorse carries a female's babies so that she can keep working on creating more. Val is a narwhal, a unicorn of the sea, while Hallie is definitely the urchin, which she takes a strange kind of pride in because everyone's afraid of its spikes. They're trying to decide which creature I would be when Tanya arrives from a beer and alcohol run. She's carrying paper bags full of drinks and snacks like chips and cookies, all the while holding the door open with one foot. Leslie gets up to help take the groceries off her hands.

"Which vodka did you get?" she asks.

"Does it matter? You're not having more than two," Tanya says.

"Buzzkill," Leslie says.

"Minor," Tanya mumbles. This whole time, she hasn't moved away from the open door, and now she turns her attention back to the group, and says, "Anyways. Guess who I brought?"

I hear the unmistakable metal click and bounce of crutches before I see her.

"Ohmygod, Jessica!" Hallie jumps off the couch and practically tramples her. Everyone gets up and makes space for her as she carefully ambles in.

"How's it going, twinkle toes?" Geoff says.

"Shut up," she replies as she brings him into a hug. She's in a wide-legged yellow jumpsuit that hides most of her cast, but her toes peek out from under the hem, and as she moves, I see the cast is peach-colored.

Val introduces us, starting with Alex and Leslie, and when she gets to me, she says, "Verónica's the one who replaced you. Verónica, Jessica's the mermaid you replaced after she broke her leg zip-lining over Magic Kingdom. She used to moonlight as Tinker Bell. You should've seen Barb the day she found out. You think she's a hard-ass now—"

"It's good to meet you," Jessica says, giving me a warm smile. She stretches her leg over the couch as she takes a seat. "And yeah. Barb called me pissed the next day. She said it was a betrayal I'd been working at Disney. Didn't even ask how I was doing."

"How are you doing?" Hallie says.

"Good. Four and a half more weeks till I'm out of this thing. The doctor said it's healing nicely."

I picture her bone slowly shifting back into place, mending itself. That's the thing about bones: they can repair themselves, and if hers does the way it's supposed to, it'll be like nothing ever happened in a matter of weeks. I wonder if she'll try to come back to Mermaid Cove when she fully heals. If not just parts of me but the whole of me is replaceable. As if he already knows what I'm thinking, Alex wraps his arms around me, and they feel like a sweater being bundled close. I sip the rest of his beer since he's driving, and soon everyone's chatting again, and Leslie's about to show me a new hat she's thinking of getting on her phone when mine goes off. It's Dani.

Where are you? I'm bored.

I tell her, and she responds, I thought you were supposed to be at Leslie's.

That's what our parents think, which is probably what they told Dani when she got home today. She wasn't around when I got ready and left.

I send her a wink and say, I am.

You could've told me.

Sorry.

I can see she's writing something in response, but she's taking forever, and in the meantime Leslie — beautiful, tireless accomplice that she is — has steered the conversation back to me.

"Okay, but wait. We were talking sea animals. Which one would Ronnie be?" She's smiling a little too wide and her voice is giddy, which is how I can tell she's drunk. Leslie's a happy drunk.

Everyone grows quiet, and of course, it's awkward, because no one really knows me well enough to answer honestly. I'm about to change the subject when Lila says, "A starfish."

Tanya gasps. "Oh my God, yes," she agrees like she knows exactly why Lila said this.

"Because of that thing you do, right after you jump into the water?"

"What thing?" Alex asks with an edge in his voice, a hint of defensiveness.

"It's so cute. You do all these backflips into a body twist and then you spread out your arms and legs and shake them," Tanya says. Geoff and all the other girls start nodding, like they've seen it too.

"It's just to warm up. The water's freezing," I say. I picture all the molecules in my body slowing down to a near stop, and I move as much as I can to bring back the heat of motion.

"It's like a little starfish dance," Lila says.

By the end of the night, the nickname's stuck with everyone except Geoff, who joins us out on the balcony wearing a beautiful fuzzy white poncho. "I prefer the term *sea star,* is the thing. Because they're not technically fish."

"Sea star's fine with me," Leslie blurts out.

"Even better," I add. "But what do you mean, they're not fish?"

"They're invertebrates. They don't have a spine or bones, even. But their bodies are basically exoskeletons made out of calcium carbonate," he says.

"So, starlike not just in shape," Alex says. I put my hand into his and squeeze, remembering the night of our first kiss under the lit-up sky.

"Exactly," Geoff says.

"How do you know so much about this stuff, anyways?" Leslie asks.

He shrugs. "It comes with the job description. When we're not performing, we're tour guides for Mermaid Cove. So I know a bunch of random water and sea facts."

"That's weird. Barb hasn't mentioned anything to me about showing guests around," I say.

"Probably 'cause you're a temp," Geoff says. Even though we all know it's true, it comes off harsh, and I must do a poor job of hiding my hurt feelings, because right away he starts backtracking. "I mean, temporarily a temp, right? For now. You never know. Nothing's for certain."

There's that phrase again. It's just like what Mami and Dani said about my surgery; there's no point in worrying about it yet. "I guess we'll just see how things look at the end of the summer. Who knows, maybe I'll get in Barb's good graces."

"If you figure out the trick, let me know, please," Geoff says.

"Why?" Leslie downs the last contents of a red Solo cup. "Does Barb not like you or something?"

Geoff shrugs. "All I know is, our entire following is practically begging her to finally give me a tail, and she won't even acknowledge it. That fan art someone posted of me a few weeks ago? They tagged Mermaid Cove in it, and by the next day, Mermaid Cove had untagged themselves."

"You think it was Barb?" Leslie leans in close like he's telling a ghost story.

"Without a doubt. She loves to pretend she doesn't know the first thing about social media, but you know she's fully in control of the Mermaid Cove brand."

"That's messed up. What does she have against you being a merman?" I ask.

"I prefer *merperson*. And I don't know." He rolls his eyes, like he's already tired of the conversation. "Barb says they don't have a tail that would fit me, and they're so expensive that they're waiting till they have more budget to get me one, and blah blah bullshit. I think she's just stuck in her antiquated, gendered ways."

"For whatever it's worth, I think you'd make a great merperson." I don't get what the big deal is about a tail not fitting him, because Geoff's size and body shape aren't that dissimilar from mine.

"Oh, I know." He grins and pulls out his phone. "Don't tell Barb, okay?" He starts scrolling through picture after picture of a dark-haired person with the most detailed makeup I've ever seen. It makes their face look like it's covered in iridescent scales and shells.

"Wait, is that . . ."

"Unrecognizable, right?" Geoff says. I notice all the pictures have thousands of likes. At the top, the bio reads simply: Phin. He/They.

"Phin. I love that," I say, "Which pronouns do you prefer I use?"

Geoff sighs and lowers his voice. "He's fine. I mean, I keep this profile separate from my work one because it gives me more freedom this way. No having to worry about the whole Mermaid Cove brand thing."

"Got it," I say, though I wish the Cove's "brand" didn't make him have to hide parts of himself.

I gasp when I get to one of him on a rock next to a blue-green spring. His back is facing the camera, and his hair is completely down, not in a ponytail or bun like he usually wears it in practice. He sits on one side of his hip and is wearing a long red and purple tail. It's nothing short of elaborate, with delicate, see-through fins dotting his knees and a fluke about the size of a boogie board.

"Wow. That's gorgeous."

Leslie looks over my shoulder. "I thought you said you didn't have a tail."

"Not a real one. This one's made out of swimsuit fabric."

"It looks pretty real to me," Alex says as he glances at the image.

"You know what I mean," Geoff says, looking at me as if only I would understand. "The ones I have are fun and all, but it's not like I'm performing in one. In front of a live audience."

I admire the craftsmanship, the way the fluke has multiple layers, colors, and textures. I can tell from the stiffness of the fabric that he's wearing a monofin underneath the tail.

It's like a giant flipper, but for both feet, and it's designed to propel us through the water. "Do you go swimming in it?"

He nods and slides the phone into his back pocket.

"Where?" I ask.

"That picture was at Wekiwa Springs. But usually I just use the university pool. They have this extra-deep one for the divers."

"And no one . . . says anything?" I can't imagine donning a tail at Palmview Lakes just for the fun of it. People would stare and think I'm too old to play make-believe. My skin crawls from embarrassment just thinking about it.

"Not to my face. And anyways, who cares? Anyone who says they've never wanted to be a mermaid is flat-out lying." He lets out a wistful sigh. "You'll see, Sea Star. When you're in the water and the auditorium is full of people in awe of you . . . there's nothing like it. Mermaids make people's dreams come true."

On the way home from the party, I can't stop thinking about Barb and how the Cove's image hasn't really evolved over the years. The mermaids may not all be white and blond anymore, but their origin stories and routines all seem to fit into two slim narratives: they're all young maidens who came from similar waters and made themselves at home in the Cove. They fall in love with a handsome boy and live happily ever after.

I don't know where Geoff or I fit into that story. I'm just

a temp, a replacement. Who knows how long Barb will want me to stay, or how long my parents would let me, if they found out.

When I get home, I start writing my origin story in my notebook.

I'm Mermaid Verónica. I came from the land of Sea Stars, where particles of centuries-old stars fell from the sky into the ocean, calcifying into caves, into holey limestone that created the foundation of Florida and birthed a daughter in its image.

Trenza: tren·za

1. (n.) a length of hair woven together
2. (n. VR) a thing woven through repetitive motion; a twisted story

Chapter 28

LESLIE'S HUNGOVER, AND IT SHOWS. We're sitting on the wicker bench on the lanai, me with my legs stretched over her lap so she can paint my toenails, and her hands won't stop shaking as she tries to brush the enamel over my pinkie.

I wiggle my toes just to mess with her.

"You're the worst. I don't have to do this, you know. I don't even like this color," she says, dipping the brush back into the bottle. It's a light shade of green that looks like the underbelly of a plant leaf when the sun shines through it.

"You're the one who gave it to me, remember?" For my birthday back in May, she got me this kit of fifty-two shades that came in a box shaped like a calendar: one new color for every week. The bottles are tiny, about half the size of my thumb, and trying them out has become a regular thing we do together. But this morning, Dani used them to paint purple and yellow flowers on her toes, and then complained that the fumes were getting to her. So we ended up out on the porch, exiled from my own bedroom.

"Whatever, it won't last. It never does on you," Leslie says.

"It's not my fault the water makes my manicure fade." I clean off the edges of my right toe with my thumbnail. My fingers are still chipped with last week's shade: Diablo Red. There's a tiny splotch on one of them that's shaped like a continent, or an island.

"So what color does Alex like?" she says.

I shush her by waving my hands in front of her face. Mami has the day off for once, so she's in her room napping, which means she's probably sitting in bed with her eyes closed, listening in on our conversation. Sometimes Leslie forgets to keep her voice down around Mami because she's never had to keep any secrets from her mom. They actually talk about things openly, like when Leslie had her first serious boyfriend. Her mom brought her the biggest box of condoms I'd ever seen, practically the size of a shoebox, with a boatload of colors, sizes, and textures. Then she took her to the doctor so she could get on the pill and said she didn't need to know when or if she was having sex—just that she wanted her to be safe when she did.

My parents. Would never.

Their only idea of safe sex is the kind you have after you're married, because it keeps you safe from going to el infierno.

God, Catholics are so dramatic.

Which is why Leslie says the box is always open to me, and I should grab protection whenever I need it. I haven't had to because I'm not ready, but I know by the way she raises her left eyebrow whenever either of us mentions Alex that she's wondering if I might be soon. I wonder about it too. But the last thing I need is my parents finding out about him and immediately jumping to that conclusion.

Twenty minutes later, I have ten bright green toenails and a practically passed-out best friend who is in serious need of hydration. She heads home, and as if on cue, I catch Mami's figure approaching from the other side of the glass door. She's wearing a sleeveless top she knitted herself out of yarn that goes from yellow to orange to red, like the fiery surface of the sun.

"¿Todo bien?" she asks, taking the seat next to me.

"Everything's fine. You?"

"I was just thinking it's been a while since we really talked. Cuéntame. How was your first week at work? And don't just say 'fine' like you did last night during dinner."

"Fine. I'm mean, all right." I try to parcel out the parts of truth I can tell her. "Work's been uneventful, but good. It was kind of slow at first while I learned my way around. But everyone's really nice."

"Do you have a desk? An office?"

I nod, thinking of my locker in the dressing room. The plastic foldout chair where I hang my purse in the corner spot by the mirror. "It's not a big space or anything. But it works."

"Good. Just keep your eyes open for anything you can do, any way you can be helpful. Tienes que ser mosca," she says, snapping her fingers. "¿Cómo se dice en inglés?"

There's never a good enough translation for our idioms. "You have to be a fly? Or maybe it's closer to quick as a fly?" I shrug. "I think it's more like the equivalent of a busy bee. Either way, some insect that buzzes around, annoying people."

"Ay, Vero. You know that's not what I mean."

"I know." But I'm tired just thinking about it. It's like no matter what we do, we're always having to prove our worth to others. I wish we could forget about it, and maybe Mami senses this, because she reaches into my open cosmetics bag on the table and takes out two hair ties and my hairbrush.

"¿Quieres una trenza?"

I nod and we both smile. Nothing has been this simple between us all summer: hair, hands, braid.

She starts by combing my ends like always. Resting her palm on the crown of my head, she works her way up and detangles my knots with a soft touch.

"Tell me the story again. Of Huacachina," I say.

"Oof. A ver. You'll have to help me." But we both know these are lines she's memorized. "There was a young princess who lived in the desert, not far from where Lima is now." She pauses.

"In Ica," I continue. "And she was in love."

"Mm-hmm. With a handsome Inca warrior who . . . well, like a warrior does. He left for war and died, probrecito. So she wept for him. Uy. Lloró y lloró y lloró." Mami stretches out the words in a songlike rhythm, her left hand running through the air as if she were tracing the path of the princess's tears. "Night and day, day and night. She cried until her tears welled in a body of water so huge, she thought she might drown in it." Her voice grows soft and wobbly, as if even this mythical sadness is too much.

"And that became the oasis. Huacachina. In Ica," I say, stepping in to help her out. "And then?"

"And then? I'm getting to it." She tugs lightly at a section of my hair that she's separated into three. "Impaciente."

I feel her start to weave everything together.

"There are different versions of the legend. Another tells of the maiden named Huacca China brushing her hair, like we are right now." I grin, remembering this line, the way Mami always loved to make me feel connected to the story. "She's looking at her reflection in the lake and catches sight of a hunter spying on her. She's so scared she drops the mirror. And then she . . . does what, again?"

"Mami! She runs away."

"Right, yes. And the shattered pieces of the mirror become the lake. And her gown blowing across the desert forms the sand dunes. And when she has nowhere left to go, she jumps into the water and hides, waiting until it's safe to come out again. But she stays under so long . . ."

"That she becomes a mermaid."

"She becomes a mermaid. To this day people hear her crying. Weeping. Some say it's because she still longs for her lost lover. Others say she lures men into the water with her song, hoping one of them will be him." Mami sighs. Her nail runs across my temple as she tries to smooth over my baby hairs.

"It's so sad," I say. "They drown in her loneliness."

"I'd never thought of it like that."

"Even her, in a way. The grief completely engulfs her." All these years, I've been remembering the story as a romantic one. As if you could love someone so deeply, losing them swallows you whole. But no matter which version of the story gets told, the princess's suffering ran so deep it literally transformed her body, down to every limb and molecule.

And we glorified it. We saw only beauty in her pain. I've heard these stories a million times, but I'd never realized this until now.

"Which version is your favorite?" I ask.

Mami grows quiet as she twists a hair tie over the tip of my braid. "I don't know. I like to think we never got her whole story. It seems unfair we only remember her for her tears." Her fingers run down the thick ridges of my braid, and then she whips the tip over her palm like it's a paintbrush. "You know, some people say her song makes young people fall in love."

This is a theory I've never heard before. I wonder if she's really heard it, or if she's making it up as she goes along. But before I can ask, she says, "Hija, have you noticed your hair's gotten dry? And lighter."

I pat it with one hand. "Really?"

"It's the pool, probably. All that chlorine, every morning you've been swimming. It's good that you won't be out in the sun as much, now that you're working."

"Right."

I turn to meet Mami's eyes, but I can't read her expression. Sometimes I think she knows the truth but she's testing me, like a teacher with all the answers, to see if I pass or fail. Other times I'm convinced she believes me, and I can't decide which is worse.

I give her a kiss on the cheek and thank her for the braid, but as soon as I'm back in my room I unravel it. Standing in front of the mirror, I split my hair into two sections and bring them over my shoulders so they cover my breasts. The lighter streaks are faint, but Mami caught them easily.

How long can I keep this secret if even the sun is giving me away?

Lie: lie

1. (n.) an untrue statement
2. (n. VR) a shield that protects you in battle

Chapter 29

WE JUST HAD OUR MOST FLAWLESS rehearsal since I started. Everyone was completely on the beat. Hallie's pike spin was a smooth, full circle. Lila cut her mermaid swim across the glass down to eight strokes instead of ten. Tanya kept her hair out of her face the entire time, and I didn't get tangled in my air hose even once. There was an energy running through us, an undercurrent of focus and excitement that we all tapped into. Even Geoff seemed to be trying extra hard to get Barb's approval this afternoon, and it worked. She called his arabesque elegant.

It feels like we're finally getting into the rhythm of being a full troupe. We get out of the water and settle into the heat of the sauna. Val unwraps her swim turban as Lila drizzles water over the rocks. Tanya sips on a bottle of electrolyte water and sighs. Like a yawn, the sensation sweeps over the rest of us in a rolling wave. I wedge myself into a back corner and place a wet towel over my face. The wood of the bench creaks against my bones.

"Did you always want to be a mermaid?" I ask no one in particular, breaking the silence with the first question that comes to mind.

Someone shifts in their seat. "If you ask my parents, I was destined from birth to be one," Lila says, a hint of pride in her voice.

I hear the soft, bristling sound of skin unsticking from the wood.

"I've always liked their fluidity," Geoff says timidly. "They're not either/or. People say they're half human, half fish, but they just are. They're both and none of those things. It feels freeing to me."

I lift my towel off my head and open my eyes. "I love that." I get the sense we're talking about different things, but I can relate to feeling caught in in-between spaces. Fragile and strong. Grounded and submerged. Real and unreal. I've always felt like I was floating through them.

"Thanks," he says, wedging his hands under his thighs. "What about you?" He turns to Tanya.

"Well, you already know my answer," she says, looking right at me.

"I do?"

"It's because of Leslie. And she was only obsessed because you were obsessed. So I guess it's actually because of you that I wanted to be one."

"Please. Leslie liked mermaids on her own, ever since

we first met," I say. No way she was ever influenced by me, when it's always been the other way around.

"Who do you think begged our mom for a monofin, even though we already had a perfectly good set of flippers, so she could show off and share it with you at the pool?"

I insert this new piece of information into the memory of our first few encounters when we were eight. Leslie was relentless in befriending me, though I would've been just as happy left alone in the water. Mostly she sat at the edge of the pool with her feet dangling in. She would tell me stories about both times she'd been to Mermaid Cove. It wasn't until she brought me that monofin that it occurred to me she might want to be friends. And I guess by that time, we already were.

"Mine's pretty boring," Val says. "I saw *The Little Mermaid* when I was eight and wanted to be Ariel."

Tanya laughs. "Don't let Barb catch you saying that name."

"What's wrong with saying—"

A chorus of hisses cuts me off.

"You've seriously never noticed?" says Hallie, waving away a plume of hot fog in front of her.

"Don't be like that about it," Val tells her. "It's just an unspoken rule. Barb doesn't explicitly recognize the Disney version, for legal reasons."

"But you have a Little Mermaid show," I say slowly.

"A version of it," Lila says. "Before the movie came out, Mermaid Cove used to have its own rendition. And it was popular enough, but then after Ariel and Sebastian"—she lowers her voice—"this place couldn't compete. So that's why our show has a sea turtle instead of a crab now. And Caribbean-inspired music. And none of the main characters have names. The little mermaid is just the Little Mermaid, and the prince is the Prince. Everything's 'inspired' by the original fairy tale, not the movie."

"Riiiiight," I say. "And you know this how?"

"There's photos of the earlier shows in Janet's office, in the archives. And I heard her and Barb talking about it a while ago. They were discussing doing a new Pirates show, but they were worried it'd look like they were copying another Disney movie all over again."

I think about the choreography showcase coming up. "Do you think Barb would ever let us do the real 'Little Mermaid'?" I say. "The Hans Christian Andersen one?"

"No way," Geoff says. "That shit's too dark for her. This is a 'family show.' She'd never go for it."

"What are you talking about, dark?" Hallie says.

"The original fairy tale," Val says. Her eyes grow wide as she leans forward, resting her hands against her thighs. "It's all about mortality. How humans have immortal souls that live on forever in the afterlife, and mermaids don't. They just turn to sea foam when they die. That's why the Little Mermaid tries to win the Prince's love. Because if he fell in love with her and married her, their souls would become one, and she'd live on with him. It's kind of sweet."

Hearing Val retell the story from memory reminds me of how I know exact lines by heart. Like her, I'd always seen it as a touching love story. Even if it didn't end happily ever after, I thought the fairy tale was beautiful. Like the sirena of Huacachina and her tragic tears—maybe no matter which culture a story comes from, we always manage to romanticize it.

"Oh, right. Real sweet, if you ignore how the sea witch tells the Little Mermaid she'll die unless the prince falls in love with her," Geoff says. I can't believe I'm sitting in a sauna full of people who are just as weirdly obsessed with this stuff as I am. "Or how she fails and then her sisters try to convince her to kill him to save her own life. Did you know in the story, she needs to stab him in the heart and let his blood soak her feet so she can get her tail back? It's sick. And *sick*."

"Like you wouldn't kill for a tail," Hallie says.

"Okay, okay, forget I asked," I say. "I was just curious if she ever changes it up."

"Nope. Which is why we need new mermaid stories," Lila says, turning up the heat on the coals until they crackle.

"Isn't that the whole point of the showcase?" I ask.

"Why? You think you have one?" Hallie says.

"And what if I do?"

"You just got here. Val and I have been working on ours for ages."

"Hallie . . ." Val says.

"And anyways, you never answered your own question," she says, suddenly cheerful like we're all friends gossiping. "Did you always want to be a mermaid? Does it have anything to do with those scars you won't tell us about?"

She points. She actually points at the side of my thigh, and it feels like every pair of eyes in this sauna follows her fingers for a brief, painfully quiet moment.

"Seriously, Hallie?" Tanya's voice cuts the stillness.

"What? I'm just saying what everyone else has been thinking. We're not supposed to keep secrets, remember? We trust each other with our lives in the water."

I wouldn't trust her with a glass of water right now. Hot mineral air fills the back of my throat. It sucks all the moisture out, the way the leftover particles of anesthesia gas leave me dry and unable to swallow every time I've come out of surgery.

"It's nothing," I say.

"It's badass," Val says. "You look like a warrior or something."

I know she's trying to be nice, but I cringe. People do this all the time. They'll say a scar is a beautiful battle mark, as if the way it tears and attempts to crawl back to its original place is a sight to behold. I don't understand their fascination with pain, as if they need to glorify it to accept it.

"Yeah, thanks. Sure."

Hallie's eyes just . . . stay there. Even when I cover it with my hand, I can feel her stare, nudging its way in.

"So what is it?" she says again, like it's an undiscovered species.

"Verónica, you don't have to answer her," Tanya says.

"It's an alligator bite," I finally say.

"Seriously?"

"Yup. There's this pond by the entrance of our apartment. And last year, there was a baby alligator there."

Geoff snorts and covers his mouth. Tanya smirks and narrows her eyes at me.

"Yeah, but it couldn't have been big enough to—ah, I get it." Realization lands belatedly on Hallie's face. "But seriously, though."

"But seriously, though," I say back to her. "I had surgery years ago for a hip condition I was born with. Not that it's any of your business."

I get up and pull my towel over my shoulders, and as I exit the sauna, I leave the door open, letting all the cold rush in.

"Why didn't she just say that?" I hear Hallie whisper behind me.

"Because . . . Just shut up," Geoff says, following me out. He catches up to me on the way to our dressing rooms and starts apologizing for her, but I cut him off.

"It's fine. Honestly. I've dealt with worse than her."

"Good. Hallie's just . . . Hallie."

"Why's she always picking on you, though?"

He rolls his eyes. "We had a thing once. Before she and Val got together." He lowers his voice. "Don't tell Barb. She doesn't like us dating each other. Says it causes drama."

"Sounds like my dad." Papi's always saying that kids in the US are so promiscuous—the mere concept of bisexuality sends him into one of his ridiculous lectures.

"But then also, a couple of weeks ago I turned her down when she asked me to be in her choreography."

"For the showcase?"

He nods.

"So you're still available?"

A look of pure delight slides across his face. "What did you have in mind?"

History: his·to·ry

1. (n.) the scientific study of the past
2. (n. VR) the stories we're made to believe, whether or not they're true

Chapter 30

ON MONDAY WE BRING BARB OUR IDEAS. While Val and Hallie pitch her an abstract dance personifying love and heartbreak, she listens and nods, listens and nods. I actually think it's pretty brilliant, but Barb only frowns and says, "It's so sad. And there's no story."

Then Geoff and I tell her ours, and she claps. Just once, loud enough that at first I think she wants us to shut up. Hand pressed like in prayer to her nose, she tilts her head back and forth as if arguing with herself. Then she sighs and rolls her eyes. "Oh, what the hell. Let's give it a shot. Everyone keeps telling me we need to try something that's really 'out there.'" She shoots her arm out as if gesturing to some faraway, foreign object.

"It's not like it's *that* unheard of," Geoff says.

Barb either doesn't hear him or ignores him. "You think you could pull it off in ten days?"

Ten days.

Meaning I'll dance it on the day of my first performance. This wasn't exactly the ringing endorsement we were going for, but there isn't much time for Geoff and me to dwell or doubt ourselves. We promise Barb we'll have it done — choreography, music, costumes — in time for a full dress rehearsal the day before.

Now we're holding our first practice at my apartment's pool, and it's nice to be swimming at home again. Even though I was supposed to show Alex another stop on the Verónica tour this morning, he doesn't mind that I canceled. Instead he showed up with water, protein bars, a waterproof sound system, and moral support.

It's the first time one of my days off coincides with my parents being at work, and the combination of having nowhere to be and no one telling me what do is intoxicating. It makes anything — even this gargantuan last-minute undertaking that I've somehow convinced my friends to help me with — seem possible. Unlike when I used to swim alone, I'm no longer marking choreography whenever I think no one's watching. Having my friends here makes me not care if people stare or judge us.

"Cut the skirt a little shorter," I tell Leslie, who volunteered to be our costume designer. We both know it should've been Dani, but lately my little sister has been mysteriously busy with her own social life instead of endlessly curious about mine, so Leslie, Geoff, Alex, and I have become our own production team.

"Shorter? Qué escándalo," Leslie says, holding Mami's fabric scissors blades up. We snuck them out of her sewing nook this morning, along with her cookie tin full of needles, pins, and thread. "But wait, what about the dunes?"

"Behind you," I say. There's a bag stuffed with sheer white fabric that Alex and I bought at Michaels on the way home last night. Leslie tugs at it like she's pulling a handkerchief out of a magician's pocket. It spans the length of four lounge chairs as the wind picks it up, creating an undulating veil over the pool deck.

"Oh my God, yes. This will definitely work. So you wear this like a dress," she says, crisscrossing the fabric over her torso. "And then after, the white kind of unwraps around you, to unravel?"

"Exactly."

"What about me?" Geoff says. We just finished a run-through of the first four eight-counts of choreography, and now he's taking a break under the tiki hut, elbows resting on the table while he checks his phone. "You said my costume would be bomb, but so far all I'm seeing is the same old, same old. A warrior and a hunter? Really?"

"I know. But trust me. The ending will make up for all of it. I just need to actually figure it out." Droplets of chlorinated water fall onto the pages of my composition notebook as I tap my pen nervously against it. As far I can tell from going through the Mermaid Cove archives in Janet's office, no one's *ever* done a show like this before. Except for one Japanese tale performed in the '80s, all the folklore retellings I found were from European countries like France, Sweden, and Norway. In them, the mermaids are either beautiful, innocent creatures who tend to their long, flowy hair, or evil temptresses who seduce men to their violent downfalls and deaths. No in-between. No nuance. They're either saints or putas, though of course there's no mention of Latin American tales, unless they somehow involve the Spaniards' "discovery" of the "New World."

"Did you know Christopher Columbus wrote about seeing mermaids in his journals? But they were probably manatees," I say. "So if having no sense of direction, claiming he discovered an entire continent when he got lost and bumped into one, then enslaving, murdering, and raping the indigenous people he 'encountered' here wasn't enough to make him the least credible source of information in history, there's that."

"If he's in our routine, I'm out," Geoff says.

"He's not in our—I was just saying. I thought it was interesting, that's all."

"I've never seen a manatee," Alex says. "Do they look like mermaids?"

"Kind of. Like if you just see their tails. And it's dark. And if you're high on opium," I say.

Leslie stops unspooling a string of elastic and turns to me. "Opium," she repeats.

"The guy was addicted," I say.

"There's actually no scholarly backing for that," Geoff says. "Speaking of credible sources and all."

"Really?"

He nods. "Unquestionably abhorrent for a hundred confirmed reasons. Just not that one."

"It's funny what makes it into the history books," Alex says. He's lying on the grassy patch just off to the side of the pool, where he's stretched out a couple of towels for us, along with several drinks.

"Agree," I say, settling in next to him. "So you've really never seen a manatee? They're cute. They come into the canals sometimes." I roll onto my stomach and pull out my notebook and pen from my bag.

"Kitten cute? Or baby alligator cute? Because I think you and I have very different definitions of that word."

"Huge, gentle giants cute. But also majestic."

He scoots close so our feet are touching, then places his chin on my shoulder. "So like Great Danes."

I grin and rest my forehead against his. "Kind of. It's hard to describe how beautiful they are."

"I know what you mean."

My whole body starts to tingle. I close my eyes, blocking out the sun, the world. Everything but the two of us. I pay attention to our breaths as they synch up.

He's chewing a sweet, fruit-flavored gum.

"Alex. I have to finish writing this thing," I whisper. He rolls onto his back and gives me space.

For a while I just stare at the blank page. The first half of the story came easy, but now that I need to write the ending, I'm beginning to doubt it's worth telling. So far, all I've managed to write at the top is *Huacachina*. *The name itself means "weeping lady."*

"Why are they always crying? It's like men can't tell legends about women unless we're pretty, evil, or sad," I say.

Satisfaction fills Leslie's eyes as she snips at the edge of a cloth and tears it straight in half with her hands. The rip is as loud as a record scratching. "That's why you're telling this one."

But it feels overwhelming when it hasn't been told before. Correction: when those in power haven't *allowed* it to be told before.

"What if I'm in over my head? What if people take it as me completely shitting over the Mermaid Cove legacy of the last eighty years?"

"Then let them. They already said yes," Leslie says. "And if it doesn't vibe with the Cove's so-called legacy, then do you really want to be a part of their future?"

"I literally just got on the troupe, Les. I can't even think about that."

"She's right, though," Geoff says. "I've been asking the same thing."

"Really?" Mr. I'm-Still-Holding-My-Breath? I've seen the hashtags people tag him in; in some ways, Geoff is more popular among the fan base than Lila and Hallie are.

"It's so heteronormative. And I don't know how much longer I can wait around to get a tail. You got fitted for yours on what . . . the second day?"

"My first," I mumble, embarrassed.

"My point exactly. All I'm saying is, the only reason I agreed to do this skit with you is because you said it'd be revolutionary. And no doubt Hallie's going to hold an even bigger grudge against me forever, so just . . . don't flinch."

We mark the next counts of the choreography two more times on the grass before taking it underwater. Without our air hoses, we have to practice closer to the water's surface so we can take breaths without it interfering with our counts. Alex presses Play on the music, and the sound dims and brightens like a sporadic light bulb as we dip in and out of the pool. The whole time, I think not only of the movements but the corresponding words. My routine, like so many others, will have voiceover narration to go with the music. It'll play over the PA system in the auditorium in tandem with underwater speakers that shoot sound through the springs.

I imagine the words I haven't even written yet booming through the space as a roomful of people take in my body and motions.

"Wait!" I pop up and nearly choke on a mouthful of water. "Who does our narration? While we're performing, I mean. Do we write a script for them? Is it Barb? In all the videos I've seen, it sounds like Barb speaking, right?"

Geoff swims to the edge of the pool. Stretches his arms like wings over the blue and pink tiles. "It's a recording. Over the music. You'll have to do your own V/O."

I'm neck deep in warm water, but I feel like my whole body just went cold.

My words. My movements. My voice. I'll have to own all of it.

I climb out of the water, dry off, and get back to my notebook. At the top, in big blue letters, I write:

Don't flinch.

Ubicar: u·bi·car

1. (v.) to find or locate, as in geographically or on a map
2. (v. VR) to find your footing long enough to make the world stop spinning

Chapter 31

IF IT WEREN'T FOR MY PARENTS being miles away, I wouldn't dream of being here.

But they are. And I do. Now that I've stepped inside Alex's apartment for the first time, everything's flipped. Not just my stomach, but literally the actual place.

"We live in the same model," I say. "Except yours is reversed."

"*Yours* is." He grins as he pushes his sneakers off with his toes and leaves them in the small closet behind the main door. I kick off my flip-flops. In our version of the A1 model, this is the space where we keep the vacuum, mop and broom, and a bunch of cleaning supplies that strike terror into my heart because seeing Mami bring them out can only mean one thing: cancel all your plans, porque hay que limpiar la casa.

I shut the closet door and take a few steps into the rest of the apartment.

Correction: it's just like ours except bigger and brand-new. If Palmview Lakes wanted to create a before and after post showing off their renovated units, they could use ours and this one. Before: dull, beige everything, and appliances from the late '80s. After: surfaces that glimmer like the cars in a fancy dealership.

"Wow. I'd heard they were going to be remodeling, but I didn't realize they'd already started." I picture the map of our complex that hangs in the leasing office, etched into my brain. The construction must've happened while I was still in school; otherwise I would have noticed them coming and going. I wonder which apartment they'll move on to next. I imagine it's a constant, long-term operation: out with the old, in with the new.

"Yeah. It kind of came with my mom's job." His eyes shift nervously from the kitchen to the lanai. It suddenly hits me that no one else is home. There's a specific silence to the emptiness, like not even the air is being shifted by another body.

Which makes me suddenly very aware of *our* bodies.

"Do you want a drink? I think we have some lemonade," Alex says.

"Water's fine."

While he goes into the kitchen, I wander into the living area. It's bathed in sunlight, and in the spots where it doesn't hit, there are several unpacked boxes, pushed aside like they're trying to hide in the shadows. The couch is a mustard yellow with deep blue cushions, and opposite there's a TV, almost as tall as I am, sitting on a stack of wooden planks.

"Your apartment's really nice."

"Thanks. My mom doesn't seem to think so. She thought this place would be . . . bigger. When we moved. It's why she took the job, because it included free rent. She wasn't sure where we'd live otherwise."

I turn in place, taking it all in. For a brief moment it gives me vertigo, like my body still has to adjust to the reversal of all that's familiar. Here, in Alex's apartment, right is left and left is right. The kitchen opens on the opposite side, and the layout of the living area mirrors ours. I take the glass of water he offers, brushing my fingers over his.

"Do you want to see my room?" He points to a door on my right, just off the sliding glass door that leads to the lanai. My knees go slightly numb at the newness of it all. Not at the idea of going into his bedroom, but the way he waits for me to nod before even shifting his weight to take a step. The way we're not having to steal time and space, sneaking off into a friend's bedroom during a party, or huddling in the back row of a movie theater.

Next thing we know, we find you sleeping with him.

My mother's words reverberate in the bare walls of this apartment. Not just what she said, but how she said it, like there was no other logical next step. As if the possibility that I'd say no to someone like Jeremy was nonexistent. As if me deciding to be with Alex would be just as bad. In the eyes of my parents, it doesn't matter what I choose to do with my body; it only matters that I do what they think is right. As if girls don't get to have a say. As if it's not really my body at all.

I nod and walk ahead of Alex into his inverse version of my bedroom. "This is me and Dani's room too, in our place."

Alex's room is full of maps. Old, expensive-looking maps in wooden frames. Kitschy maps, like the kind you'd find on a diner's paper placemats, pinned to the walls. Folded-up road maps of Texas and globes in the form of two stress balls on his desk. They're everywhere.

"Explain?" I gesture at the maps and lean gently into him so that my forehead rests against his chin.

He chuckles silently, but I feel the tremble in his chest. "My dad was always on the road when I was little. He was a truck driver, so when I missed him, I'd draw all his routes on a map. It made me feel closer to him, I guess. Eventually my mom didn't want him being gone all the time, so he got a desk job. I think that's when he figured out that he didn't want to be home. Not in Texas, anyway."

I trace his journey along a map of the Southern states, thinking of how Alex steered the moving truck from Texas to Florida. He drove all those miles, just like his father used to, in the opposite direction. "That's when you came here."

"All nine hundred and twelve miles." He starts sifting through a stack of papers on his desk with one hand, avoiding my eyes. "But by that time, my obsession had stuck."

From between the pages of a worn Moleskine notebook, he pulls out scraps of maps. Some look like shavings of a shredder, while others are cut into odd shapes. They're the pieces that were missing from the maps in the storage unit. He clears the space to reveal what I thought was a desktop calendar. It's a portrait of a family of three—*his* family, judging by the younger version of Alex being embraced by a pale woman with light curly hair and a darker-skinned man in glasses and a mustache. I gasp as the shapes of their features settle. Every line, curve, color, and hue is composed entirely of maps.

"You made this?" I lean in close to make out the details. The earth-colored mountains of Mexico fill in Alex's and his father's hair. Stretches of desert lend shading to their similar bone structure. Bits of the ocean live in his mother's eyes.

"They're just these collages I got into years ago."

"*Just?* They're breathtaking." Different maps create different effects. City transit maps are mostly sharp, bold lines of grey, while less populated areas are softer greens. Each cutting is as precise as a brushstroke.

He runs a finger over his father's smile. "I tried to use maps of where we've been. So the places tell the story."

I think back to that day in the storage unit, all the art he wasn't ready to revisit yet. "Are there more?"

He looks down. Crinkles a piece of map into a marble-size wad into his palm. "They're in boxes. We had a den before, which I used as a studio. But here there's not a lot of space." He gestures at his bedroom, same as the space I share with Dani. None of the art pieces hanging on the wall are his creations. I try not to think of them sitting in a dark box.

"Which one's your favorite?" I sit on his bed and lean back on my hands, crossing one leg over the other.

"Map?"

"Mmm–hmm."

He moves his lips side to side, probably chewing on the inside of his cheeks as he thinks it over. It's so quiet we hear the neighbor's water pipes roaring through the walls. Finally he picks up the Moleskine again and holds it open over my lap.

"Actually, I've been thinking a lot about these two. How their shapes look almost the same. Except flipped, and a little bigger." He points at one page and the one across from it. Two maps are glued side by side. Florida. And Peru.

A lump forms in my throat. I'd never thought of them as anything but far apart, never felt much other than torn between them. On one page, there's a birthplace I can barely remember. On the other, the home I know like the back of my hand, even when it doesn't know me. Somehow, Alex saw them as linked. I put my hands on them. Hold the notebook close.

"You're making art again?"

"Kinda," he says. "They're just maps."

"They're more. Similar, but flipped. Like our homes."

A sadness sweeps over his smile, and I want to ask if that's the right word. Does he think of this as home yet? He is already home, to me.

"What are you doing tomorrow? Maybe after I'm done at the Cove, we can find you some new favorite places."

"Currently"—he takes a seat a couple feet away from me on the bed, then lies on his side—"I'm liking right here."

I tap the space between us. "Right here?"

"If you want."

I shift closer. "How about here?"

"Even better."

I lie on my side and face him. Our bodies are two parallel lines, barely any distance between us. "And here?"

"Almost perfect."

We kiss, and I roll onto him. I start to feel distant from everything but us. From the voices that tell me it's wrong to want this. From the voice that didn't listen when I said no. From my fears that say this body is too flawed to be desirable. They're all here, but they start to fade, or maybe it's my voice that is finally the loudest.

I slip my hair out of its scrunchie and let it cascade over my shoulders onto his face. It creates a cave of us: all I see is his deep brown eyes and his curled lips, which he briefly presses together, softening them in anticipation of mine. I place my hands just above his shoulders and sink closer. He pulls me in, and my consciousness blurs at the edges, feeling so much and nothing all at once.

We get lost, and we find each other. Follow hands and touch and breath. We peel off each other's shirts and then I'm in my bikini top, with all its knotted strings at my neck and back. I stop and then he stops, until I breathe and tell him to pull. The air hits my skin, which is now freezing and scorching and screaming and sighing, and we dip under his sheets until there is nothing but white and light and each other.

He asks if I'm okay as I start inching out of my shorts. His hand has stopped over the line above my hip bone, the ridge of skin that has always been an afterthought, a scar unseen by the sun.

It's five inches in diagonal with two marks at the end that look like a dotted line. Like a stone being thrown across water, gliding and then bouncing twice before its final plunge.

I tell him how far I'll go and close my eyes as his hands become a part of me.

In a room full of maps, we explore.

Release: re·lease

1. (v.) to allow to escape confinement
2. (v. VR) to escape your fears, doubts, and body, even if only briefly

Chapter 32

ALEX OFFERED TO WALK ME HOME, but it's already a quarter past five, which means Mami gets off work any minute now. On days when Papi's shift doesn't end until late, she takes the bus and gets dropped off a block from Palmview Lake's south entrance, passing Alex's apartment on the way to ours.

I wouldn't be caught dead within a five-mile radius of him at this hour.

Or, rather, I would be caught with him. It'd be just my luck. And then my parents would kill me. Either way: dead.

Instead of cutting through the grassy patches behind the buildings, I take the longer route along the sidewalk so I can stop by the mailbox hut. I'm not in a hurry to be back in our apartment yet. Spending time at Alex's was like being in an alternate universe. A world in which everything looked nearly the same except felt completely different. Fear and guilt lifted. The air was easier to breathe. Tucked away in his not-my-bedroom that my parents don't even know exists, I didn't have to worry about them finding us out. I felt an all-consuming freedom. Down to my last nerve. A relief. An exhale.

His touch lingers on my skin as the wind envelopes me. It feels crisp and light, like I just got out of the shower. I turn the key in our mailbox and find it's stuffed. Credit card offers, coupons, and circulars wrap themselves around bills from the electric company, notices from our health insurer, letters from important-looking offices of government I know Mami will tear open eagerly. I've started sorting the junk, tossing it in the trash bin at the edge of the hut, when I see two letters from colleges. They're thick and sturdy; I've received enough of these to know they're promotional packages designed to pique my interest in applying. One is from a state school that was already on my list; the other is in California.

All the way on another coast. Another ocean.

I'm about to throw both away when I catch something move in my periphery.

It's small. Just a body sunken into the folds of the hammocks among the trees, readjusting itself. The body goes still, but the hammock keeps swinging, and I'm about to look away but then I notice the feet sticking out of one end. Two pairs of feet.

The purple and yellow flowers painted on the toes.

"Dani?"

It's like watching the world's clumsiest butterfly emerge

from its cocoon. Limbs stir and stretch the fabric until finally my sister's head pops up, terror-stricken, followed by that of the second guilty party. Jason Parker.

"Oh thank God, it's just you," she says, the skin all around her lips inflamed pink.

"What are you doing here? Out like this?"

"Relax, Vero." She climbs out of the hammock and straightens out her clothes.

"Mami could've seen you!"

"I was being careful."

"Oh yeah, good job looking out from behind Jason Parker's face."

His eyes narrow, and his chin shrinks into his neck. "Hey, it's not like—"

Dani puts one hand in the air, and he goes quiet. I start walking away, and she follows me.

"What is up with you?" she says.

"Nothing."

"We weren't doing anything wrong."

"With Jason Parker?" I scoff. "Doubtful. How could you be so careless? On the hammocks? Right next to the mailboxes? When you know Mami gets home any minute—"

"Just because *you* got caught with his stepbrother—"

"This isn't about that. And you have no idea what really happened that night."

"It's not any different—"

"It's totally different. I was humiliated."

"And you think I'm not? By you?"

"That's real cute, Dani. You don't even know how lucky you are. You don't have to worry about some jerk making fun of your butt or people acting like your skin is disgusting because it's scarred. You can go around hooking up with his stepbrother, or anyone else for that matter, without having to even consider how guys like them treat girls like me."

Dani slows down. "I'm sorry, I didn't know."

"Of course you didn't." We pass the pool, the vending machines. Cars amble along the road in front of the leasing office, but none of them are my father's. "You can make out with Jason in a goddam hammock in broad daylight like it's nothing. Because if you got caught, they'd simply blame it on me. You know that, right? They'd say I was the bad influence. I'm the one who's promiscua and setting a bad example. I'm the one who'd have to deal with them, not you."

"Oh my God." A growl rises out of Dani's throat. "This isn't about you. For once. Please, stop making this about you."

"I don't make things about me."

"No, but they always are. You're the center of Mami and Papi's universe, and you're too busy feeling sorry for yourself to notice."

"Oh, right. Sorry you never got to experience the joys of being in and out of surgery, Dani. How selfish of me."

"That's not what I meant. I know parts of it sucked, but—"

"Parts of it?" It's like she's looking at a storm and telling me to be glad for the silver linings. "You don't know the half of it."

"But you and Mami got to spend all those days together.

And then I'd come home from school and the two of you had another inside joke I didn't get. And Papi's always worried about you. How you're feeling, how you're walking, whether you're pain."

"You're seriously jealous? Of their attention? Trust me, you don't want it."

"You don't know what I want."

"And you don't know what you're asking. You don't think I'd like their actual attention on *me,* for once? Me as a person, not me as a body, and what it needs, or what it doesn't. As if they get to decide everything."

"Like what you do, and who you do it with?" Her voice gets pitchy, and I know she's mocking me.

"Yes, fine. What are you getting at, Dani?"

"You're being just like them. All you can focus on is how *Vero* feels. It might come as a surprise to you, but you actually ruined a big moment for me, with Jason."

I shake my head, eyes up to the sky. "You'll have plenty more, I'm sure."

She stops at the corner of the sidewalk, just before we turn onto our street. "You know what? You're being worse than them. I thought you of all people would understand. Put yourself in my place for once."

"*Your* place? You think my whole life I haven't imagined what it's like to be you?"

"Not in any real way. Just because you've had it hard doesn't mean everything for me is easy."

I gasp, my hand landing with dramatic flourish on my

chest. "Oh, I'm sorry. Did my existence make things diffi-cult for you?"

She narrows her wet eyes at me. "You always do this."

"Do what?"

"Twist things around and put words in my mouth. And then you expect me to play along with your bullshit stories and lie for you? I'm done." Her arms flail in the air in sur-render. I rush toward her as if she just dropped something I don't want to fall.

"Wait. What are you saying? Geoff and I are performing next week. Don't fuck this up for us. I swear, I'll tell Mami and Papi about you and Jason if you do."

"You are such a self-absorbed liar. And no pretending to be a mermaid or anything else you're not is going to change that!" She yells so loud it stuns both of us into silence. We wait. For one of us to speak, for our parents to come out and tell us to stop making a scene in the middle of the street. When nothing happens, Dani takes off toward our building, and for half a second, I actually expect her to cartwheel.

But she just leaves me there in her wake.

Transformation: trans·for·ma·tion

1. (n.) a change that occurs at a foundational level
2. (n. VR) a change that happens somewhere so deep, it can never be undone

Chapter 33

MONDAY I WAKE UP KNOWING TWO things: I'm getting my tail today and there's rain coming. Probably a storm. I never sense the quick, light showers that fall even with full sun out. And the heavier downpours will often make themselves known, the pressure slowly sinking into my bones as I go about my day. But it's a rare one that alerts me before I've even gotten out of bed. It wraps itself around my hip joint like a vise and squeezes each time I make the slightest move. My insides feel like they're screaming in protest.

I get up anyways. We have our last big rehearsal before the show in two days, and since neither Alex nor Leslie were able to get a car, I asked Lila if she could pick me up. When we hit the Turnpike, there's a massive dark cloud miles ahead of us. We're driving straight toward it.

"You think Barb will cancel rehearsal?" I ask.

Lila leans into the steering wheel to get a better look at the sky. "If there's lightning, then yes. Let's hope it doesn't come to that. But if it only rains . . . nah. Rain doesn't change anything when you're underwater."

"Right."

"Wet's wet, you know?"

Except when it's not. Except when the humidity seeps into your bones instead of wicking off.

It starts falling just as we get off on the exit toward Mermaid Cove. At first the drops are shy taps against the windows, but without warning they're a deluge of stones, heavy and impatient.

"When do you think it'll let up?"

"I don't know. Here—" Lila reaches into the backseat and tosses an unopened package at me. "If it really bothers you that much."

I recognize the raincoat from the Mermaid Cove gift shop. Folded into a perfect rectangle, it's green with the words *Mermaids dance daily, rain or shine!* in cursive reminiscent of the '50s. Even though we don't dance daily anymore, no one's ever updated it. I remember begging Papi to buy me a raincoat when I was little. He said no, of course, pointing at it like it was an overpriced trash bag. But now that it's in my hands, I can't help wanting to unwrap the raincoat with the same joy of opening a long-awaited Christmas present.

"Very funny," I say. "It'll match my tail perfectly."

Lila fidgets in her seat and clicks the car locks open. "Did you see Barb's text? We're meeting in the theater first." She bobs her eyebrows at me twice. "Who knows. Maybe she's canceling practice after all."

Inside, the others are already sitting in a circle on the mini stage in front of the center glass. There's no sunlight coming through the water, so Barb signals for someone to turn on a spotlight and claps three times for us to quiet down.

"Morning, everyone. Obviously, it's raining, and I'm waiting to hear from a friend at the news station on the latest weather report to make sure it's safe for us to be out there. So you'll be practicing in here today. And in the meantime—" She curls her finger at someone offstage. There's a very loud rustling and then Janet shuffles in carrying an iridescent purple tail across both arms. It's so long and majestic it trails behind her like a bridal train as she moves across the stage. A collective gasp sweeps over us.

"Gorgeous, isn't it?" Barb says, her eyes aflame with mischief as they meet mine.

"Is that . . ."

"Yes, yours, Verónica. And not a moment too soon. T minus two days now," she says.

Janet extends her arms toward me, thrusting the tail into the spotlight. I've seen it before, looking cold and lifeless under the fluorescent glow of Janet's office, but here on the stage, it's transformed. It has sparkles of blue in it, dark as night, and neon pink glimmers that turn green when the light hits it, all engulfed by the most beautiful shade of purple I've ever seen. It reminds me of the inside of a purple potato, how when you cut into it, it reveals a bright magenta that seems to defy nature.

"I don't even know what to say." I run my fingers down to the fins, then scoop my palm under them. They're translucent, with just the right amount of light passing through.

"Say you'll be ready in ten," Barb says, shouting over my head at everyone else in the room. "I just got a text that there's no storm expected till this afternoon. So we have time for two run-throughs, but I need you in the water stat."

Everyone disperses while I gather my bag and the tail. It's deceptively heavy, like a sequined dress, and I relish its weight because it reminds me this isn't a fantasy anymore. This has presence, mass. It exists in my world, and soon I'll be a part of it, and the tail will be an extension of me, a thing that can't easily be taken away.

I run my fingers over it as I walk, every inch new to my touch. Even as I rush so Barb won't have to wait, I try to commit this moment to memory.

"You still want them to cancel rehearsal?" Lila teases. I shake my head, too happy for words. She laughs and offers to help me into it.

The transformation happens fast. Sitting just off the side of the tube, I lie on my back and slide into the tail like it's a pair of jeans fresh out of the dryer. The material is cold against my skin, almost like a waxy plastic. Lila gestures for me to turn on my side as she zips me up. I lean against my right arm, glancing back at her over my left shoulder.

"Look at you. Already striking a pose."

This is what it's like. To hold something that commands

people's awe and admiration. To bask in their attention rather than fear it. I feel warm inside. Safe.

"How's the fit?" Tanya asks.

"A little tight."

"It's supposed to feel that way. It'll feel better in the water."

In the water, I can't really feel my legs.

I swim through the tube and up to surface, floating on my back and spreading my arms like wings as I take in the colorless sky. The clouds cluster all around us, and soon it starts to sprinkle. A microdrop lands on one of my lashes, and I close my eyes and go into a dolphin spin, using my arms to propel myself into a circle several feet underwater.

It's like stepping through a mirror. When I look up, I can still see the world above me, blurred and distant, but I'm no longer of it. I go still, letting out small bursts of breath that allow my body to sink deeper into the spring. When I glance up one last time, rings the size of my hands appear and disappear from the surface as the rain hits. The water catches them like an invisible shield. But within seconds they start growing larger and faster. Everyone takes a sip of air and gets into formation.

Everyone gets into formation just as the familiar intro of the Little Mermaid show flows through the speakers. I play one of her sisters, so most of the time, I'm in the background and Hallie's front and center, except for when we all spin around her at the end.

We're just two eight counts away from the final water

curtain when Barb starts yelling. It's not the usual cues or choreography—it doesn't even sound like she's speaking to us. I hear her say, "Excuse me?" And then, "How did you get in here?"

Someone responds to her in the background with a muffled voice that seems familiar. Something about its rhythm makes me stop mid-spin and drop my air hose.

The music goes quiet. Lila, Hallie, and Tanya turn their heads toward Barb's control center, signaling with their hands that they can't hear anything. But there's no one in there anymore, and the music is no longer playing, and we're floating aimlessly, wondering what just happened. I try to read their body language, but all I see on the other side of the glass are fuzzy silhouettes. My chest starts closing in, like two hands squeezing at my lungs, and I go searching for my hose.

When I find it, I take a deep breath and swim up to the glass, cupping my hands over it. At first I don't believe what I see. Don't want to believe.

There's not enough clarity to know for sure, and maybe my eyes are just playing tricks on me, all my greatest fears imagining the worst.

Two figures approach the front, both of them dark except for an orange-red top that looks like an ember in the dark. It gets closer and grows into a sun.

A voice comes back over the sound system. "Verónica, please come out. Your parents are here?"

I feel like I could drown.

Liable: li·a·ble

1. (adj.) obligated by law to be held responsible
2. (adj. VR) held responsible even (or especially) if it's not your fault

Chapter 34

IN THE HALF SECOND WHERE ALL logic escapes me and I'm operating on fear alone, I try to make myself invisible. I look around for places I might hide before they see me — behind one of the logs on the set, inside the sandcastle prop like a scared fish. The panic takes over, but I can't move. I start sinking and all I can focus on are my legs and how they feel disconnected from me, like I couldn't will them to push me out of the water if I tried.

In an instant, Lila and Tanya scoop their arms over mine. Their touch is a jolt through my spine. I twist out of their grasp and push off the glass toward the water's surface.

I hear Mami's voice out by the deck. "I'm not talking to you. I need to speak with my daughter. Right now." Her words sound harsh; gone are the soft cushions between each syllable, the melody in her accent. Her voice is a weapon she's not afraid to use.

"We've called her, Mrs. Rentería. She'll be here any second," Barb says.

"Sonia, tranquilízate," Papi whispers.

"I am perfectly calm," she responds. It's jarring to hear Mami speak to him in English. The anger in her voice is steady, solid. It makes the air shake inside of me.

"I'm here," I say, pulling myself onto the deck. My tail slaps against the wood as I stretch my body out, propping myself up on both arms.

Mami's eyes meet mine and then I see them travel the length of me, all the way to the tip of my fins.

"Verónica."

My name is just a word now. The way she just said it, full but somehow empty. Like all the tenderness and history are gone. The way a stranger would say it, because that's how she's seeing me.

"All these days. Puras mentiras."

I wish there really were such a thing as pure lies. Lies you could tell without hurting anyone, least of all yourself.

"See? This is what you get for telling her all those stories. She lives in a fantasy world," Papi says. They start arguing a mile a minute in Spanish, and my face turns so hot, I feel like I could evaporate from embarrassment. So much for being "good immigrants" that never call attention to ourselves. People are staring. The other mermaids stand by the theater entrance pretending not to listen. The groundskeepers tending to plants have turned off their hoses.

"Excuse me!" Barb's voice drops between them. "Will

someone please explain what's going on here? How is any of this a surprise? Your parents signed all the liability forms. Did they not?" Her last three words are low and emphatic. She looks at each of us as she says them, like they're rocks she just thrust into our hands.

Mami doesn't miss a beat. "Of course. This is just a misunderstanding of another matter. A *family* matter."

Her lips curve into a thin, sharp smile. "Get out of that thing and get dressed, and we'll discuss this at home."

I've never understood until now when people say they feel claustrophobic. Like the world is closing in on you. We've had this car since I was eight, and my sister and I used to be small enough that I could lie across the backseat while Dani stretched over the floor, placing two pillows behind the front seats so the bump in the middle wouldn't dig into her. I'd stare at the sky out the back window. I'd count raindrops against the glass and run out of numbers when it poured.

"Get in," Mami says, flipping the front seat forward so I can climb into the back. It's like crawling into my own prison.

I try to curl into myself. Grey clouds chase us as we pull away from Mermaid Cove, growing darker with each passing mile. I used to love this car even though it was old before we bought it. But now the clutch is so stiff and heavy, I know I wouldn't endure more than thirty minutes driving it. The pain of holding down the clutch only to have its weight shoot back at me the second I press on the gas would be too much. I've begged my parents to get an automatic car, but they say they can't afford it.

Now this same car that I can never take anywhere feels like a holding cell.

"First thing tomorrow, you go and tell Barb or whoever that you're quitting," Mami says.

Desperation tightens my throat. "But we have a show the day after tomorrow. My first performance."

Papi actually chuckles. "No, you have your MRI that day."

"It's not until August," I say.

"They called this afternoon," Mami says. "Someone canceled, and we took the appointment."

"Without even asking me?" This can't be happening. Please, God, make it happen any other day but this.

But Mami ignores me and yells, "Who signed those papers?"

"What?"

"The ones esa mujer said."

"Her name's Barb." I don't know why I say that. Probably because I'm trying to brace myself for what's about to come next. "And I did."

"As me." She already knows the answer. She just needs me to say it out loud.

"Yes."

In the mirror I see her eyes widen. Black pebbles sinking in a sea of white. "You didn't." She lets out a slow, shaking breath, and it's like watching a statue disintegrate, all the perfect shapes and surfaces crumbling under their own weight. The only thing worse than me forging a signature is someone with power finding out about it. And to Mami, anyone outside our family is powerful. Everyone has more of it than we do.

I look away. Damage done.

"What were you thinking?"

"It was just a liability form, in case—"

"In case you got hurt? In case you injured your hip and needed surgery? So they wouldn't have to be held responsible and we'd be left on our own, picking up the pieces?"

I hadn't thought of it that way.

"I'm not that fragile. I can do this. Trust me."

"Trust you? How are we supposed to trust you? You put yourself and this entire family at risk. Forging our signature. Faking documents. We do any little thing wrong, se jodió todo. Do you want us kicked out of this country?"

"We're permanent residents now."

"How many times have I told you? It's not a promise, Vero."

"Sonia," Papi says. "Don't put that on her. It's one form."

"One form is all it takes! How many forms do you think I've agonized over all these years? How many scrutinized, down to every last box, every little detail? You're not the one who holds her breath, waiting for them to come back just to be disqualified over one mistake, one checkmark, or one name spelled with an accent that they don't know where to place. Don't talk to me like you know, because you don't. None of you do."

She sinks back into her seat and turns her face toward the window, but I can tell by the tendons that tighten around her neck that she's trying hard not to cry.

"Mami, I'm sorry. I didn't know." She waves me off, and I wonder if I'd just told her about being a mermaid to begin with, if I hadn't lied or signed that ridiculous paper, then maybe, maybe she would've been on my side. But how was I supposed to take that risk when she always agrees with Papi?

We're finally parked in our mismarked spot, but my parents don't move or say anything. They just stare ahead without acknowledging my existence, like they're guarding a locked gate. And maybe they are. I can't leave this two-door trap until they do. I can't get out unless they let me.

"Why are we staying in here?" I'm in the middle seat, arms crossed over my chest, waiting for either of them to get out so I can escape.

Papi scratches his temple and sighs. "Look what you started."

"Me? If you'd just let me be who I am from the beginning, none of this would have happened!"

But Papi's not even listening. He says to Mami, "See? You can't even talk to her. Everything is our fault, according to her."

"I'm right here. Stop talking like I'm not."

"This is very simple," Mami says, in a calm, measured

way that is scarier than her shouting. "You're going to quit the little mermaid place yourself, or else I'll call this Barb and tell her Dr. Brown said you need to quit. Punto. Your choice."

"That's not a choice. That's a threat."

Mami turns to look at me so fast, I'm surprised she doesn't pinch a nerve. "Oye. Estás recontraatrevida," she says.

So I'm being too bold. Good. For once, I'm more scared of what'll happen if I stay quiet than whatever they'll do to me for talking back.

My hands turn into stiffened claws as I grasp at air. "You can't do that. Dr. Brown's always said the water's good for me."

A look of satisfaction flashes across her eyes. "Bueno. We'll see what he says once we get the MRI."

"Sonia . . ." Papi says.

"Oh my God. You want my hip to get worse, because without that, you'd have no other way to control me."

"That's ridiculous." Mami snaps open her seat belt and gets out. I push down on the handle behind the seat, and it thrusts forward. "¿Tú sabes qué? Haz lo que quieras. Ruin your body, for all I care."

It's like a punch in the gut as I get out.

Do whatever you want means the opposite. It's neither an invitation nor an allowance; it's a warning and a dare. Haz lo que quieras and just pray you choose wisely. It's somehow worse than telling me what to do.

"Te dije que one day you'd take this too far," Papi says

as we make our way toward the apartment. "First it's kissing boys in a hot tub. Then it's lying behind our backs and forging papers."

"What's next?" Papi asks. He raises his voice toward the sky, as if he were asking God or some other invisible entity.

I say nothing because I don't know. I try to picture my so-called near future, but it starts to fade like a foggy mirage. The only thing I know for sure is that Papi's idea of my going *too far* is just me daring to live my life on my terms. It's so completely unfair.

I make my way toward our apartment. There's a shadow by our kitchen window that I know is Dani's, but she scurries away the second I look at her.

Pucha maaaare.

The whole ride home, it hadn't occurred to me to ask how they found out.

I run after her and slam our bedroom door behind me. She's standing with her back to me, completely still, but I can see her muscles flinch.

"Why'd you tell them?" I ask.

"I swear . . ."

"You ruined everything."

"You're not listening."

"I can't believe you told them."

"I didn't. I swear."

"No seas mentirosa."

Her hair whips the air as she turns to look at me. "That's your job, remember? I'm not as a good a liar as you."

She goes to our desk and opens our laptop, typing some-thing into the browser. Fingers shaking, she has to press De-lete several times before she gets it right.

"See for yourself. I was here. I was looking at this photo, and Mami came in to use the laptop super agitated, needing to fill out some forms to confirm your appointment. And I don't know, she has laser vision or something. But she saw you. In the picture. And before I could close the tab, she was all over it. She even sent it to Papi."

"What the hell are you talking about?"

She turns the screen so I can get a better look. Tiny tiles made up of Mermaid Cove's photo feed stare back at me, but immediately one catches my attention. It's a candid shot of me and Geoff on a day we were going over our choreography out on the grass.

"I don't remember anyone shooting this," I say.

"Probably some social media intern."

"There's no intern. There's just Barb and Janet." I must've gotten so into practice I didn't notice them taking pictures. "Dammit, Dani. How could you let Mami see this?"

"I'm sorry! I swear I didn't do it on purpose. It all hap-pened so fast. And you're missing the whole point. Look," she says, pointing at the screen.

I sit down and look closer. I'm in my red one-piece suit, and I'm standing on my right leg, my back arched as I pull my left ankle toward my forehead. My one best move.

The caption reads: *Coming soon to the Cove. The dawning of a new mermaid story.*

I feel a rush of pride and then it drains out of me. "Wait. Did they . . . ?"

"That's what Mami noticed, honestly. Before anything else."

I want to cry. "I never told them to do that. I never told them they could."

"I'm sorry, Vero."

She goes to close the laptop, but I stop her. Where my scar should be, there's just skin. Only because I know to look for it do I notice the blurry edges, the remnants of a botched photoshop.

Endure: en·dure

1. (v.) to remain strong or firm under suffering
2. (v. VR) to continue in pain for the benefit of others, but rarely for yourself

Chapter 35

SOMETIMES THE WORST KIND OF PAIN happens in the after.

It takes its time sinking in. It has to be processed before it can really register.

By then the catalyst might be gone but the sensation has made a home for itself. In the frictionless spaces between my bones. The damaged relic of my pride.

Everything that happened yesterday throbs inside of me. I can't tell if it was the rain or the fact that I ignored it and pushed through anyway that makes today's ache echo. And then there's the picture. When I signed the liability form, I gave them permission to post pictures of me on social. But I never said they could edit me. Who gave them the right? I want the original picture that was taken of me. Taken *from* me. It's mine, and they don't deserve to have it.

Minutes after my parents leave for work, Leslie's at the

door to our lanai. This means she probably hid behind our building, waiting for their car to pass.

"How long have you been there? You could've gone through the front," I say.

She looks disappointed. "But that wouldn't have entertained my super-spy fantasies, Ronnie. Anyways, I've come to rescue you."

"Rescue me?"

"Yeah. When you didn't answer my texts this morning I figured your parents flushed your phone down the toilet and put, like, tape on the door so they'd know if you got out."

"Close," I say. Mami might've said haz lo que quieras, but she left two baskets of laundry on my bed for me to fold, and Papi finally got on YouTube and figured out how to track my phone. They took my keys to the apartment too, as if the fear of leaving our home unlocked would keep me inside until it's time for my MRI appointment tomorrow.

Leslie sits on my bed and starts rolling the socks into balls. "I won't do underwear," she says. "But if it helps you get out of this lint trap faster . . ." I start to smile, but my chin starts to quiver. "Oh, Ronnie. I'm so sorry. Just tell me whose notifications I need to change to fart noises."

"Me muero," I say, laughing so hard I'm actually on the floor. I picture Leslie dressed in all black, sneaking into Barb's office and my parents' bedroom to change their phone settings like some sort of vigilante prankster. "You'd text them over and over again, wouldn't you?"

"Well, yeah. Can you imagine their phones going off

while they worked? It's the best kind of revenge. Harmless but embarrassing." She sits down next to me and puts her head on my shoulder. "But seriously."

"Seriously," I say. "How am I ever going to go back there?"

"To the Cove?"

"They must think I'm a child. Getting pulled out of the water by my parents like that."

"Honestly, they're just worried about you. Tanya says Val thought you had a death in the family. And Lila is telling them not to jump to any conclusions. But Geoff wants to know if you're still performing tomorrow."

"I know. I saw his messages." I haven't been able to answer them. "I'm still trying to figure things out."

"Your parents are really that mad at you?"

"Worse than you can imagine."

So I tell her everything. About my hip and the necrosis and how it's unpredictable. How there are stages of it, and tomorrow they'll take an MRI to see which one I'm in. As I've researched, I've learned there's four, and the last is basically the bone collapsing. I feel like a walking hurricane, my future caught in a forecaster's cone of possibility.

"Ronnie," she says, more sad than anything else. "You've just been carrying this? All alone? Why didn't you tell me?"

I start giving all the usual excuses. Nothing was certain yet. I didn't want her to worry. But then I stop and say, "I was scared. I wanted to ignore it so it'd go away."

"Has it?"

"What?"

"Gone away."

"I don't know. But it's about to *take* away everything I've worked for."

She pulls her legs in so she's sitting cross-legged, back straight. "Says who?"

"My parents. Who else?"

"Yeah, but what are they really going to do? Lock you up and make you do the dishes, too?" She gasps dramatically.

I'm about to explain that she doesn't understand; it's not that simple. But the more I think through my parents' logic, the more it starts to fall apart. They can track me on my phone and tell me not to leave the apartment, but I'm not some stack of papers they can lock in a fireproof box in their closet.

"You're right. And I love you," I say. "But I have to go."

A short walk later, I'm at the door to the racquetball court, out of breath from having hurried over.

When I open the door to the racquetball court I find Alex reaching for the knob on the other side.

"I heard you coming," he says, smiling like this is any other day. I haven't told him details, so all he really knows about yesterday is that it was the worst, that I'm in huge trouble with my parents because they found out I'm a mermaid, and that I'm not even sure if I'll be able to perform tomorrow.

I burrow into his chest. The sound of his heart beating calms me.

"It sucks that they don't get what this means to you," he

says, then he holds me and just lets me feel like shit. No attempts to cheer me up or assure me it'll all work out in the end. He kind of just . . . accepts that I'm not okay right now.

It feels good. Not better. But good.

I kiss him. Long and so soft that our lips are barely touching. We lock arms and let the weight of our bodies support each other.

After a while, Alex cups my face with his hands and asks if I want to talk about it.

"Let's go for a walk," I say.

I head out the door and let him follow me toward the canal at the end of the road, the dead end where a barricade seals it off like a worn Band-Aid over a cut. He sits on top of the barricade and offers his lap to me.

I shake my head. "I just feel restless. I don't want to sit right now. I haven't left my room all night, and for all I know, my parents are never going to let me leave the house again."

"I thought you said they don't ground you."

"This feels different." This will be worse than any guilt trip they've ever given me. This will be a grand tour, a purgatory of blame.

"I don't get it. I mean, okay. So they didn't want you to be a mermaid and you did it anyways. But you got a job. That's really all it comes down to."

I try kicking a rock across the pavement, but all it does is scoop a bunch of pebbles into my flip-flop. "It's bigger than that."

"How?" The wind in that word sounds like a storm being

pushed out of his lungs. Answering it would stir up everything. I let the silence last too long.

"Is there something you're not telling me?" he says.

"Only if you assume I have to tell you everything," I snap.

"Whoa. Okay." He brings both hands up.

I step over the barricade. The ground is soft and grassy, and it curves downward toward the edge of the canal. I sit and try to hug my knees as Alex's steps crunch toward me. It feels like there's a gulf stretched between us.

"So," he finally says. "Is this another one of your favorite places?"

A cloud covers the sun as it glides across the water. There's no sound but the bristling leaves of trees that lean like curious bystanders over our bodies. I wish he already knew everything. I wish I didn't have so much to explain. I'm arranging the words in order in my mind, starting with the surgeries I hardly know about to the one I know is in my near future, when something stirs in the water.

It pinches the surface, rippling in perfect circles. A large, shapeless mass floats just underneath it.

Alex takes my hand and I squeeze it.

"It's okay. It's just a manatee."

She moves in practically slow motion, so much that the water stills enough for us to see her clearly. Her nose presses so far her into her face, her eyes are nearly squinted shut. Her flaps are like giant flower petals fluttering on each side of her body.

"I didn't know they're so big," Alex says.

"They're the cows of the sea," I coo.

She starts turning, exposing her belly to us. It's marked like a loaf of artisan bread: three cuts that baked onto her skin over time.

"What happened to her?" Alex says.

"They're scars. Probably from boat propellers. People aren't supposed to go above a certain speed, or even enter parts of the waterways with their boats, because the manatees get caught in them. But they do it anyways."

"That's messed up."

"It is." I run my finger over the edge of the scar that peeks out of my shorts. It's slippery, like a wet, polished rock you try but fail to find your footing on. It makes me want to slip into the water with her. Tell her not to be afraid, she's safe. But I know I can't make that promise. "People say it doesn't hurt them because they have such thick skin. But still."

"Doesn't make it less cruel."

I look down at his hand in mine. "The other day in the sauna, Val said my scars make me look like a warrior. It made me so angry. I never asked to be in any fight."

He sighs. "People think they're saying the right thing sometimes. But usually it just makes them feel better, not you."

"Exactly." Maybe I say this too loud, because the manatee starts floating away from us. "It's not some metaphor to me. It's my body. My life. And everyone always looks at scars as survival marks, and healing. But they never really want to see the hurt that caused them."

"That would be too honest," he says.

My gut clenches. "That day my dad saw us at the pool, it wasn't just a normal checkup. They told me my bone might be degenerating. Maybe eventually collapsing." I refuse to look at him, but I feel him come closer. His figure reenters my periphery and then pauses, waiting. "I didn't tell you because I didn't want to believe it. And I didn't tell my parents about becoming a mermaid because they would've told me I couldn't do it. But I knew I could. So I pretended none of it was happening. I wanted to feel alive instead of knowing my cells were suffocating. That's how they die. The blood flow gets cut off and they don't get enough oxygen and no one really knows how bad it can get, or how fast. It's just . . . up to my threshold of pain."

He blinks several times, taking everything in. "How bad is it?"

"I don't know. They have to take an MRI tomorrow."

"I meant the pain. How do you feel?"

"I don't know." It's such a strange thing to admit, but it's true. "People talk about pain like it's measurable. They'll ask me to put it on a scale from one to ten. But I've been pushing it away so long it's like my barometer's broken. I don't know if I can trust my mind. Or my body. I think part of me thinks I deserve it. Like I should endure it, because that would be the brave thing to do. To be strong."

"For who?"

"What?"

"Who are you being strong for?"

Instinctively, I think to say *Myself.* But the word trips over itself in my mouth. "Nobody. Probably everybody. I don't know." I get up and start pacing the grass. "And you know what the messed-up part is? It doesn't even matter. I can pretend to be a mermaid all I want, but it's just that. I'll never be good enough. Perfect enough. I can put on the costumes and the tail, but Barb will still photoshop me out."

"Wait, wait, what? She photoshopped you out?" Alex says slowly, as if he doesn't want to believe it.

"Not all of me. Just my scar."

But it hits me that it feels that way. I've spent my whole life thinking my hip dysplasia is one part of me, and it is. But how long can you hide the same part of yourself before realizing you've never once felt whole?

Leap: leap

1. (n.) the act of springing free from the ground
2. (n. VR) to trust in yourself, to have faith

Chapter 36

IT'S TWO IN THE MORNING, AND I'm in bed with our laptop open, the picture still on the screen. I've been zooming in and out for at least an hour, but I can't bring myself to stop. It's strange. My whole life, all I wanted was to cover up my scars. I used to wish them away. Pray.

Please, God, make them disappear. Make the world not see.

I didn't know that in the same stroke, I'd be making the world not see me.

Mermaids are fantasy made real.

These were some of the first words Barb ever said to us the day of auditions. Like a spell cast over me, they filled me with awe and longing.

We give the gift of escape. We help people forget the world and all their troubles, if only for one twenty-minute show.

Was my scar one of those troubles?

A pressure throbs behind the bridge of my nose. I try to

blink back the onslaught of tears, but it only makes things worse. I don't want to cry, because more than my greatest sadness, I'm angry. Angry at the photo. Angry at all the lies.

Mermaids are perfection in the flesh is what she always said.

So I thought that was what I wanted to be: perfect.

I tap two more times on the image, and it grows bigger. It is the farthest thing from perfect. Whoever did this didn't even get the right colors for my skin. They really thought they could promote our showcase and erase me from my own story with one shitty, clumsy Photoshop job.

"Vero?" Dani turns over in her bed, half asleep. "Are you still looking at it?"

I snap the computer shut. "Sorry. I didn't mean to wake you."

She comes over and sits next to me, curls into a tight ball. Dani's always been so little and nimble. When we were kids and Mami took us to the park, we'd spend nearly all our time on the swings, competing to see who could get higher. It was always her legs that swung her closest to the sky, so far up I thought she might come all the way around. Just when I'd get scared she could fall and would start begging her to come down, she'd leap through the air and land safely on the ground.

I pull on the sleeve of the oversized red and yellow jersey she's been secretly sleeping in, wanting to read the back. She leans forward into the glow of the streetlights outside of my window. It says *Parker*.

"Tell me how it's going with you and Jason."

She gives me a dubious look, like she's unsure I really want to know.

"I'm serious. And more importantly, you seem serious. So what's he play?"

"Fútbol. He's a midfielder."

"Really? Papi would love him. Or at least, he would—"

"If we weren't dating."

"Bingo."

She grabs a lock of her hair and runs the ends over her palm, like she's painting circles with them. The stories our hair could tell, with all we share as we brush and braid. Except lately, she's grown quiet.

"We're lucky we're nothing like our parents. It's not like one of us walked in on you with your boyfriend and completely lost her shit," I say.

That gets a half laugh out of her. "No jodas. I think I saw my life flash before my eyes, for that second and a half I thought you were Mami. You even sounded like her."

"Oh, God. I'm so sorry." I remember it felt that way for me, too. When my parents saw me with Jeremy, I knew a part of me died in their eyes. I could see it in the way they looked at me. "Seriously, I'm really sorry. I wasn't thinking."

"I wasn't either. When I said what I did about them giving you all that attention. I think it was just easier to say it to you than them. But it's not your fault. It's not like you control them."

"Believe me. I wish."

"So what are you going to do about the show tomorrow?"

"Technically, today," I say, glancing at the clock on my screen. Time feels meaningless this early in the morning.

I run my hands over the mini sequined pillow wedged between us. The colors flip between blue and green with my touch. I've been going back and forth like this all day, trying to figure out what my future at Mermaid Cove holds. What my near and far future holds, period. But everything feels like it's being compressed into one day, volatile and charged, like a star that is either burning out or being born. I have no idea which way it'll go. I'm just so tired of waiting. For results. For plans. For approval from my parents and Barb and the world. The show's at noon today, and my MRI is scheduled for three. I picture my body floating through two large, dark tubes, and I'm more scared of not knowing what's on the other side than I am of never going through them.

"I need your help with something," I say.

Dani agrees before she even knows the plan. Then I text Alex and Leslie to see who will have a car.

It's so simple it's terrifying, but it's the only true way to do this.

In the morning, we wait for when our parents are in their bedroom, and we just go. I'm not hiding from them this time. I just need a window, a head start.

I leave them a note on my bed where I'm sure they'll see it.

I'm not going unless you come find me.

Voice: voice

1. (n.) the sound produced in a person's larynx and uttered through the mouth
2. (n. VR) the sound of yourself reverberating through your bones

Chapter 37

I'M SO NERVOUS I THINK I'LL forget everything. It doesn't help that my last chance to rehearse was disastrously cut short. Now I run the choreography over in my mind, as if it were a video on replay. I take the ten slow, deep breaths Papi's always talking about. I feel like my insides want to be on my outside. I'm stretching in my tail just a few inches from the tube, trying to touch my toes, which are actually my fins, and I keep picturing my spine curling like a snail's shell over the rest of me.

I'm jealous of them. Of all the creatures — like turtles and snails — that get to carry their homes on their bodies. They always have somewhere to go that no one can take away from them. I thought I had the Cove, but it doesn't really belong to me. Not if it won't accept me as I am.

Before getting ready for today's show, I stopped by Barb's

office to confront her about the picture. I told her I wanted it taken down, and that I want the original, too. At first she acted like she didn't know what I was talking about, but when I explained, she said, "We didn't think you'd mind."

"Why would you ever think that?"

"Oh come on. You're always trying to cover them up. You shouldn't, you know. Your scars are beautiful."

It made me so angry. It made me want to tell her she's not allowed to say that. I hadn't realized this until she erased one, but I don't want my scars to be seen as beautiful, or ugly, or strange or badass. I just want them to be allowed to be.

I knew my words would be wasted on her, so I said the next best thing. "I'll quit if you ever erase them again."

She only looked at her watch and told me I had twenty minutes to get ready.

Now it's possible this first performance will be my last.

The preshow music emanates from the tube. We sit with our fins and legs hanging over the edge of the entrance, holding hands. Geoff is on my left, and next to him are Val, Hallic, Lila, and then Tanya completes the circle on my right.

Geoff points and flexes his toes, warming up his ankles. "You think it'll work?"

I didn't realize he had it in him to be tense. "Do I think what will work?"

"You know. Our routine." He stretches out his legs, pressing them tightly together. All I can see through my tail of my own legs is the outline of my kneecaps.

"Oh." We stare at our limbs like we want them to do

311

something extraordinary, perform some kind of magic. I nod because I recognize the hope hanging in the way Geoff just said *work*. Like if we really pull this off, maybe it'll change everything, fix everything. About how people like Barb and my parents see us.

About how we feel in our bodies.

Except I'm okay in my body. Sometimes it's my body in the world that isn't.

With a flick of my foot, I slap him lightly with my fin—a poor attempt to shake off my mounting nerves. "Honestly? I don't know how it'll be received. But I know we're giving it from a place that's completely ours."

He takes a deep breath. "That's true." He nods several times like he's processing this idea, turning it over and over in his mind. "Okay. We can do this. We *know* this."

We start wiggling around anxiously just as Lila tells everyone to get ready. In an instant, the whole group goes quiet, and it looks like they have their eyes closed, but then I realize they're just staring down the darkness.

After a beat, she clears her throat and says, "To a good show. A safe show. To showing the world what's in our hearts." Then she plops like a fish out of a plastic bag into the tube, and one by one, the others follow.

I must be squeezing Tanya's hand extra hard, because just before she lets go, she shakes it and startles me out of the death spiral playing in my mind. "When the water hits, you'll be fine."

And then she's gone and I'm jumping in after her, and it

turns out she was right. The water washes away every hesitation. It's like a switch flipped inside me. My mind goes blank, but it's also set free, and I move through the music and water on pure instinct. I'd never known that body memory could take over like a current carrying me to safety. I get swept away in it, and it's only when we're done with the Little Mermaid routine, holding our final pose and waving at the crowd beyond the glass as the air curtain settles and clears, that I feel the energy coming through the other side.

They're stirring. I can't see their faces, but I know they're applauding. Even though there's glass between us, we're all connected. I drink it in. In exactly two counts of eight, I'll swim out of sight into the air tank, where I'll change into my costume for the Huacachina routine. I try to search the rows of seats for my parents, but the crowd is faceless, and all I know, because they texted me, is that the three waving figures in the front are Alex, Leslie, and Dani. I smile and wave back, but behind my cold teeth I feel my fear resurfacing. Suddenly I'm more afraid of my parents missing my performance than I ever was of them finding me out. It's funny how that works: the thing I most feared is now the thing I most want.

I want them to come.

I want them to see me.

I take a breath from my air hose and start swimming away. Before I dip into the air tank, I take one more glance over my shoulder. There, ambling into the empty spots in the front row, are two new figures.

The long note of the pan flute comes on.
Time to tell a story.

I read somewhere that the reason our voices sound so different in our heads is because of our bones; the waves travel and vibrate through them, making our voices sound deeper. So I almost don't recognize myself at first. The audio blares loud and clear through the water. Geoff and I sit still on a limestone rock.

Like so many mermaid stories, ours begins with a young woman and a man in love. She a Peruvian princess, he an Inca warrior.

We hold hands and push off the rock toward the glass. I sip from my hose and try to release any thoughts of who is watching. I'm no longer in my tail but a tan one-piece bathing suit with a long, sheer piece of fabric wrapped around me. It loops over my neck, crosses over my chest, and wraps around my waist and hips. It flows and undulates with my body as Geoff and I twist in and out of each other's arms. I stretch into an arabesque, and he does the same in the opposite direction. We float toward each other, linking one hand to each ankle so our bodies are a full circle, spinning slowly as one.

But an ill-fated battle tore them apart.

Geoff goes motionless and sinks out of sight. I swim across the glass in search of him, finally giving up as I lie across a rock and bury my head in my arms.

She cried day and night until the desert filled with a lagoon of her tears. Huacachina, whose name means "weeping lady," never stopped mourning and awaiting her love. One day, as she bathed and braided her hair, she was startled by a hunter who she saw watching her in the reflection of her mirror.

I turn over my shoulder and feign shock. Geoff's figure peeks at me from behind an underwater palm tree. He's in dark green pants now, and his legs shoot through the water as he comes after me. We take off in swirls and circles. I twist and untwist from my air hose, and as I do, the white fabric unravels, stretched like a cape behind me.

As Huacachina ran away, pieces of her mantle came loose by the wind, creating the sand dunes along the lagoon that we see today.

I make my way unseen to the air lock tank, where Tanya waits for me with my tail.

She stayed in the water so long, she became a mermaid.

Cue my reentry. Tail and all. I do a fifteen-stroke mermaid swim across the glass, almost close enough that I can read everyone's body language. Hands to mouth, eyes wide in wonder.

The music picks up, and I begin twisting and spinning to its beat. My voice grows stronger and more dramatic over the PA.

It's said she sings for her lost love every full moon.

And that whoever swims in her tears drowns in them.

I start reversing the direction of my movements.

Or that she tries to entice men to join her.

I stop and bring my hands to my head, looking confused by the words blasting through the speakers.

Or that she sings to couples in hopes of making them fall in love.

My arms go up in exasperation as I wave to the sound engineer to stop. The sound of a record scratching fills the water. And though I can't actually see them, I can practically feel the audience gasp. Wondering if I really just broke character, or if this is all part of the story.

Wait, wait, wait . . . which one is it? I wave my arms and look in the direction of the audience, speaking directly to them. The silence stretches as I swim across the glass, like a teacher waiting for a response from her students. Then, right when it becomes uncomfortable, the music comes back on, and my narration continues.

Like too many legends, Huacachina's has changed with the whims and wishes of whoever tells it. No one actually knows her true story. Maybe it's time she told her own . . .

In our rewritten version that we dance in this cave in this water, Huacachina didn't drown in her own tears.

She didn't just wait for someone else to join her. She came to the water's surface.

Under the light of the full moon, she saw the sand dunes that her mantle had created and took in the body of water that now lived outside of her.

But the hunter waited for her. She cried out for him to leave, but he fell to his knees and begged forgiveness. He hadn't meant to scare her. He had only seen her sorrow and recognized his own. He had seen her tears and wished he could cry too. He had also a lost love, but he was so ashamed of his grief that he tried to hide it from the world. Now it was drying him up inside, suffocating everything that was once alive. He didn't want to hunt anymore. He didn't want to hurt.

So Huacachina told him to swim in her tears.

Day and night, she sat on the rocks' edge and listened to him release his sorrows. He swam and danced and let the water's gentle hold take over him. Until the morning came that they found they'd switched places. He was a merperson now, and the sun had dried her tail back into legs.

Huacachina began walking the desert again, exploring the sand dunes she'd created. And the merperson found a home in the lagoon, where he saw his truest form reflected in its waters.

Topography: to·pog·ra·phy

1.   (n.) the study and mapping of surfaces
2.   (n. VR) a map of my body

Chapter 38

GEOFF SWIMS IN MY TAIL like it was made for him. The beads that hang in a thick, curved line from his neck to his chest accentuate all its beautiful colors. I'm back in my white mantle and tan suit, and our bodies float in place as we take a final bow. The fabric jellyfishes all around me. Breathing. Flowing. It rises toward the water's surface, unveiling my bare-skinned legs beneath it.

Not naked. Nor calata, the coarseness of the words implying a body's been stripped of something.

Somewhere on the opposite side of the glass, my parents are finally seeing me the way I want to be seen. No more hiding, no more pretending to blend in. Just a girl in an imperfect body, refusing to swim any further in shame. Telling the stories of her ancestors on new shores and in a new home. Telling legends of her own.

My heart is still beating as if my chest were underwater when I leave the dressing room in search of them. I'm freshly showered, wearing a diagonal-hem skirt Mami made me and a white, sleeveless bodysuit with flat teal strappy sandals. Outside the auditorium entrance, a small crowd of people holding flower bouquets and stuffed animals wait to congratulate the mermaids. Geoff sits on the giant stone, flipping his tail back and forth as he poses for pictures and videos. Children wave drawings of us and ask for our autographs. I sign two little girls' blank notebooks with the words *Hugs & Wishes, Verónica.* I let the accent over the *o* in my name create a shooting star.

I'm standing with a pen still in my hand when I see my parents by the partition ropes leading up to the ticket booth. They're leaned in close to each other, their body language all whispers and worries, while next to them are Dani and Leslie, carrying a bunch of flowers and a balloon. Alex paces near them at a close but safe enough distance. He has what looks like a packing tube in his hands, which he taps nervously against his palms.

I let myself be pulled into Dani and Leslie's embrace, knowing my parents will discreetly wait. "You were incredible. I cried the whole time," Dani says, while Leslie spouts every pun imaginable, including the cringe-inducing *mermazing.* Their arms are so warm around me, like anchors keeping me steady in a tide of rising panic. I take their gifts and start to pull myself out of their hold. We exchange a couple of brief, knowing glances as my chest fills with air.

"Verónica." Mami's voice is shaking. When I turn to

meet her eyes, they're wet and unsure. "You took all our stories," she says, and I can't tell if it's accusation or a celebration, because she's trying so hard not to cry that she just keeps swallowing her words, holding back.

Papi grows tired of waiting for her to finish. I can tell from the rigid stance of his shoulders that he doesn't know how to react. With one arm crossed, he rests his elbow on top of it and brings his hands to his lips. "It was a good show. Original and daring. We'll talk more on the way to your appointment."

They start walking, but I don't follow. Instead I turn to face Alex and place my hand in his. We don't say a word, but we don't have to. He just kind of nods, and I can see in his eyes he's anxious, trying hard not to detach from this moment. Three short steps is all it takes for my parents to realize I'm not trailing them.

"Verónica. Por Dios. We're going to be la—"

It's the same look in Mami's eyes at first, but different. Disbelief and then a quiet settling, as if something inside her just became disarmed. Papi shakes his head. He blows air through his teeth and says, "So that's it. She's just going to do anything she wants from now on?"

I ignore it. I have flowers from my best friends in one hand and Alex's steady grip in the other, and their unwavering faith in me makes me want to be strong, for no one else but myself.

"Mami, Papi, this is Alex. He just moved into Palmview Lakes from Texas."

He stretches out his hand. "Good to meet you. Good to see you again, Mr. Rentería."

Mami looks to Papi, confused, but then she shakes her head as if resetting her brain. "Wait a minute. I don't understand. You knew about this?"

"I found them in the pool," Papi says, keeping his voice low. "Doing God knows what."

"Doing nothing!" I say. "And even if we were, you act like liking him is the equivalent of killing puppies or something."

"Like him all you want," Mami says, looking Alex up and down like he's a used car. "It's what you do next that's the problem."

"What we do? With our bodies, you mean? My. Body?" I know I'm crossing a line right now, but I can't stop myself. I can't keep staying quiet.

Mami hikes up her purse and starts walking away from me. "I don't have to listen to this. Get into the car, and we'll talk about this after your appointment. Or did you forget?"

"Of course I didn't. But Alex is taking me."

"But we've always gone—"

"Déjala," Papi says, cutting her off. "We'll go in separate cars. You said so yourself, we're going to be late."

He walks away without another word.

In Alex's car, once we arrive at the hospital, we take a moment to collect ourselves. We drove forty-five minutes with the windows down, in a spent state of clarity and silence. We had more time than my parents estimated, or maybe Alex drove faster or they got caught in traffic that we missed, because we arrive first to the parking lot outside the imaging center.

I know this because my parents have yet to text me that they're here or that they're checking me in. And though we've never gone separately to one of my appointments—always the three of us, always them both taking time from their work—there's no doubt in my mind that this is a thing they'd do.

I explain this to Alex, and he says, "Really?"

"Yes. Why?"

"It's just not something most parents would do. Or could do. At least, not mine. They always took turns. But maybe that's just us."

I think back to what Mami said the last time we came here, when she tried to reassure me things wouldn't be as bad as I thought.

We have always gotten through it together, as a family.

Except together hasn't always meant the same. I think of the photo taken the day of my first surgery in the US: four people holding the weight of different emotions. They shouldered all of it for me then, kept the hard, scary truths hidden. They described it to me like it was a fairy tale: you'll sleep, and then you'll wake, and your hip will feel so much better. I didn't have to fear the things they did. That it wouldn't work. That it'd make things worse. Or that maybe, possibly, they'd lose me, somewhere in the foggy state between sleep and nothingness. But I'm not that little girl they need to shield from the truth anymore. I want to be the one who protects my body.

"We should probably go in, like, five minutes," I say, rubbing my arms for warmth. After the show, I skipped my usual twenty minutes in the sauna, and now the chills are surfacing. Alex offers me his burgundy zip-up hoodie from the backseat and in the same movement retrieves the cardboard tube he had at the springs.

"Real quick. I meant to give this to you after the show." He pops the top off and tilts the opening over his hand. Out slides a rolled-up sheet of paper. I hold one end against my thigh and stretch out the other.

I gasp.

It's a portrait of me made with maps.

I recognize the image he must've referenced, a picture he took of me by the pool. I was stretched out on a lounge chair on one side, with my head propped up by my elbow. My eyes are closed because the sun was so bright and the wind was blowing my hair across my lashes.

I run my fingers over its many creases, all the intricacies he filled with places. It's a mixture of Peru and Florida, of the desert the Huacachina legend was birthed in alongside a tourist map that pinpoints Mermaid Cove. There are patches of the Pacific and the Gulf of Mexico, and lines formed by the Turnpike and depths of the ocean. There are even pieces of

the map of Palmview Lakes, the scattered bits of all our favorite places. The racquetball court and the pool and the ponds,
the canal where we saw the manatee. They become my neck,
my smile, my navel and thighs and scars. A living collage of
my body and all the places it's called home.

Trust: trust

1.   (n.) a firm belief in the truth of something
2.   (n. VR) a fragile thing that needs time to heal when broken

Chapter 39

I'M TOLD TO HOLD STILL THE entire thirty minutes I'm in the scanner. The MRI machine is basically a hard-surfaced stretcher tucked into the hole of a giant O, so I lie there in its mouth like some sort of offering while the radio waves scan my femur to create images.

I'm not afraid, but I'm not relaxed. I close my eyes, but I don't fall asleep. There's a loud humming all around, but eventually I can tune it out and hear my silence. It's a low, pale static. My breath becomes light and shallow until soon I feel my consciousness pulling away from the back of my eyes. I compartmentalize my body. I feel like I can study it, like it's only a part that's apart from me.

When it's over (in a flash? in an eon?), I make my way back to the exam room with my parents, and we wait. Papi asks how I'm feeling in whispers as Mami picks bits of lint off my gown. I start to slowly piece myself back together.

"How do you feel?" Dr. Brown says, his voice a foghorn in a chamber.

I startle and tell him that I completely zoned out. Everything felt both clear and vague.

"You were probably meditating."

"I don't know how to do that."

"You don't have to. Your mind figures it out," he says, making a clicking noise as he gestures, turning a dial over his temple. Then he pulls up my scans, side to side with last month's X-rays, on his monitor.

"How have you been feeling?" His voice is low as he studies the images of my hip.

"Fine."

"Define *fine*," he says, as if it's a word that only I can tell the meaning of.

My mind goes blank. For all the pages of words I've written and rewritten, this one hasn't entered my dictionary. "What do you mean?"

The monitor creaks as he angles it toward me. "Have you been feeling any pain?"

A voice inside me thinks, *Almost always.* But I haven't admitted that to anyone, especially not myself. I nod and say, "In various degrees. Sometimes it's pretty pointed, and sometimes it hardly registers."

(Translation: sometimes I push it away to be brave.)

He takes a deep breath. "Let me show you what we have here."

My parents lean in, but he looks mainly at me as he talks.

"Do you see how your femoral head looks kind of cloudy here?" He traces its curve with his pinkie. "This shade here. This shape that looks like a crescent moon . . ."

My parents nod. He shifts his head to one side as our eyes meet, and I realize he's waiting for me to acknowledge I see it. "Oh. Yes."

"That's late-stage necrosis. I'd say about stage three."

Mami places a hand on my shoulder. "What does that mean, Doctor?"

"Will she need surgery?" is what Papi wants to know.

"So here's the thing." He clicks off the monitor, and it goes blank. All their eyes turn to me. "Surgery is very likely. Typically, an open reduction is an option, where we rotate your femoral head to put a less damaged part of it in contact with the joint. But you know we've already done that."

"I didn't, though. Not really. I mean, I knew you put screws in but not that that's what you did." Suddenly I'm very aware that this is the most I've ever said to my doctor, and the longest we've ever sustained a conversation, just us two. I wonder if he felt bad about last time, realizing how little I knew about my own bone.

"Yes. Well . . . we did that twice, as you know."

He's talking very slowly now, dragging this out, and I feel

like my blood is rushing to my feet and the floor is melting under me as I wait for him to say arthroplasty.

"Typically, at this stage I would suggest replacement—"

My parents both let out a sigh. They start saying something about how he knows what's best, but he only smiles and pauses, like he has more to say. They grow quiet.

"But that's only if you're in severe discomfort. A lot of patients are, with images like yours. But some aren't. So it's not a matter of if you'll need a replacement, but more like when."

I don't get it. None of this sounds like new information, and I just spent the whole summer worrying about a *near future* that is just as vague now as when this all started. I want answers. I wish he would just tell me what I need to do. "What do you recommend?"

"I guess I should make this clearer. It's up to you. Really. If you're in so much pain that you'd rather do it this month, or this year, then great. If it's not really bothering you and a replacement would be a greater intrusion at this point than the ways your pain affects your day-to-day life, then it can probably wait."

My parents look at me, confused. I let the meaning catch up to all the words he just said, to me and not to them. I think this has to be a mistake, because this has never happened before, this eye contact and trust and choice.

"You're saying I get to choose."

Papi makes a croaking sound, like he's sure that's not what the doctor meant.

"I'm saying, since you say you're not in any significant pain"—he lengthens out those words, languishing on pain—"that you should listen to your body and decide what feels right, and when."

And damn.

If that wasn't the last thing I ever expected him to say.

Honesty: hon·es·ty

1. (n.) the quality of being free from deception; genuine and sincere

2. (adj. VR) the scariest thing to be to yourself, the bravest

Chapter 40

I FIND ALEX WAITING FOR ME where I left him, at the far end of a row of empty chairs. He stands as soon as he sees me and kisses my forehead. Without asking how it went or how I'm feeling, he looks into my eyes and says, "Ready?"

All this time my parents are strangely silent. They stand in a far-off corner as if giving us space, trying not to watch. But there's something in the way they hold each other that makes me tell him I should go with them.

In our car, I sit in the back in the middle seat, in the space that's never felt big enough for a whole person.

"It wasn't the mermaiding that made it worse, if that's what you were thinking," I say when the hospital is just a dot in the rearview.

Papi keeps his eyes far too focused on the road. Mami brings her thumbnail to the edges of her mouth and sighs.

"I was thinking that if we'd only caught things sooner, this wouldn't have happened."

"I've only been there a few weeks. It couldn't have affected it that much." I think of all the rehearsals we did out of the water. The aches I made a home for in my body. If I'm being completely honest, I've been doing it for years, ignoring this expanding pain. But the water has been the only place that dampened it.

"That's not what I meant, hijita. I was thinking, your hip. When it's caught early enough in babies . . ."

She doesn't have to finish for me to know what she means. It could've just been fixed with a brace. It's not a lifetime of surgeries for everyone.

"It's not your fault," I say. "I don't blame you. And I don't regret it. That'd be like me wishing I wasn't born in Peru, or that I didn't have a little sister. I wouldn't take away any part of me, because that would mean erasing all of me."

Mami reaches her hand back and rubs my shin. "I was so angry when I saw that picture."

"They deleted it," I say, but I check my phone just in case. There's fresh content from today's show, but no pictures of our Huacachina routine. It's disappointing, to say the least. I thought we were leaving our mark. I thought were telling a new story.

"So what now?" Papi says. "We just let you go and do whatever with whoever, and we're supposed to pretend everything will be fine?" He sweeps his hand through the air across the windshield. Like he's throwing me out into the world. And in this moment I can see his pain, clear as the worried eyes in our picture.

I try a joke. "You have to trust me. It's doctor's orders."

"Ay, Vero. We've just always wanted what's best for you," he says softly.

"I know. But I need to decide for myself for a change."

Which means no more lies, no more hiding. No more trying to prove myself to others. How have we been doing this our whole lives? How hasn't the pressure ruptured something deep inside of us? Maybe it has, and we've been too busy pretending we're fine to even notice.

Define fine.

"And what about las sirenas?" Papi says. "You lied to us. You expect me and your mother to simply . . . let that go?"

"I'm sorry," I say. "I messed up. And I know it doesn't excuse it, but I felt like I didn't have a choice."

"There's always a choice, Vero," Mami says, the firmness coming back to her voice.

"Is there? When you and Papi left Peru, was it really a choice, or did you run out of options?"

"That was different," Papi says.

"It's not, though. You always say you left because you wanted Dani and me to have opportunities you didn't. But what good is that, if you're just going to narrow down our choices to what you think is best for us? How is you deciding for us any better than the life you left behind?"

"You just . . . you have so much potential, hijita. We don't want to see you wasting it," Papi says.

"I'm not wasting anything. And it's not forever." Saying it out loud, a sadness settles over me. Even if Jessica never came back to reclaim her place at the Cove, I know now I wouldn't be able to stay past summer. Not with my pain ebbing and flowing the way it is.

We let the car grow quiet for the rest of the trip. I click through Mermaid Cove's feed again and check if anyone else has tagged us in their posts. Dozens of tiles fill my screen. The majority of them are of Geoff and me—him in the tail, me in the sheer fabric. Not a single one is photoshopped.

So . . . you think it "worked"? I text Geoff.

I think WE worked it, he writes back. Then he sends me a link to the Cove's profile, where they finally posted a picture of the two of us. I click through the tags and notice Geoff has a new bio: Merthey Geoff at Mermaid Cove, also swimming as @Phin.

Perfect Merthey is perfect, I text them.

Thanks. It felt right. It was time.

Has Barb said anything?

No. But let her. I can't bring myself to care, they text back.

You're a Phin-spiration, I write, adding several heart and mermaid emojis.

They reply with a kiss, and I go back to the picture of us, staring until it dims. I tap it again to bring it back to light. I may not be in costume or underwater anymore, but I feel like I'm still that girl in the story. Tired of weeping and hiding. Ready to explore a landscape of possibilities she didn't know could be hers.

I scroll through the dozens of comments the post has received in not even an hour. People are calling Geoff's and my choreography a revelation, the best that Mermaid Cove has ever seen. They want to know how long our showcase will last, and someone, probably Barb, has taken great care to tell them to get their tickets before they sell out—we're performing seven more times before the showcase switches over to Tanya and Lila's routine.

Near the end, there's a long thread of people commenting on my scars. They say I'm an inspiration and they want to congratulate the Cove for giving me the spotlight.

Giving?

Last time I checked, I tried out like everyone else for the spot. Their comments make me feel like a spectacle, like the real attraction isn't my art but the fact that I'm doing it in the first place, as if they never expected I could.

We arrive home an hour before the pool closes. I change into a suit to meet my friends, who are waiting for me.

"Will that boy be there?" Mami says.

"His name is Alex, and yes."

She takes my hand and picks at a blotch of polish on my nail. "It's just that . . . there are mistakes you can't take back, you know."

"I know, Mami. Trust me, you and Papi never miss an opportunity to remind me." I keep my voice soft and playful because the fear I've always had at "talking back" to her is gone. For once, it feels like we're just having a conversation, and I can tell all of Mami's defenses are down, because she looks at me like she's the child instead of the adult.

"We're your parents," she says, squaring her shoulders. "It's our job to take care of you."

"Mami. You can't control everything that's going to happen to me. Or everything I choose, either."

"Dios mío. No me digas que you're already having—"

"That's not what I'm saying! I only meant I'm going to be eighteen. I'm going to college next year. And even if I go somewhere close by or, God forbid, if I end up on another coast, I need you to trust me to know what's best for me."

"Ay, hijita, another coast?"

"Mami, focus. You can't treat me like I'm eight forever."

She takes a few strands of my hair and starts twisting them into a loose braid. "But you are, in my eyes."

And for a millisecond—just long enough to replay my whole childhood in my mind—I remember what it was like to be that age again. Not the surgeries or the pain or the horrible ways kids stared at me. Just the way it felt when she and I were home. When she'd dab my toes with a sponge, careful not to wet my cast. When she made a song and game out of everyday errands so I wouldn't feel bored being in the house all day. Those days are some of my hardest and yet they're full of my happiest memories. They were sweet, fun. Safe.

"I know, Mami. Te prometo. I'll love you like I'm eight forever. K?"

She gives me a tight, long hug, and by the time she lets me go, her eyes are glossy but dry. "You are a stunning mermaid," she says. "And that tail. ¡Asu, qué bella!"

I smile but I can't stop wondering how much longer I'll get to wear it. How much longer I'll want to. A seed of an idea pops into my mind. "Mami, can you make me one? We can go this week, to pick out the fabric."

"I guess I can try."

She's being modest, but I know whatever she makes will be more beautiful than any tail the Cove could ever give me. I kiss her on the cheek. "Gracias, Mami."

"Go. Swim with your friends. Pero pórtate bien," she says, like she can't help sneaking in one last *behave*. "Your father knew about este Alex, didn't he?" I can tell she's only half teasing, that she still feels hurt that Papi didn't say anything the day he caught us by the pool.

It feels like ages ago. Not just in time but distance. The fear that rushed and rose through me that day is gone. In place there's just relief.

From the kitchen we hear Papi open the refrigerator. He's pulling out limes, red onions, fish and cilantro. He tells me to be sure Dani and I are back in an hour and a half, when the ceviche will be perfectly cooked and ready. Mami's looking at him with her mouth open, waiting for an answer to her question.

He lets out a tired sigh. "I didn't want you worrying about it, viejita. You worry about so much. We both do. Maybe we try"—he lowers his palm flat toward the floor, like he's pushing down an invisible force—"un poquito menos."

He looks flustered, like he's trying to say something but he never learned the right words. I think of how Dani and I used to laugh when Papi got a word in English wrong, and he'd shake it off and say *¿Me entiendes, o no me entiendes?*

I understand him now. Not completely, but enough. I give Papi a gentle kiss on the cheek and leave them to talk amongst themselves.

Minutes later, I'm approaching the gate to the pool when I hear the sound of Dani's laughter, followed by a massive splash. Leslie yells that she wet her toes, and Alex and Jason tease her with deep, long *oooohs*. I'm already peeling off my shirt as I walk onto the deck, smiling at how right it feels. How good it feels to come home.

"Here, I got you something," Leslie says, pulling a hand-made card out of her tote. "I was supposed to give it to you before your appointment, but I left it in the car. So to make up for it I had everybody sign it."

By *everybody,* she means Alex, Dani, and Tanya.

In huge bubble letters on the inside, it says:

We'd tell you to break a leg. But that'd be blas-femur.

Something between a laugh and a gasp escapes me. "You thought of this one yourself, didn't you?"

She pouts her lips and gives a proud, mischievous nod. Alex pushes himself up out of the pool and sits next to me. Tanya, Dani, and Jason swim over to the pool's edge. They're all watching me, waiting.

"So how do you feel?" Alex asks.

No *what did the doctor say?* No *how is your bone?* All he really cares to know is how I am. Amidst all the chaos of today and the ups and downs of this whole summer . . . where do I stand?

"I feel . . . exhausted," I say. "But excited. I don't need surgery. Not right away, anyways. One day, eventually, I will."

"When?" Dani says.

"I don't know. But I'll know when I'm ready. I never knew it was my decision to make, and that somehow changes everything."

"That's amazing," Tanya says. "Barb is going to be so thrilled. We've been flooded with comments and messages about your routine. She's floating around the idea of keeping it going for at least the rest of the summer . . ."

"She told you that?"

Tanya nods excitedly, clearly expecting me to mirror her emotions. But I'm thrown by Barb's sudden change of heart—one day she's erasing me, and the next she's using my body to sell more tickets.

"I guess it's convenient for her now," I say.

"What do you mean?" Tanya asks. "We thought you'd be happy."

I did too.

But today everything feels different.

"I just need some time to think," I say, and so I dive into the water and let the noise of the world disappear somewhere far above me. I sink to the bottom and look up at the sky through the rippled water. It feels like everyone on the other side wants a piece of me, wants me to do something for their sake instead of mine. Go to a good school not too far away. Be the kind of daughter that makes her parents proud. Help Mermaid Cove sell more tickets. Perform, perform, perform.

Every footstep felt *as if she were treading on sharp knives and spikes, but she bore it gladly.*

I think of the question Alex asked me by the canal when we saw the manatee, a question I so quickly brushed off.

Who are you being strong for?

Which was really *who are you enduring pain for?*

It's been for everyone else but me. If I've endured it, it's because I didn't want to be a bother. Didn't want to disappoint. I used to think strength was about proving all the things I could do, but maybe it's also about voicing the things I can't. Saying I don't want this. For myself and my own body.

I come back up to the surface just before my lungs start stinging.

"The thing is, after Geoff and I finish performing our showcase this week and next, I'm not going back."

"You're giving up being a mermaid?" Tanya asks.

I debate how much I want to explain. If Geoff were here, they'd tell me it's not the Cove that makes the mermaid. I have this pool and Florida's springs. A whole ocean, if I really want it. Soon, I'll have my own tail, one I'll always know was made for me, not altered after the fact.

"I'm not giving up. I love it. But this is as far as I'm comfortable going with it."

"But I thought you said you were fine," Tanya says.

Define fine.

I think of all the words I've written over the years in my notebook. This dictionary that's helped me make meaning of the world. There are words I've left untouched because I didn't think they belonged to me. I didn't think they could say enough.

"I don't know what fine looks like yet, for me. I've spent so much energy trying to convince everyone else I was fine that I didn't stop to think if it was true or not. I just need time to figure things out."

Time to listen. Time to learn what I want, what I need, what I'm ready for. One day, the doctors will cut my scars open again and replace this part of me that's been flawed and pained and mine all my life. I want to choose that day. I want to choose all my days.

They nod and say they understand. They go back to the games they were playing in the water. I start to resubmerge myself into the deep end. I push off the wall and swim to the other side in a single deep breath. I don't know why I ever thought being here wasn't enough. The underwater lights switch on even though the sun hasn't fully set, so I can't see my own shapes and shadows. But I open my eyes anyways and see Alex swimming toward me. I smile, and the water isn't cold and biting against my teeth. I come up for air, and I can breathe again.

Author's Note

Although Mermaid Cove is fictional, it was very much inspired by a real place: Weeki Wachee Springs in Florida. Named by the Seminole Indians to mean "little spring" or "winding river," the spring is the site of an underwater mermaid attraction created in 1947 under the same name. What started as an eighteen-seat theater carved in limestone became a world-famous attraction over the decades. Today, Weeki Wachee Springs is part of the Florida State Park System. Its main attractions include mermaid shows, water slides, a lazy river, and of course, the clear water springs in which visitors swim. The mermaids perform several underwater shows daily, and the park's beautiful and rich history has enchanted people for generations — myself included.

When I started writing what I initially called "my mermaid HIPpy novel," I knew I wanted to base it on Weeki Wachee and my experiences being born with and living with hip dysplasia. But soon the park in which Verónica performs evolved into a fictional place that provided me with just the right amount of artistic license. Whereas at Weeki Wachee, mermaids train for months (even becoming scuba certified) before their first show, Mermaid Cove is on a shorter schedule. Weeki Wachee is open year-round, while the Cove is more seasonal. To be eligible to be a mermaid at Weeki Wachee, performers have to be at least eighteen, while Verónica is a year younger. By the end of the first draft, I'd reimagined not only the setting, but how I defined the setting. It became a fluid place, made up of a physical body of water but also of Vero's actual body and the lands she seeks to feel at home in. I consulted experts in both orthopedics and immigration to explore these dynamics; any deviations from their valued insights were carefully weighed. Ultimately I tried to tell this story in the language my body is most familiar with: an intentional blend of facts and fictional truths.

Similarly, in retelling the legend of Huacachina, I was struck by how many versions there are. Often, the variations are small but not insignificant. In one she's a young maiden; in another, an Inca princess. Sometimes Huacachina refers solely to the oasis, whereas in other legends, it's also the mermaid's name. Rather than choosing any single legend as the One, I decided to embrace the nature of oral storytelling. The narratives we tell evolve, shaped by our inner and outer worlds. So it made sense to me that Verónica would question the legends she's heard all her life and weave her own story into them.

With these artistic choices and deviations, I hope this novel captures a longing that so many of us hold in our hearts from a young age: the desire to be a mermaid—free to swim and dance and play—and be seen as we truly are.

Acknowledgments

I've been dreaming up this book my whole life. When I was eleven years old, I wrote an essay about my hip dysplasia and various surgeries that I sent to either *YM* or *Seventeen* magazine (I don't remember which). What I do remember is wanting to tell my story, to have these hidden parts of me seen on my own terms. I have so many people to thank for helping me make my younger self's wish finally come true, all these years later.

To my agent, Laura Dail: thank you for being a safe, nourishing support when my ideas are barely seeds and for being a light and a force when they're grown. Thank you for helping me keep believing—especially throughout 2020 and beyond—that my stories will find homes.

To my editor, Jennifer Greene: this book wasn't even finished when you read the first pages, but you already saw what it could become. Thank you for giving me the guidance, support, and space I needed to make it a reality. I'm a better writer with each book we work on.

I'm so lucky to have trusted friends who are my first readers, who know when to tell me to keep going and when to reassess. Barbara Sparrow, Demery Bader-Saye, Everlee Cotnam, and Kate Cotnam: the journey of not just this book, but this writing life, could not have happened without you. I'm eternally grateful for our ten-plus years of sharing beautiful moments and difficult ones over chips and queso and cake.

To ire'ne lara silva, my compass amidst the fog of self-doubt and life's hardships: there were so many times I doubted I could write this story, so many times you reminded me I could. Thank you for being the one I trust when I start to lose faith.

I had just begun writing this book when the pandemic started and we went on lockdown. There were days when creating through all the grief, fear, and uncertainty felt impossible. I wouldn't have gotten through it without friends like Désirée Zamorano and Erika T. Wurth: what a blessing it is to be in the thick of it all with you two.

My most heartfelt thanks to spaces like Las Musas and Disabled Kidlit Writers who remind me of the power of community. To Mia Garcia, for being a constant, supportive voice that actively checked in on me as I stressed over deadlines and reminded me to let go of my self-judgment. To mi familia of writers (there are so many of you, but you know who you are!) who recognized that we need space to share and commiserate and energize one another when the world feels heavy: thank you for the Zoom meetings that never felt like Zoom meetings. To Moira Muldoon, for sharing parts of your story with me when I called to ask about local swimming holes; that conversation made my inner child feel so much less alone.

So many, many thanks to Dr. Raúl Gösthe, Dr. Mara Karamitopoulos, John Athanason, and Stephen Robbins for lending their time and expertise to Vero's story. My work as as a fiction writer inevitably involves fictionalizing, but I try to do so in ways that ring true. Thank you for helping me ground this story in both reality and possibility.

Pınar Yaşar and Amy Bowen, I can't thank you enough for reading this book so thoughtfully. Thank you for seeing my hopes and intentions for it, and for helping me make sure that they were coming through on the page. Your comments, insights, and words of encouragement were a light that kept me going when the writing left me scared and vulnerable.

Publishing a book is a team effort and I'm so blessed to have had such amazing people working on this one. Celeste Knudsen and Loika: words can't describe what this cover means to me. You both manifested the heart of this story so beautifully and vibrantly. Taylor McBroom and Tara Shanahan, thank you for championing *Running* and now *Breathe* as they make their way into the world.

I don't know why I thought writing this part last would make it any easier to put into words. To my family and friends: so much of what should have been hard was instead joyful because I had a home full of cousins, aunts, uncles, and grandparents who reminded me I was loved and supported. To my parents: los quiero hasta el cielo. Thank you, Ceci, for our afternoons watching *Who's The Boss* and pranking my teacher in our living room on April first. Thank you, Ramón, for always believing in my stories and giving me the space to write this one, quite literally, when life was in chaotic transition. Ushu, I admired you so much that I followed in your footsteps. You have always been wise and loving enough to encourage me to find my own path. I love you. Thank you also to my primos, Frankie, Flavia, Aldo, Piero, and Bianca, for playing mermaids and make-believe with me. To my nieces, Sofia and Olivia: I can only hope to make you as proud as you make me every day!

I'm so happy to not only have found my life's love in Eric, but to have gained a whole family with the hugest hearts. Thank you to my in-laws, Odalis, Rey, Kathleen, Ily, Lissy, and Sean, for always being there for us no matter where our next adventure takes us.

And Eric. My love, mi amor, my home. Thank you for dreaming up this life with me.